MISTRESS OF PEACOCK WALK

by
Kate Sweeney

MISTRESS OF PEACOCK WALK
© 2014 BY KATE SWEENEY

ISBN 10:1935216597
ISBN 13:9781935216599

FIRST PRINTING: 2014

THIS TRADE PAPERBACK IS PUBLISHED BY
INTAGLIO PUBLICATIONS
WALKER, LA USA

WWW.INTAGLIOPUB.COM

CREDITS

EXECUTIVE EDITOR: TARA YOUNG

COVER DESIGN BY TIGER GRAPHICS

ACKNOWLEDGMENTS

Once again, I'd have to thank my sister Maureen, who is always there when I need to bounce something around when we Skype. While I had the idea for this story, Maureen came up with the title. Thanks, Mo.

And of course, to my editor Tara, who always keeps me thinking, which is not an easy task, and sometimes very painful.

Chapter 1

"I love to come to Chicago in the spring. Though it 'tis a wee bit chilly." Kathleen took a deep breath, letting it out slowly. "Do ya know what I mean, cousin?"

"Yes. And you're nuts, cousin. A wee bit? We could still get snow," Rose said.

"I know. But it smells so fresh and new. Sometimes, I wish our lives were different and my parents emigrated to America and not yours. Did ya ever wish that?"

Rose laughed and pulled her sweater around her. She slipped her arm in Kathleen's as they walked along the paved bicycle area of the beach. "Well, Kath, if that was the case, then you wouldn't be the mistress of Peacock Walk, the Culhane ancestral home, which by the way, I won't get to see until the fall now that you've disrupted the natural order of things. It was my turn to spend spring in Ireland. And don't worry, someday, I'll get tired of the snow and cold, and come and live with you and the kids and Aunt Vivian. So be careful, I might make a good mistress." She wriggled her eyebrows for effect.

Kathleen smiled wistfully as they watched her two children running ahead of them. "I think that would be grand. The children love you. I think ya need to retire soon."

Rose laughed at the idea. "If I don't get a promotion soon, I just might. Though truly, this job is just a means of paying the bills, putting a little away each month, and making sure I have enough money to come for a long visit every year with my family across the ocean."

"Well, I'm glad you can do that. Right now, I wanted Donal and Caitlin to have a little away time to come see their favorite second cousin."

"You mean their only second cousin."

Kathleen laughed. "Too true. No one would ever believe between our parents we'd be the only two offspring."

"I know. What ever happened to the big Irish Catholic family scenario? It's just as well. I wouldn't want to share my only cousin and my only second cousins."

"And they do love you. They're always askin' when Rose's comin' for a visit."

"I love to come to Ireland to see you." Rose glanced at Kathleen, whose red hair blew wildly in the wind, as she pensively watched the kids. "So when you called and wanted to change vacation plans, it concerned me. Is everything all right? I know it must be hard with Desmond gone."

"It's getting better. Time helps. It's been over a year now. The kids are coping better, as well. Donal, being older, is a bit more sullen."

"You mean more than he usually is?"

Kath smiled and bumped shoulders with Rose. "He gets that from the Flaherty side of the family. Not happy go lucky as we Culhanes. And Caitlin, well, she's missin' Des, but she's still so young. Ya know, Des never spent any real dad time with them. But the world is different to a seven-year-old."

"I know. How are those violin lessons coming?"

"Och, please don't bring it up. Me ears can't take it anymore. And now she's taken up step dancin'."

"Oh, God."

"I know. She sounds like a herd of buffalo. She's not the graceful one, my Caitlin."

"Yes. My godchild is not light of foot." Rose laughed while watching Caitlin run with her red hair, like her mother's, blowing wildly. Donal, who was fourteen now, protectively pulled her close to him when a cyclist rode by. "He's a good brother."

"He adores her."

"How are you, Kath?"

Kathleen took a pensive breath. "I'm better. I know things were bad between Des and me. He was such a complicated man."

When Rose snorted sarcastically, Kathleen chuckled. "I know Des Flaherty was a wild Irishman who could be very self-centered and childish."

"He nearly put you into bankruptcy," Rose said softly.

"I know. And thank you for the investment tip. It surely turned things around. We got back most of what Des squandered."

"And you were right not to tell him about that. I know you felt guilty."

"Not for long. He angered me so, but he didn't deserve... Well, it's over, and he's at peace. I want that for my family, as well."

"Speaking of family, didn't Aunt Vivian want to come with you this time? She hasn't been to Chicago since right before Desmond's accident."

"I think she's getting a little older. Besides, it's spring and she loves to clean and air out that old musty house of ours."

Rose watched her as Kathleen seemed miles away. "You seem preoccupied. What's going on?"

"I've done some thinkin'. And there are things that just don't sit well about Des and how he died."

Rose led them to a park bench. "Sit and tell me."

"It's nothin' I can put my finger on. And to tell ya the truth, if Meghan Quigley hadn't shown up at the door—"

"Who's she?"

"It's a long story that's all jumbled in my head. I still can't wrap my mind around it all."

"All what? You sound so mysterious."

"It's not my intention, but I don't want to go into anything just yet. Meghan is a good woman and I trust her. And," she added with a sly grin, "she's gay."

"Well, that's out of the blue." Rose raised an eyebrow. "Something you'd like to share, cousin?"

"Not for me, you *amadan*."

7

"Don't start calling me an idiot in the Irish," Rose warned playfully.

"Sorry. I've got Donal sayin' it now. I mean, she's gay and she's single. You'll meet her when you come in the fall. By then, maybe I can know what…"

When she didn't finish her sentence, Rose watched her. "Know what?"

Kathleen looked as though she didn't hear Rose. Then she blinked and smiled; she reached over and patted Rose's hand. "I'll know more about everything. Including Meghan Quigley. I'll talk ya up nice." She wriggled her eyebrows.

Rose smiled, but she saw the uneasiness behind Kathleen's eyes. There was something she wasn't telling her. And it wasn't about Meghan Quigley, though it was curious. But beyond the concerned look, Rose saw the Culhane stubborn jaw set. And Rose knew what that meant. Whatever it was, her cousin wouldn't say anything until the right time. Rose would have to be patient and wait.

With a nagging feeling of dread, she sat back, and with Kathleen, she watched Donal and Caitlin running along the beach.

Chapter 2

"Daydreaming again, Rose?"

Rose stared out the window at the Chicago skyline. From the twelfth-floor office, she had a great view. She sighed and looked at Sharon. "I guess I was."

"About what?"

"Oh, nothing really, I suppose." Though in truth, Rose had been thinking about Kathleen's visit two months earlier. It'd been on her mind since. She'd talked to Kathleen in that time, but nothing of any importance had been discussed. Rose hadn't heard from her in three weeks, which was not unusual. It just constantly nagged at her.

"Maybe you need another vacation," Sharon said.

"I just took one a couple months ago." Rose slipped on her glasses and tried to concentrate on the reports on her desk.

"Remember when I came back from that glorious vacation?" Sharon sat back and swiveled in the chair in front of Rose's desk. "It was seven days in heaven. Cancun. Remember?"

Rose laughed again. "I do. You were insufferable for a week."

"Yes, but what a vacation I had."

"Sex all week? With a stranger?"

"He wasn't a stranger after the first night," Sharon said in defense. "You should try that kind of vacation, instead of always going to Ireland. I mean, I get it. Your folks were born there and you have relatives, but geesh, go somewhere warm and sunny and have sex. Or at least find a lesbian in Ireland."

Rose immediately thought of the woman Kathleen spoke of. Meghan something-or-other.

"What's wrong? Didn't you have fun when your family visited? Come to think of it, you usually talk more about your vacations."

Rose shrugged. "I don't know. This time was, I don't know. Something was just off. I mean, Kathleen was okay, the kids were fun. I don't know. Just odd."

"Well, they are still getting over his death."

"I know. That must be it. When Kathleen's husband died… even though Desmond wasn't a very good provider—"

"Well, given the fact that your cousin is wealthy."

Rose snorted sarcastically. "I don't mean to speak ill of the dead, but Desmond Flaherty never held a job for long, but he spent money like he was the heir and not Kathleen."

Sharon rocked dreamily in her chair. "An heiress to a mansion in Ireland. And I love the name, Peacock Walk. Sounds so…"

"Peacocky," Rose said dryly.

Sharon laughed. "Don't be so sarcastic. Where did they get that name?"

"Back in the day, my ancestors used to have peacocks roam all over the property. I think they got them from someone in England, who got them from India, I believe. It was more for ornamental purposes, and supposedly, it meant you had money or royalty of some sort. A crazy idea that some exotic birds protect your property or some such nonsense. Actually, my great-grandfather had them trained, well, as much as you could, I suppose. They would stay on the grounds near the house, as if they were protecting it."

"Do you still have them?"

"Of course. It's one of those stipulations that's handed down generation to generation. Kathleen feeds them and keeps them. They stay close to the house and walk the grounds. Hence the name, Peacock Walk. They're beautiful actually, well, the males are."

"Interesting. And just think. If your folks stayed in Ireland and Kathleen's moved here, you'd be the mistress of Peacock Walk, in…" She looked at Rose. "Where is this mansion?"

Rose raised an eyebrow. "Trahern, County Donegal."

"You'd be the mistress of Peacock Walk in Trahern, County Donegal," she said in haughty fashion, with her nose in the air.

"Number one, there is no great wealth. Number two, it's not a mansion. And number three, I'm no mistress, and number four... I...oh, hell, I forgot my point."

"Senility," Sharon mumbled. "At forty-eight."

Rose wasn't listening; her mind was back in Ireland and the conversation she had with Kathleen. "She just sounded so mysterious when I talked to her three weeks ago," she said absently. "I know I shouldn't be bothering you with this."

"Hey, we've known each other for five years. I tell you a lot of what's going on in my life. Sometimes it helps to say things out loud. So give. What's bothering you? What do you think is wrong?" Sharon sat forward in her chair, eagerly waiting. "Who wants to work? Give."

"She just said the strangest thing." Rose absently tossed her pen on the desk. "She said she trusted me. Always has since we were little girls. And her kids love me, which I knew, because hell, I love them. But the last few years when I would visit, Kath and her husband always seemed to be drifting apart, you know? And then when she was here, we were sitting on the couch. The kids were asleep and we were having a glass of wine. She said she knew Desmond was into something."

"Into something? Like what?"

"She didn't or wouldn't say. I thought the wine would loosen her up, but it only made me tipsy."

"That's because you're a lightweight. So she didn't say anything else?"

"Only that she made some changes and would let me know soon. Whatever that meant."

"Changes in what?"

"I don't know."

"Hmm. I can see being so vague how that would be disconcerting. How did her husband die again?"

"Car accident. It was late and they think he was drinking, and the car skidded and hit a stone wall, then crashed over a cliff."

"Do you think someone, like, ya know…?"

"Oh, God, no. If you've ever been to Ireland, especially where they live, the roads are so narrow, and it's scary how close you drive to the edge of some of those stone walls. I'm surprised there aren't more accidents like that. It was just tragic." Rose shrugged and sighed deeply. "Oh, well. At least Kath has the kids and Aunt Vivian. I think I'll talk to her and go there before November. Maybe we can take a train to Dublin and have a little adventure."

"That's a great idea. Give them something new. Do they love a good adventure as much as their cousin Rose?"

Rose laughed along with Sharon. "Yes, they do. I do love a good adventure."

"You're a kid at heart, that's why. So shouldn't we be getting back to work? You called me in here for a reason."

"Oh, skip it. We'll do it tomorrow. I can't get into these reports right now. If I read one more Excel spreadsheet, I'll scream. You can leave early. Go ahead."

"Great, thanks. I have an apartment to look at."

"Oh, you're still looking?"

"Yes. You know how I hate my place. And I refuse to spend money on good furniture when I'm looking for something better. The only thing good about it, it was furnished, as meager as it is. I want something closer in the city. It's just too long of a drive from the burbs."

"I wish there was something for rent in my building. They're small but cozy. And you know me, I don't need much. Just the extra room when my family comes to visit."

"This is true. I've known you for five years, and you've never purchased anything new. What's up with that?"

Rose laughed. "I don't know. I'm content with what I have."

"Which isn't much."

"Well, like I said, I don't need much. Now get out of here before I change my mind and make you muddle over these spread—"

Sharon was already out the door.

After a tedious afternoon of ridiculous spreadsheets, Rose

finally got home. She kicked off her shoes at the front door of her second-floor apartment.

"Ah, relief." She sighed and leafed through her copious amounts of mail. "Junk, junk, junk. ComEd, gotta keep that one. Don't want them to turn off the electricity."

She walked to the kitchen and tossed the junk mail in the trash and the bills on the table. Then she opened the kitchen window slightly, letting in the summer fresh air. She took a whiff and smiled. "Love the summer in Chicago."

She unbuttoned her blouse, then unzipped her slacks as she made her way to the bedroom. She slipped into her favorite pair of shorts and Cubs T-shirt and barefooted it back to the kitchen; she opened the refrigerator, realizing she hadn't gone shopping this week.

"Okay, Chinese it is," she said. "Last night was pizza."

The delivery boy was very glad to see her; that concerned her. Did she eat out that much? She gathered her feast, a bottle of water, and settled on the couch. With TV tuner in hand, she put her feet up, ready to spend the next few hours catching up on the latest episodes of *Castle* and whatever British mystery on PBS she missed.

"A good English whodunit and a fun murder if there is such a thing," she said, plucking the dumpling out of the box with the chopsticks. "Maybe Sharon is right. I should go somewhere warm and have wild sex." She dipped the steamed appetizer in the spicy sauce first. This is something they really don't have in Trahern, Ireland, she thought, savoring the bite.

It dawned on her that she hadn't had a real date in over six months, even longer for wild sex. When did that happen? She used to go out all the time. Visit the local pubs and bars with friends and have a great time. Sometimes she'd meet a nice woman and sometimes not. Her mind wandered back to the woman she met while jogging along Montrose Beach. That was a steamy month, then poof, the woman, what was her name? Lee? Lydia? Rose shrugged. She was gone as quickly as she came into Rose's life.

"And when in the hell did I become forty-eight?" she said to the TV. She dug into the box of shrimp lo mein, pulling out the chopsticks full of noodles.

Three hours later, she woke up in the dark with only the TV illuminating the living room. She groaned and gathered the Chinese remnants, putting them in the refrigerator, then headed to the shower.

"I need to cut my hair," she said, looking at her reflection in the mirror. "And maybe another rinse to cover the gray." Her shoulder-length brown hair had streaks of gray once again. She looked closer at her hazel eyes, which were bloodshot. She lightly slapped her cheeks to make them rosy, then saw the new laugh lines at the corner of her eyes and waved disgustingly at the mirror. "Hit the shower, then hit the sack, Culhane."

After the shower, she slipped naked beneath the sheet, letting out a contented sigh while trying to ignore her vertebrae creaking as she stretched.

As she drifted off to sleep, Kathleen's words echoed through her mind. *He's into something. I've made some changes, and I'll let ya know, Rose.*

Rose fell asleep hearing her cousin's soft Irish brogue.

She had no idea how long her cell had been ringing or what time it was. She bolted up and grabbed at her cellphone on the nightstand. "Hello?" she mumbled, looking at the clock. It was three a.m.

"Rose? It's Aunt Vivian."

Rose tried to wake up; her racing heart helped. "Aunt Vivian? Hi. What's wrong?" She tried to think of the time difference. It was nearly nine in the morning there. When she heard Vivian sniff as if she were crying, Rose jumped out of bed. "Aunt Vivian?"

"It's Kathleen," she said, trying not to sob.

"What? What?" Rose frantically reached for the light on her nightstand; she fumbled with the switch and turned it on.

"She's dead, Rose. An accident, the police are sayin'."

"What?" Rose nearly screamed. "That... How?" Her mind raced, as well as her heart. She felt nauseated and swallowed back the urge to vomit.

"It was the same as Desmond," Aunt Vivian whispered into the phone. "The same way." Then she let out a sob. "The children are so upset."

Rose frantically ran her fingers through her hair as she looked around her bedroom. "I'll get a flight out as soon as I can and I'll let you know. I'll call you back. Oh, Aunt Vivian, this is…I can't believe it." Rose sat on the edge of the bed and cried, along with Vivian.

"I know, darlin'. I know. Just please get here as soon as ya can. That Quigley woman is here now."

Rose wiped her eyes. "She's there?"

"Yes," Vivian said. "She's the one who found Kathleen."

All sorts of scenarios ran rampant through Rose's brain. "I'm so sorry. Please try to keep everything together until I get there."

"I will, darlin'. Just hurry. This is so heartbreaking."

Rose tried not to break down again. "I know. I'll be there soon. I love you. Take care of the kids."

"I love you, too."

Rose didn't care about the price; she called and booked the next nonstop flight to Ireland. She called Sharon and left a message, explaining as best she could. She showered, threw clothes in a suitcase, closed up her apartment, and in thirty minutes, she was in a cab headed for O'Hare Airport. She didn't have time to think of what happened; she tried to keep a logical thought as she ran though the airport to her gate.

As she buckled her seat belt, she looked out into the darkness of the early morning. The sun had not even risen, and Rose's day had begun—and her life forever changed.

15

Chapter 3

Rose touched down in Ireland, grabbed her luggage, rented a car, and was on her way. And exhausted. She tried to sleep on the seven-hour flight, but her mind wouldn't let her; she had cried off and on the entire time. She glanced at the countryside as she drove. The sun was shining, and it was unseasonably warm for Ireland. Since she got the phone call from Vivian, Rose's mind had been in a tailspin. Looking at her watch once again, she knew it was a three-hour drive; there was no quick way to get to the house. She had thought of flying into Londonderry or Belfast, but with no direct flights, she knew she'd be in the air for at least a year. So she opted for the safest route. Her reliable way, the way she always flew on her vacations to see Kathleen and her family.

Tears welled in her eyes as she remembered all the years of traveling back and forth. One year, she'd go to Ireland, then the next, Kathleen would come to the States.

How could this have happened? she thought as she drove, too fast, down the narrow roads north toward County Donegal and the village of Trahern. Her next thought was of Donal and Caitlin.

"Oh, those poor kids," she said, trying once again not to cry and not drive too fast. What would happen now? And then, Meghan Quigley's name invaded her thoughts. Who was this woman and what did she have to do with whatever happened?

She obviously had some connection with Kathleen if she was at the house right now. Why did the idea of Meghan Quigley worry her? She only wished Kathleen would have confided in her more in recent weeks. As she got closer to the house, the sun was setting over the Atlantic, and with all this, Rose had forgotten how ruggedly beautiful the west of Ireland was. Though now, it seemed to lose its magic. Rose reached up and wiped the tears from her eyes and tried desperately to concentrate on the narrow roads. When she got within a mile or so of Peacock Walk, she saw it. The yellow tape cordoning off an area of stone wall on the curve of the road. As she slowed down, she noticed a lone police car and two young uniformed officers standing guard over the skid marks and the remnants of broken glass; her stomach began to churn.

When Rose stopped, they walked over to her car.

"I'm sorry, ma'am, but you'll have to move along."

"I understand. Is...is this from the accident this morning?"

They both leaned down, shining their flashlights in her face. She held her hand up to shield the light. "If it is, I'm Rose Culhane. Kathleen Flaherty is my cousin. My aunt called me this morning."

"You're a Culhane? Yes, ma'am. It 'tis. I'm very sorry."

"Is there anything you can tell me?" Rose felt like vomiting when she saw the stones all over the road where Kathleen's car must have hit the wall.

"Just that we suspect she lost control. It was a bad storm, windy and rainin' early this mornin'. That's all I know. I'm sorry."

"Was it an accident?"

"Yes, Miss Culhane."

Rose looked at the yellow tape. "Then why do you have the tape up?"

The officer looked behind him. "Just procedure. They were investigating most of the day, miss. They just came and took the car away a little while ago, but there's a lot of broken glass everywhere. We don't want any more accidents."

"I understand. Thank you," Rose said and slowly pulled away.

She was sick to her stomach at the idea of Kathleen dying like that, just as Desmond had a year before. And if she was not mistaken, his car had crashed somewhere in the same vicinity. When she saw the familiar old sign *Peacock Walk* and underneath

Private Road No Trespassing, the ache in her heart was so palpable, she caught her breath. She turned onto the narrow gravel tree-lined road and slowly drove to the house. And while she wanted so badly to see the children, she dreaded and hated the reason for being here.

In the clearing, the old two-story Georgian house came into view. She stopped for a moment and looked at the familiar gray-bricked home she visited all her life. Well, that wasn't entirely true. When she was a child, it was just too expensive, and her father was too proud to let his brother pay for them. Once, maybe twice, but that was all. It wasn't until he was dying did her father, Daniel Culhane, allow his brother, Jeremiah, to pay for their airfare for one last visit. Rose's mother had died years before, and she supposed her father wanted one last look at the home of his childhood.

Taking a deep pensive breath, she drove up on the circular driveway, hearing the familiar crunch of the gravel under her tires as she parked near the front door. The old brass porch lights illuminated the large stone stairs, welcoming her as they always had. She sat for a moment, collected her resolve, and looked through the floor-to-ceiling windows to see Vivian sitting in the big chair. She looked so much older than the last time Rose was here. She noticed Vivian look up when she heard Rose's car door slam and met her at the big wooden door.

"Rose," she said with a sob and pulled her into her arms, not wanting to let go.

"Aunt Vivian," Rose said, crying, as well. She too held on to Vivian, who smelled of perfume and the heady aroma of the ubiquitous peat fire; it was familiar and comforting, just as it was when she was a girl. Rose hung on and sobbed into her shoulder.

Vivian pulled back. "All right now. Enough of the cryin'. We've got the little ones to think about."

Rose nodded and wiped away the tears. "How are you holding up?"

"I'm fine. Just so incredibly tired and sad. One suitcase?"

Rose laughed sadly. "I just threw it together. I have no idea what's in there. I don't even remember packing it."

"Well, you and Kath are the same size, if ya need anything. Come now, let's get off the porch."

Rose followed her into the foyer; she smiled at the old furniture Kath didn't want to get rid of. A lot of memories and family in the mahogany bookcase in the foyer and the deacon's bench opposite that. The double doors to the library across the hall were closed now; the vision of Rose as a little girl peeking into the room flashed through her mind. Vivian took her jacket and hung it on the old coatrack by the door.

"Are the kids sleeping?" Rose asked, following Vivian into the living room. Even though it was summer, there was a chill in the air. Vivian had the enormous fireplace glowing with peat.

"Yes. They wanted to wait for ya, but they just couldn't last, poor darlin's," Vivian said. "You must be starving."

"I'm fine. Sit down, Aunt Vivian. Please tell me exactly what happened."

Vivian eased back into her chair; Rose watched her with concern. Her stone-white hair was always in place; her watery blue eyes sparkled from the tears she had shed all day. She wore the wool slacks and Irish knit sweater, making her look like a typical country estate owner. "You look so tired."

Vivian smiled. "I'm fine now, don't bother." She took a deep breath and let it out slowly, as if giving her time to collect her thoughts. "This mornin', about seven, I was just up and makin' tea when the phone rang. It was Meghan Quigley. She said Kathleen had been in an accident." Vivian looked right at Rose. "I didn't even know she was out of the house."

"What do you mean?"

"The night before, she put the children to bed, and we sat right here. I read as usual, and Kathleen was on the phone. I didn't know with who. I went off to bed around nine, and she said she would lock up and come up in a while." She swallowed her tears. "The last thing she said was she loved me, and I said the same. As we always did." Vivian stared at the fire looking deep in thought. She cleared her throat and continued. "So Meghan said she called the police, and she would stay there until they arrived. My mind was on the children. I had no idea what in the world to tell them.

It was over an hour before the police and Meghan came here and told me she must have lost control of the car. It was windy and storming, and she more than likely hit that stone wall about a mile or so down the road." She looked at Rose then. "Just like Desmond."

Rose nodded, trying to take all this in. "Where is…Kath now?"

"They took her to the medical examiner in Donegal. I suppose they want to make sure there's nothin' more to it than an accident. I had to go and…make sure it was Kathleen."

"Aunt Vivian, I'm so sorry. I wish I could have been here sooner."

"Nonsense. You came as quick as you could. Meghan Quigley took me. It was kind of her. Such a tragedy. I finally told the children. It was horrible, Rose. I wanted to wait and tell them when you arrived, but it would just be unkind to make them wait. They saw the police who were comin' and goin' all morning."

Rose reached over and took her weathered hand. "I feel so bad for those kids."

Vivian nodded. "Caitlin is so young, and Donal is just withdrawing. I could see it in his eyes as I talked to him. His wall went up, then he cried and sat with Caitlin all day. They're sleeping in the same bed right now. Oh, then I called Sorcha."

"I haven't seen her since…"

Vivian snorted rudely. "She only shows up when someone dies. You can say it."

Rose chuckled. "Aunt Vivian."

"Oh, it's true. She's an old biddy and a distant relative, but a relative just the same."

"I remember Mom getting mad at me when I couldn't pronounce her name."

Vivian giggled. "You mangled it, for sure. When you called her Scorcha, I thought I would wet meself."

Rose laughed then. "The Gaelic pronunciation is ridiculous. Mom made me say it over and over. Surika, Surika…God, I used to say it in my sleep. I thought I'd go crazy."

"She said she would be here for the wake. So start practicing again."

"Well, we don't have many relatives," Rose said tiredly.

Vivian nodded. "Oh, I called Desmond's brother, Brendan. You remember him."

"Yes. Isn't he in London or something?"

"He is. Said he would come here in a day or two for the funeral."

Rose closed her eyes, fighting the tears, as she had all day. She was exhausted. "Where is this Meghan Quigley now?"

"She left about an hour ago. She was going to stop at the police in Donegal, then head home. Said she'd be back in the morning."

"What is she doing here?"

"I'm not sure. She showed up here almost four months ago or so. She and Kathleen have been discussing something since, but Kathleen wouldn't tell me. They were thick as thieves those two but seemed to get along well."

"She mentioned Meghan Quigley to me, too, but was very vague. I wish she would have confided in me, as well."

"Every time I asked, she would smile and kiss my forehead." Vivian grunted angrily. "And ya just know how much I love to be treated like an old woman."

Rose hid her grin. "Well, you are…"

Vivian shot her an angry look, then she laughed along with Rose. "Hush now. Don't sass me. Ya get that from your father." She stood with a deep groan. "Come on with ya. Let's get you something to eat."

Normally, Rose would argue, but right now, she knew Vivian needed to keep busy, and truthfully, she was starving.

She sat at the long wooden table, affectionately running her fingers over the top, feeling every nick and every line carved where someone had cut a slice of bread without the breadboard and Aunt Vivian would scold and shoo them out of the kitchen. Vivian took out the leg of lamb and the loaf of homemade bread.

"Don't you ever go to the store?"

"Why? When I can make better bread than they sell in the store? And Mr. Murphy keeps bringin' me lamb."

"Well, that was the deal he made with Kathleen. She allowed

his sheep to graze in the fields free of charge, and in return, you get lamb and goat cheese. Seems fair."

"Yes, it does. He's got himself a fine business with the cheese and the goat's milk. The restaurants in the bigger cities love him." She cut a thick slice of lamb, then two pieces of bread. She then set the plate in front of Rose. "Hmm," she said and got a bottle of sherry. "I think we could both use a wee bit." She poured two small glasses. "Not too much, I'm dead on me feet already."

Rose ate the sandwich, realizing how hungry she was. Afterward, she sipped the wine, which immediately warmed her to her toes. And now, like Vivian, she was exhausted.

"What happens now?" Rose gazed out the window into the darkness.

"I don't know, darlin'. How long can you stay?"

"I'll stay as long as I'm needed. I don't care about anything right now but those children."

"I'm glad to hear ya say that. Now your room is ready for ya. Go take yourself a nice long bath. I left a robe in there for ya. Then have a good night's sleep. We'll gather our thoughts in the mornin'."

Rose put the plate and glasses in the sink and followed Vivian down the hall. Rose locked the door, turned out the lights, and retrieved her suitcase. They walked side by side up the old mahogany staircase. At the landing, Vivian turned to her, pulling her once again into a fierce hug.

"Good night, Rose. I'm so glad you're here."

"I am, too, Aunt Vivian."

"You have a good rest, and we'll tackle the day." Vivian patted her cheek.

"And I want to meet this Meghan Quigley and find out what her deal is."

"Deal?"

Rose laughed at the confused look. "What she's up to."

"Ah, yes. I'm curious, as well. But she seems like a very nice woman. And Kathleen trusted her."

"Yeah, well, we'll see. G'night," Rose said, kissing her cheek. "I love you."

"I love you, too."

"I'm just going to look in on the kids," she said.

Rose quietly opened the bedroom door; the light from the hallway illuminated their sleeping faces. Her heart broke when she saw Caitlin cuddling her stuffed bunny while she slept close to Donal, who in his sleep frowned deeply. She wanted to go in and kiss the life out of both of them, but she knew there would be time for that later. For now, she quietly closed the door.

Rose set her suitcase on the chair. She laughed ruefully when she opened the suitcase. A couple of sweaters, jeans, socks, and underwear, practically her entire wardrobe—which pathetically fit in one suitcase—that she had grabbed out of the drawers in haste. "Good grief."

She crept down the hall to the bathroom and sighed when she saw the old claw-footed bathtub. Steam rose from the hot water as she eased into the old tub. She put her head back and sighed once again; for a moment, all her aches faded away, and for that moment, she felt peace.

In the back of her mind, she had a feeling that peace would not last long.

Chapter 4

Rose had a restless night, as she knew she would. She tossed and turned throughout. And she knew it was not the jet lag or the bed, which was extremely comfortable with the eiderdown comforter and pillows. Finally, she fell asleep around three, so when she woke with a start at seven, she did feel rested but disoriented. When she realized where she was and the reason, her heart grew sad once again. She quickly showered and dressed. Heading downstairs, she heard no sounds of anyone being up.

She made a pot of coffee on the stovetop. Aunt Vivian did not own a coffeemaker. Then she relit the peat fire in the kitchen fireplace to take the chill off the room. As she waited for the coffee to brew, she looked out at the foggy morning. By ten or so, the sun would have burned off the fog—unless it was going to rain, which could happen at any moment no matter what the forecast.

It was then she heard the sound of tires on the gravel drive out front. And immediately, she heard the peacocks screeching, another familiar sound from her youth. The peacocks always scared her. They put up some squawk whenever anyone came close to the house as if they were protecting the property, but truthfully, they were just annoying because they didn't like people. Or maybe they just didn't like Rose.

"Crazy birds." She ran to the living room just in time to see a Land Rover with mud splattered all over it pull up next to her rental. Rose held her breath as she waited to see who it was.

When a woman got out of the car, Rose knew it must be Meghan Quigley. She watched this woman as she looked over the rental car. Rose took in her appearance: she wore jeans, hiking boots, and an Irish sweater with the sleeves pushed up. She had her curly jet-black hair styled a little shorter than Rose's shoulder-length. Her complexion was typical Irish—alabaster white with rosy cheeks. Rose noticed her frowning expression; she looked tired.

Rose then lost sight of her when she mounted the porch stairs. She waited for the soft knock, then took a deep breath and opened the door. Rose was not prepared for the smiling blue eyes that greeted her. Nor was she prepared for the fluttering in her chest when she looked into those eyes. For a moment, she just stared at her, and the woman seemed to do the same.

"You must be Rose?" she finally asked in a soft but thick Irish brogue.

"Yes." Rose thought she noticed a look of surprise on this woman's face as she held out her hand.

"I'm Meghan Quigley, a friend of Kathleen's. I'm sorry. I don't mean to stare. It's just that Kathleen described you perfectly."

Rose shook her hand, which Meghan held on to for a moment longer. Rose eased her hand away. "Yes, I've heard of you." She didn't mean to sound so suspicious, but she was caught off guard, and there was just far too much she didn't know about Meghan. And she didn't want to be distracted by the compliment, if it was a compliment.

Meghan raised an eyebrow. "May I come in?"

"Oh, I'm sorry. Certainly." She backed up, allowing Meghan into the foyer.

"I told Vivian last night I'd stop by. I hope I'm not too early. I hesitated, but I saw the peat smoke from the fireplace, so I figured someone was up."

"No, not at all. I was just making coffee," Rose said, leading her to the kitchen. "No one is up yet. I'm hoping they get some rest."

"And you? Have you rested?"

Rose offered her a chair at the table. "Yes. Thank you." She took two cups out of the cupboard along with the sugar. The cream she found in the refrigerator. "And I have to thank you,

Miss Quigley, for taking my aunt into Donegal. That had to be difficult for both of you."

"I couldn't let her go alone. I'm-I'm very sorry about Kathleen."

The compassion in Meghan's voice had Rose fighting back tears once again. She found it difficult to speak; she merely nodded her thanks.

"Must have been an exhausting day." Meghan accepted the cup of coffee with a tentative smile as Rose poured.

"It was. And very sad." Rose sat opposite Meghan. "It must have been hard for you, too. To find my cousin."

Meghan frowned as she poured cream into her coffee. "It was."

"Seems strange you being out there early in the morning. Do you live nearby?"

Meghan looked up, searching Rose's face. "No, not really. I live in Sligo. Ya know, Yeats country. But everything seems nearby in Ireland. I understand you're from Chicago?"

"Yes," Rose said. Nice turn of topic, she thought. "But my family is from here."

"Right. Kathleen told me. The Culhane family is very close-knit."

"Can we get back to the topic?"

"Which was?"

"How you found my cousin early in the morning. Not living in the area, it's curious how you were here."

A dark look shrouded Meghan's face. "I only wish I was here sooner. This might not have happened."

"How could you stop an accident? From what I understand, it was a bad storm, raining and windy. Did you have a difficult time driving?"

"Rose…may I call you Rose?"

"Certainly."

"Rose, I hear a distinct accusatory tone."

Rose drank her coffee. "I'm just having a difficult time with this, Miss Quigley."

"Meghan, please. And I don't blame ya in the least. I know

how close you were with Kathleen and the children. I'm sure you must be devastated."

"You see, that's what I mean. You sound like you're very familiar with my family. And the last time I spoke with Kathleen, you were just someone that showed up on her doorstep."

Meghan again searched her face. "And what else did she tell you?"

"Why?" Rose leaned forward. "What else is there to tell?" When she saw the hurt look on Meghan's face, she sat back, calming her anger. "I'm sorry. I'm not angry with you, Meghan. It's just so sudden and tragic. I just talked with Kathleen three weeks ago. She told me she trusted you, and she had made changes that she'd tell me about soon. Do you know what changes she was talking about?"

Meghan shook her head. "I honestly don't. But at some point, we do need to talk. I know this is horribly sad, and it's not the right time." She stopped and ran her fingers across her brow. "There's so much you're thrown into right now. Perhaps after, well, in a couple days, we'll have a chance to talk."

"You sound so mysterious. Just like Kathleen."

"And I don't mean to be. I—"

"Well, good morning," Vivian said softly from the doorway. "I thought I smelled coffee. Good morning, Miss Quigley."

"Good morning."

"I see you two have met." Vivian looked from Rose to Meghan.

Rose was angry and now confused, and she knew her face showed it. "Oh, yes. We've met," Rose said. "G'morning, Aunt Vivian. Coffee?" When Vivian pulled a sour face, Rose laughed. "I'll put on the kettle."

Vivian sat at the head of the table. "I checked on the children. The poor things are still asleep."

"It's best for them," Meghan said.

Rose set the copper teapot on the stove but said nothing.

"It's a horrible thing," Meghan continued.

"Yes, it is," Vivian said sadly. "And as much sleep as I got, I'm still exhausted. How are you, Rose? No jet lag?"

"No. I slept just fine," she said over her shoulder.

"So I wonder what happens next," Vivian said. "Thank you, Rose."

Rose set the brown bread on the table, along with the butter and jam. Meghan held up her cup.

"May I?"

Without a word, Rose refilled her empty cup. She caught Vivian's raised eyebrow. The kettle started to whistle angrily, mirroring Rose's state of mind at the moment. She prepared the pot of tea, retrieved a cup and saucer, and placed them on the table.

"It's not every day when an American can make a proper pot of tea," Meghan said.

"Oh, Rose has had a lifetime of experience." She winked at Rose, who smiled and kissed her on the side of the head. Vivian reached up and held her hand. "I'm so glad you're here."

"I am, too." Rose no sooner sat down than they heard Donal and Caitlin running down the stairs. Rose's heart was in her throat wondering what to say to them. They were still in pajamas, hair disheveled and barefoot—Rose never saw anything so wonderful in her life.

When they came into the kitchen and saw her, they both ran to her. Rose opened her arms, and Caitlin launched herself onto her lap.

"Rose!" she cried and hugged her around the neck.

Donal hugged her, as well. It saddened Rose to see tears in his eyes.

"Donal," she whispered, trying not to cry. She reached up to cup his face. "I'm so sorry, honey."

He nodded, his bottom lip quivering. He looked down at Caitlin and put his hand on her red head.

"Mam's gone," Caitlin whispered to Rose.

"I know, sweetie," Rose said, sniffing back her tears. "I'm so sorry. I'm here now. And we'll all get through this, I promise."

Donal nodded again, then he threw his arms around her neck and held on tight as he sobbed. Poor Caitlin, seeing her brother crying, cried, as well, burying her head against Rose's chest. She silently rocked them, murmuring words of love and reassurance. She looked over at Vivian, seeing her wipe away the tears that streamed down her face. What shocked her was Meghan Quigley's reaction. Rose saw the tears well in her blue eyes, as well. Her face was beet red from the effort, Rose thought, not to cry.

Meghan cleared her throat and stood. "I'd better be on my way. I just wanted to stop by and check in on everyone." She looked at Rose and smiled slightly before regarding Vivian. "You'll call me if you need anything."

"I will. Thank you for all you've done," Vivian said. "I'll be in touch with you when we…"

Meghan nodded. "I know. I'll stop by now and then, if that's all right."

"Of course. I know this had to be hard on you, as well, Ms. Quigley."

"Meghan, please. Well…" She looked at Rose. "I'll see ya soon. I'm very sorry. I'll let myself out."

As she clung to Donal and Caitlin, Rose watched Meghan as she walked out of the kitchen; she wanted to reassure her, as well, but she didn't—she wasn't at all sure that Meghan Quigley wasn't involved somehow, if there was indeed something.

It was all so confusing to Rose, and though she wasn't sure— she would find out.

Chapter 5

"Well," Rose said, clearing the breakfast dishes. "Let's go for a walk and find the peacocks. They've been squawking up a storm ever since Meghan pulled up. I've missed them."

Caitlin wiped her face on the napkin and jumped off her chair. "I have to get dressed." She ran out of the kitchen and up the stairs.

Donal helped Rose by putting the plates in the sink. They stood side by side; Donal reached over and held Rose's hand. "What are we going to do now?"

Rose put her arm around his shoulders. "We take it a day at a time. And you must tell me what you're thinking and feeling. Always. Whenever you want, you know I'm here for you and Cait." She looked down into his blue eyes, seeing so much pain and something else, Rose thought—hesitation, as if he wanted to say something but held back. "Anytime," she whispered and pulled him closer.

"I will," he whispered, then pulled back. "What do you think of Meghan?"

"Well, I don't know her at all."

"I like her," he said with a shrug.

"That's good. And I'm sure once I get to know her, I will, too," Rose said, washing the dishes. "I wash, you dry?"

Donal picked up a towel. "Mam liked her. They talked all the time."

"About what?" Rose asked absently.

"Da mostly," he said with a shrug.

Rose handed him another plate. "They talked about your dad?"

Donal nodded. "Mam was mostly upset when they'd talk. She'd always tell me to go and play, so I never heard much."

Rose glanced at him; he had a faraway look as he dried the dish. "I know it's tough when you want to be treated like a fourteen-year-old…"

"And ya get treated like you were Caitlin's age. I know she didn't mean it. I even heard Meghan tell Mam she should talk to me. But she never did." He put the plate on the table but didn't turn back to Rose. "I know she was probably protectin' me."

Rose dried her hands and watched him. He hung his head; when she saw his shoulders sag, she wanted to hold him like she used to when he was a baby. Instead, she placed a hand on his shoulder. "It's so hard for you. I can't imagine going through what you kids have to deal with. But you know I'm here. Always."

"But you'll go back to the States," he said softly, still not looking at her.

"Let's not think of that right now. I'm here, and we'll get through this."

"I'm ready!" Caitlin announced as she walked into the kitchen.

Donal laughed and rolled his eyes.

"I know. She's a kid," Rose whispered.

Donal nodded emphatically.

"Dishes can wait," Rose said, taking the towel from Donal. "Let's go exploring."

On the way out, Rose found Vivian in the living room reading. "We're goin' esplorin', Auntie," Caitlin said.

"Are ya now?" Vivian looked over her reading glasses. "Well, you explorers have a good time. Ya might want to bring an umbrella, looks like rain."

"Oh, explorers don't use umbrellas, Aunt Vivian," Donal said in manly fashion.

"They do if they want to keep dry," she replied, turning a page in the book.

Rose had to admit the peacocks were beautiful. They ran and skittered away as she and the kids walked toward them. Well, Caitlin ran after them. It was amazing how these birds would congregate around the front and side of the house, just wandering and foraging for food. Rose always thought it was so funny when people came to the house; they'd see the beautiful peacocks but never made the attempt to pet or go to them. Something about a peacock—they were beautiful to look at but always seemed aloof, if a bird could be aloof. Once in a while, the male would spread his beautiful feathers and strut his stuff, but that was it.

They could still hear them squawking as they walked from the house. The gray clouds drifted in as they walked around the property of almost forty acres of green rolling hills dotted by Mr. Murphy's sheep; the low stone walls leading nowhere in particular gave it that definitive Irish look. In the distance, a grove of oak trees gave the family cemetery shade and a sense of peacefulness.

Donal had given Rose a walking stick he found; she absently hit the ground as she walked, watching both children climb the rock walls. She was happy to hear them laughing, if only for a little while, and dreaded the time of Kathleen's funeral.

Last year was hard enough when Desmond died. Now with their mother gone, Rose couldn't imagine what was going through their minds, especially Donal's. There was something there, Rose was sure of it. But it was far too soon to pressure or ask him. He said he liked Meghan and that Kath liked her, as well.

"Rose!"

The sound of Caitlin's happy voice brought a smile to her face. "What?"

"Mr. Murphy's here!"

Rose looked beyond them to see the old man waving and smiling, and right behind him was his sheep dog Salty, the black and white border collie. With a couple of whistles, the dog herded the sheep up the rolling hill. By the time Rose got to them, Salty had chased them almost out of sight.

"Mr. Murphy," Rose said. "It's good to see you again."

He took off his cap and shook her hand. "And the same to you, but I'm sick about the reason, miss."

Rose's smile faded as she watched Caitlin and Donal follow Salty up the hill. "Don't go too... Oh, what am I saying? Let 'em run."

"How are they farin'?" he asked as he too watched them. "Poor darlin's."

"They're still in shock, I'm sure. So much tragedy in their young lives."

"Too true. But it's good you're here now for them. Did ya happen to meet the Quigley woman?"

"I did. She came by this morning. What do you know about her? I heard so little from my cousin."

Mr. Murphy shrugged as they walked toward the hill. "Not much. Seems like a nice woman. Educated as well. Went to a big fancy school in Dublin, I hear. She's been around for a few months or more. Some say snoopin', but ya hear that from the old crows in the village."

"Snooping around Trahern? Why?"

"Oh, I don't think it's anything to worry about. She's just tryin' to get acquainted, I suppose."

"Hmm. Well, Kathleen liked her. So does Donal."

"Yes, she and Donal have become fast friends, which as it turns out, could be a good thing," he said sadly.

"Yes, it could be," Rose said. "I hope it is."

Mr. Murphy stopped and wagged his finger in her direction. "None of that now. You'll be soundin' like the rest of them."

Rose laughed. "You're right."

"Well, I'd better get to the sheep before they're scattered all over Donegal."

"I'd better do the same with the kids. Have Salty herd them back here, will you?"

As if they heard them, Caitlin and Donal ran over the hill.

"Speak of the devil," Mr. Murphy said. "Well, I'll be gettin' back. If you need anything at all, you come get me. Tell Vivian I'll have some goat cheese by the end of the week for her."

"I will, Mr. Murphy. Thanks."

He ruffled Donal's hair as he passed and gave Caitlin's red head a kiss before he went on his way.

With a clap of thunder, Rose looked skyward. "That figures. Looks like we should have brought the umbrella. Let's get back before it starts. I don't want to hear 'I told ya so' from Aunt Vivian." The rain started one big drop at a time. "Last one home is an old maid."

Rose took off with both children right beside her. By the time they got to the house, it was pouring, and all three of them were soaked and laughing as if they hadn't a care in the world. Rose truly wanted to bottle that feeling.

"I won," Caitlin said.

"Ya did not." Donal shook his wet head. "I did."

"Well, I know I was last," Rose said, running her fingers through her wet hair. "So I guess I'm the old maid." She reached for the door, but it was already open.

Meghan Quigley smiled. "You're too hard on yourself."

Caitlin giggled along with Donal, both scooting by after a happy hello to Meghan.

"Wipe your feet," Rose called to them.

Meghan stepped away to allow Rose inside. "We should have taken my aunt's advice about the umbrella. As many times as I've been here, I'm always caught off guard by how quickly the weather changes." Rose knew she was rambling; she had no choice. Meghan smiled but remained silent while she helped Rose with her wet jacket.

"Thank you." Rose caught Meghan glancing at her breasts; she quickly turned her back. "I'd better go change. I'll be right down."

"Rose, there's an inspector in the parlor," Meghan said.

Rose turned back. "Police? What does he want?"

"He called me earlier," Meghan said, looking into Rose's eyes. "Said he had a few things to discuss. I said I would meet him here. I hope ya don't mind."

"Oh, no. Of course not. Thank you."

"Would it be all right if I put the kettle on?" Meghan asked.

For some reason, her soft voice sent a chill through Rose, and she knew it wasn't from the dampness. "Certainly."

When Meghan turned, Rose put her hand out to stop her. "Meghan, I'm sure Kathleen wanted you to feel at home here. So, please, I hope you still do. I-I'd like you to."

"Thank you. That means a great deal to me."

For a moment, they continued to look at each other until Rose shivered.

"You'd best get out of those wet clothes," Meghan said.

"I'll be right down," she said, scampering out of the way.

She dressed in the only other pair of jeans she brought with her and a sweater. She made a mental note to go into Donegal later in the week. As she walked downstairs, she heard a man's voice.

When she walked into the living room, she noticed a deep scowl on Meghan's face, and Aunt Vivian looked as though she was about to faint. The young man turned around when Rose walked up to them.

"Hello," she said, glancing at Meghan.

"This is my niece, Rose Culhane. This is Inspector Russell."

Rose took his offered hand. "How do you do?" she said cautiously.

"Fine, thanks. I was just telling your aunt and Miss Quigley about your cousin's car."

"What about it?" Rose walked over and stood by Vivian. She noticed Meghan now stood facing the window, her hands shoved deep in the pockets of her jeans as she watched the rain.

"Well, the mechanic tells me the brake line might have been tampered with," he said, watching her.

"What?" Rose asked. "Are you saying what I think you're saying?"

Inspector Russell absently scratched the back of his head. "Well, Miss Culhane, all I can do is tell you what I've found. It could be someone cut those lines. Though we have no proof or reason why someone might do that. Do you?"

"No, of course not." Rose looked at Meghan, who still looked out the window.

"When was the last time ya talked with your cousin?" he asked.

"About three weeks ago." Rose still glanced at Meghan.

"And how did she sound?"

Rose gauged her answer. "The last time I talked to Kath, she sounded worried, or maybe preoccupied is a better word. She's been dealing with the death of her husband. It was hard on her and her family." She put her hand on Vivian's shoulder. "I assumed this was an accident. And now you're telling me…"

Russell held up his hand. "I'm not tellin' ya anything just yet. I just want to keep ya informed when we find anything." He glanced down at his notes. "How well did ya know Mr. Flaherty?"

"Desmond? He was my cousin's husband. I knew him as well as I could living in America and only visiting once a year. Why?"

"I'm just gathering information. It's a little coincidental that he died a year ago almost the same way as Mrs. Flaherty. There's nothin' else you might know?"

Again, Rose glanced at Meghan. "No. There's nothing more I know." She saw Meghan's shoulders straighten as she gazed out the window.

"And, Miss Quigley? We have your statement. Anything you care to add or might remember?"

"No, I told ya all I know," Meghan said over her shoulder.

"So are ya saying this was not an accident?" Vivian asked; Rose heard the impatient tone.

"No, ma'am. Like I said, I'm just gatherin' any information I can. They could be wrong about the car. It's an older model. And if Mrs. Flaherty was driving in rough terrain or off road, it's very possible something sharp hit the line, causin' a slow leak of brake fluid." He put the notebook in his breast pocket. "Well, I'll be goin'. If ya think of anything, just give us a call." He handed Rose his card. "I'll be in touch. Good day. I'll let myself out."

Rose watched Meghan in silence until she heard the car pull away.

"Meghan, would you please tell me what statement you gave to them? I've been curious how you came to find Kathleen on the road," Rose asked.

When Meghan turned to face her and Vivian, the tears that rolled down her cheeks stunned Rose. "Meghan, please tell me what you know."

"Yes, I think you're right. I wanted to wait and give you some time. But it's better that we talk now."

Rose felt that sick feeling once again. She only hoped Meghan was right, and now was the time.

Chapter 6

"Let's go into the kitchen," Vivian said, ushering both women.

Meghan sat at the kitchen table along with Vivian sitting once again at the head of the table.

"We'll have a cup of tea and discuss this." Vivian poured the steaming brew into a teacup.

Rose sat opposite Meghan, avoiding her as she stirred the sugar in her tea.

"Before you go on, Meghan, I called the funeral home earlier," Vivian said. "They said they would call me when they released Kathleen's body. We'll make plans then." Vivian's voice faltered as she drank her tea. "She'll be put to rest in the family cemetery."

Rose's chest felt tight while listening to Vivian. She took a drink of tea, hating how her hand shook.

"Kathleen spoke so fondly of you, Rose," Meghan said quietly. "She talked about you all the time."

Rose smiled and nodded. Her throat ached so, she could hardly swallow; she took another sip from the teacup.

"She told me how she loved it when you visited, and when you got your new job, you were able to come at least once a year. She truly loved that time. And loved to come visit you in Chicago."

"You seem to know a good deal about me." Rose looked into her eyes, not knowing what she was looking for. But she did see kindness in Meghan's blue eyes. And she wanted to get the suspicious feeling out of her heart for this woman. Kathleen trusted her—Rose wanted to do the same.

"Kathleen loved you. She loved talkin' about you and how well ya got on with Donal and Cait. You were a good godparent, she'd tell me. And I can see the children love you, as well."

"I do love them. Speaking of them, where are they?" Rose was very conscious of Meghan watching her; it was becoming a little unnerving.

"They're in their rooms. Dryin' off," Vivian added with a touch of sarcasm.

Rose laughed along with both women. "Okay, okay. I should have taken the umbrella."

When the phone rang, Vivian stood. "I'm sure it's for me. Meghan, I've heard this. So you tell Rose what you told the police…"

"She's still so tired," Rose said as Vivian walked out of the kitchen.

"This is taking its toll on everyone," Meghan said, toying with her teacup.

Rose saw the blank look as Meghan absently ran her finger on the rim of the cup. "Meghan, I'm not sure what, if anything, was going on between you and Kathleen."

Meghan took a drink of tea. "She called me that mornin'. She was on her way home and told me she wanted to meet me here. I asked her where she'd been already it bein' so early, but she said she'd tell me. It was rainin' so bad she wanted to get off the phone and I agreed." She laughed sadly. "That's the last thing she wanted, she said, was to have an accident."

They sat in silence for a moment to let that particular irony set in.

"What did you do?"

"I drove here. When I pulled up, I didn't see her Land Rover, so I waited. It seemed like hours. But after a few minutes of waitin', I tried her cell. It went straight to voice mail, and that terrified me. So not knowin' where she was or what direction she'd be comin', I just took the south road first, and that's when I found her. The car was still smokin'. She'd run off the road and hit the stone wall. I called the police, but she was already gone."

"I'm so sorry you had to find her."

"That she was all alone…" Meghan said softly, her bottom lip quivering.

"What was she into?" Rose asked.

Meghan looked up. "Ya believe me?"

"Yes," Rose said, quicker than she thought she would. And she did believe her. "I do. I'm not sure why, but I do."

"You could have told the inspector about the changes that Kathleen said she was makin'. I know you have your suspicions, Rose. Why didn't ya tell him that?"

Rose looked into her eyes and searched her face. She then looked down at her teacup. "I don't know why I trust you. We've only just met, but something tells me that I should. I see a kindness in your eyes that I'm sure Kathleen saw, as well."

"Thank you. I cared for Kathleen. We—"

"I think I've known there was something going on with you and Kathleen."

"What makes ya think there was?"

"Because I know my cousin. She sounded vague and almost confused when we last talked, but she didn't sound like that when she talked about you. It's none of my business what you two were doing and…" She stopped, then blurted out, "She told me you were gay."

Meghan's head jerked up. She looked comically stunned. "What?" Then it dawned on her. "Wait a minute. Ya think I was after your cousin?"

Rose winced at the angry, incredulous tone. "No, of course not. Though, now that you mention it…"

Meghan shook her head. "I was not after Kathleen." She looked as if she just swallowed spoiled milk. "She was a widow with two children, for heaven's sake." She leaned forward then. "And what's more important, Rose Culhane, she wasn't a lesbian."

"I'm sorry…"

"Good grief, woman. What opinion must ya have of me? To think I'd go after…"

"I said I'm sorry," Rose said again. "We're getting off topic."

Meghan's eyes blazed with anger as she went on, "Kathleen told me you were gay. So I suppose ya think now I'm after you, as well?"

"No. I do not," Rose said, astonished. But then she smiled slightly. "Though that would probably make more sense."

For a moment, they looked at each other. Meghan's blue eyes danced with anger.

"Well, I'm not," she said, still angry. "For the love of..."

Rose couldn't help it. What a stupid conversation. She started chuckling. Meghan watched her curiously, as if she were crazy. Then she grinned and started to laugh, as well.

"What an odd thing to talk about amidst all this." Meghan shook her head. She chuckled nervously then. "I'm sorry. Ya just caught me off guard. All right now. Back on topic."

"Yes," Rose said, still watching her. "Back on topic. I just think there was something going on that she wanted to tell me but didn't get the time. That's all I'm saying. And if there was something you wanted to tell me, well, please know you can talk to me. That's all."

"Rose..." She stopped and sat back. "I—"

Vivian came in, halting any further conversation. "That was the funeral home." She sat down, looking so worn out. "They've released Kathleen's body. The wake will be the day after tomorrow and the funeral the next day. Oh, and I called Brendan, Desmond's brother, again to let him know. Brendan said he would come for the funeral. Did I mention that before?"

"Yes. That's kind of him to come from London."

"I told him he could stay here." She reached over and held on to Rose's hand. "I hate to ask this of you, Rose, but we're short on rooms. Would you mind taking Kathleen's room and letting Brendan stay in yours?"

"Of course. I—"

The phone rang again. "For the love of St. Peter," Vivian said, scurrying out of the kitchen once again.

"Have you ever met Desmond's brother?" Meghan asked.

Rose smiled sadly. "Yes. When Des and Kath got married, then when Des died. He seemed like a pleasant enough guy. I think he's a writer or journalist. I remember him saying he left Ireland to pursue this."

Meghan raised an eyebrow. "Ireland, the haven for writers, and he leaves to go to London?"

"I know. That sounded strange when I said it." She looked at Meghan, who looked deep in thought, if her frown was any indication. "So were you about to tell me something when Aunt Vivian interrupted…?"

On cue, Vivian walked into the kitchen once again.

"Ya mean like now?" Meghan asked; a small grin tugged at the corner of her mouth.

Rose grinned but said nothing; she found Meghan's smile very engaging.

"That was Mr. Downey, our family solicitor, lawyer to you, Rose." She grinned and patted her hand. "Apparently, and I never thought of this, we need to hear what's in Kathleen's will after the funeral. She made…" She stopped and looked at Rose with wide eyes. "Rose…"

"How stupid of me not to think of that. She made some changes," Rose whispered and sat back.

"Do ya think that's what she meant?" Meghan asked.

"Possibly. Whatever changes she talked about were changes to her will?"

"I suppose we'll just have to wait until after the funeral to find out."

Chapter 7

The afternoon, thank God, was uneventful, but she and Meghan were never able to really talk. Meghan had been called away; her job, she said. She had things to do, as she put it, but Vivian invited her back for dinner, which Meghan agreed to. So the rest of the day was quiet and rainy. Rose took care of some laundry, put fresh sheets on the beds, and cleaned the bathrooms, not that they needed it. Vivian was a stickler for cleanliness.

Donal and Caitlin spent time in front of the fireplace, staying close to each other. Vivian leafed through the mail, and Rose wandered around the house from room to room, remembering the few times when she was a girl and she and her family would visit. Then, when she was older—and her parents passed away, after Kathleen married, and the kids came—she visited at least once a year. They were happy times. Desmond was hardly around; he was always into something. Always looking for the perfect job or at least the perfect quick fix. It would annoy Kathleen to no end. But somehow, he was always there for birthdays and anniversaries, never forgetting them. But then he was off on something else, gone as quick as he came.

Kathleen had told Rose it was the day to day that frustrated her. But Desmond always seemed to have money. It was then Kathleen realized he was dipping into her inheritance. Nothing major, but a few thousand here and there. Always promising to turn it into more but always falling short. There were times when Rose was torn between feeling sorry for Desmond and hoping for all their sakes he'd pull through and wanting to strangle the life

43

out of him. She could well understand how frustrated Kathleen was. It bothered Rose like nails on a chalkboard, but Kathleen had to live with it every day.

It was in the last couple of years they really hit a wall. She was constantly on the phone with Kathleen, calming her down or just listening to her lament over his "chasin' the rainbow for the pot o' gold." It wasn't that Desmond was neglectful or abusive, he was just self-centered and did not have any type of work ethic. Kathleen said many times, if it wasn't for Peacock Walk and her inheritance, they'd be living like the tinkers—Irish gypsies traveling around in a horse-drawn caravan. Rose thought that was a slight exaggeration, but she got Kathleen's idea.

Though he may have had the gypsy in his soul, Rose didn't think he deserved to die so young. But who knew how long Kathleen would have lived with Desmond the Wanderer, as she called him. Rose remembered how he would argue and say he was more the Wild Colonial Boy from the old song. Kathleen wouldn't give him that credit—at least the Wild Colonial Boy had a purpose, she'd say. Rose thought that was a low blow, and after Kathleen took the time to cool off, she would agree and apologize.

And now? Kathleen was gone, as well. Leaving two kids behind. Rose stood in the living room doorway, watching Donal and Caitlin stare at the fire, their sad faces illuminated by the glowing peat.

"Well, it's time to start supper. Meghan will be back around six, she said. Caitlin, why don't you help your old auntie in the kitchen?" Vivian winked at Rose, who smiled.

Donal nudged Caitlin, who seemed as though she wasn't listening. "Auntie Vivian needs your help with supper."

Caitlin jumped up. "You need my help?"

"Of course I do." Vivian held out her hand, which Caitlin gladly took. "You can tell me all the things I'm doin' wrong."

Rose walked into the living room and sat in the chair by the fire. "Certainly is chilly for June. Must be all this rain."

Donal nodded and sat Indian style, still gazing at the flames. "I love to look at a fire."

"Me too."

"Meghan says if ya look long enough, the flames stand still. I've tried it. Doesn't work."

Rose laughed. "Well, maybe Meghan was, ya know..." She mimicked someone taking a drink and rolled her eyes.

Donal laughed along. "I don't know about that. She's pretty smart, though."

"She is? That's right. Mr. Murphy said she went to school in Dublin."

"Yeah. She went to university and everything. Mam said she had PH something..." He shrugged.

"PhD?" Rose offered.

"That's it. What is that?"

"It means she went to college, and whatever she was studying, she went as far as you could. It's called a doctorate."

"She's a doctor?"

"Well, not a medical doctor but a doctor in the field of whatever she studied. That takes a lot of schoolwork. That's very hard to do and takes a lot of focus and passion in what you're studying." Rose wondered what Meghan did for a profession. Was she a teacher? There were things she didn't know about Meghan, things she wanted to know.

"Do you think she liked Mam?" Donal asked softly.

Now here was the thing. Rose could take this question one of two ways. First, Donal knew she was gay; Kathleen sat him down the year before and told him. Basically because someone at school had made a joke about gays, and Kathleen wanted Donal to understand how important it was not to judge and to be accepting. Rose wasn't sure it was a good idea at the time, but she soon realized she hadn't given her young second cousin enough credit. Donal didn't mind at all when he found out. He almost wore it as a badge of honor; it seemed not too many classmates had an American second cousin who was wealthy and gay—go figure. Rose often wondered where he got the "wealthy" part. But he and Rose had a very good talk after Desmond's funeral. Donal was a bright young boy who had a mind of his own, much like his mother.

So did he know about Meghan? And was that his question? Or did he just want to know if Kathleen liked Meghan in general? Rose gave herself a headache trying to quickly sort all that flashed through her mind.

"Um, Rose? Did I ask something wrong?"

"Oh, no, no, honey. You can ask anything you want about anything and anybody and any…" She felt as if she was heading right for a cliff and couldn't stop. Poor Donal just watched her with the oddest look.

"I mean the same way Meghan would like you," he said.

And there it was…

"No, sweetie. I don't think Meghan liked your mom that way. I think she was just a good friend. That's all." Rose laughed and let out a sigh of relief; her palms were sweaty. "You're too old for me."

"So ya like her?" Donal laughed along with her. "Because Rory at school has an uncle who's gay, but he doesn't have a partner yet. And if you like Meghan and she you, then I'd be the first at school."

"Whoa, whoa, Donal. It's not a competition." She tried to sound logical, all the while she was screaming in her mind to shut up. "You see, when two people—"

He jumped up when someone knocked at the door. "I'll get it."

She sighed and put her head back. "I think I'm having a stroke." She smiled when she heard his cute voice. "What a kid."

"Hi, Meghan. Rose and me were just talkin' about ya. I was wonderin' if you like Rose because I think she might like you. And a friend at school—"

"Oh, shit." Rose jumped out of the chair. "Donal!" She ran to the door to see Meghan standing there with a bottle of wine in her hand, her blues eyes wide and her mouth on the floor. She looked like a statue.

Donal looked from Rose to Meghan. "What?"

"Nothing. Go see if Aunt Vivian needs help," Rose said quickly. When he opened his mouth, Rose clamped her hand over it and pushed him roughly toward the kitchen.

Meghan put her hand up. "Maybe I should leave. He'll have us married in a minute."

"At least leave the wine." Rose laughed and stood back. "You might as well come in. What else could happen?"

Meghan cautiously walked in and looked around.

"What are you doing?"

"Lookin' for the priest," she said. "Or Vivian with a shotgun pointed at me middle."

Rose laughed along with Meghan, who handed her the bottle of wine. After a moment, Rose stopped and cleared her throat. "That's the most I've laughed since all of this happened."

"Laughin' can begin the healing process. It's been my experience anyway," Meghan said. "So…that must have been some talk you had with Donal." She followed Rose into the living room.

"It was enlightening, let's leave it at that."

"He's a smart boyo. Like his mam. And his cousin," she added quietly. She sat by the fire, putting her hands up to warm them. "It may be summer, but the nights are still a little chilly. More with the rain." She frowned, as if she knew she was making small talk.

"Who are you kidding? It's always damp here." Rose grinned, and for a moment, she enjoyed the conversation. "So Donal tells me you have a PhD?"

Meghan looked up. "That boy talks too much."

"Well, somebody has to," Rose said, offering a smug look.

"You're a sarcastic woman, Rose. Kathleen warned me about that. Yes, I'm a geologist." She laughed when Rose's mouth dropped. "What did ya think I was?"

"I have no idea. But a geologist wasn't even on the list. How did you get into that field?"

"My father taught history and archaeology at Trinity. When I was a kid, he used to take me to all the ancient sites around Ireland and the British Isles. It fascinated me, still does, but as I got older, I was more fascinated with the geological side of it."

"Rocks?"

Meghan laughed. "I'd like to think there's a little more to it than that, but yes, rocks."

"Meghan, I thought I heard you," Vivian said with towel in hand. "And wine? Wonderful. Dinner is ready. Hope you're hungry."

"I'm always hungry, Vivian. Thank you."

"Let's eat in the dining room," Vivian said. "We haven't eaten in there since…"

Rose put her arm around Vivian's shoulder. "That's a good idea."

Donal and Caitlin set the table with little arguing. Meghan opened the bottle of wine and poured three glasses.

"Can I have some?" Caitlin asked, leaning her elbows on the table.

"May I have some?" Vivian corrected her. "And get your elbows off the table."

"May I have some?" Caitlin asked eagerly.

"Of course not. What a silly question," Vivian said simply.

"Listen to your aunt, darlin'," Meghan said, tweaking her nose. She looked at Donal. "Don't even bother."

As they took their places around the table, Vivian, sitting at the head, reached her hands out to Meghan on one side and Rose on the other. They in turn held the children's hands.

Vivian bowed her head. "For what we are about to receive, we are truly grateful."

"And hungry," Caitlin said, looking up. She stopped grinning when Vivian gave her the eye.

"This is delicious," Meghan said, taking a spoonful of stew. "And bread? Vivian, you'll have me as fat at Paddy's pig." She laughed along with Cait, who giggled happily and ate her bread.

Rose looked at Meghan, thinking she'd have to go a long, long way to that. Meghan was in very fit shape. She wore a dark blue sweater that made her eyes look darker, almost a midnight blue. Her short black hair fell in waves around her face, a stark contrast to her white complexion, and her lips had a natural red hue; she was very attractive and…

"Rose?"

When she heard Meghan's soft voice, she blinked. Meghan held the plate of bread up to her; a slight smile crossed her lips. "Bread?"

"What? Oh, I'm sorry," Rose said. "My mind. I was…" She quickly took the bread. "Thanks."

"Your face is all red, Rose," Caitlin said, eating her bread.

"Must be the wine." Meghan leaned down to Caitlin's level.

Rose playfully glared across at Meghan, who laughed and continued eating. She caught the curious expression from Vivian, who looked from her to Meghan; Vivian picked up her wineglass. Rose thought she grinned slightly as she drank—at least she hoped so.

After dinner and the kids helping with the dinner dishes, they finally made their way back to the living room where Donal stoked the fire; he and Caitlin took their place, lying in front of the fireplace. Meghan sat in the old chair next to them, smiling as she drank her coffee. Rose sat on the couch with Vivian in her usual chair by the window.

"My, that was a good stew, if I do say so myself." Vivian let out a contented sigh and put her head back. "And you children did a marvelous job of cleaning up. No broken dishes this time. You're gettin' better."

"It was marvelous on all counts," Meghan said. "Thank you again, Vivian."

"You're welcome in this house anytime, Meghan. Isn't she, Rose?"

"Of course you are," Rose said, watching Meghan. "So tell us about being a geologist."

Donal perked up. "Is that why you're a doctor?"

"Geology?" Vivian said. "What a fascinating subject."

"You're a doctor? Can ya fix Bunny?" Caitlin held up her ratty stuffed animal, showing Meghan the tattered long ear.

"Uh, well, no. I'm not that kind of doctor," Meghan said, looking uncomfortable. "Sorry about Bunny."

"What does a gee…gee…" Caitlin stammered.

Donal leaned into Caitlin. "Geologist, ya *amadan*."

"I know, Donal," Caitlin insisted.

"Donal, don't be callin' your sister an idiot. Even in the Irish," Vivian said sternly.

Caitlin still regarded Meghan. "What is it?"

49

"Um…" Meghan looked around at the array of curious expressions patiently waiting.

"Rocks," Rose offered simply before taking a drink of coffee.

Caitlin frowned deeply as she watched Meghan. "You fix rocks?"

"Well, no. I…" Meghan glared at Rose's smiling face. "I study them."

"Why?" Caitlin asked, still enthralled.

"Because they tell us about the planet," Donal said to Caitlin. "Right?"

Meghan smiled. "Right. It's amazing the story they tell."

"Rocks tell a story?" Caitlin now looked very dubious with one arched eyebrow. Rose thought how much she looked like Kathleen.

"They do indeed." Meghan leaned forward. "They tell us how the earth began. And all the plants and animals that lived millions of years ago. And we know this because when they died, we found their skeletons in the rocks."

"Fossils," Donal offered eagerly.

Vivian and Rose exchanged grins as they listened.

"Yes. Very good. Fossils show us how old the planet is. And the rocks tell us what we've done to the planet, and we can see what we have to do to fix it."

"My teacher says we're going to ruin the planet one day," Donal said.

"We might. We keep strippin' it away, layer by layer."

"Rock by rock?" Donal offered.

"Exactly. And one day, the earth will say, 'Enough, you've taken all I'm gonna give ya.'"

"And what will happen?" Caitlin asked, sitting up.

Donal rolled his eyes. "We'll blow up the earth and die," he said dramatically.

"Donal," Vivian said, shaking her head. "Don't tease your sister."

"I don't wanna die," Caitlin said.

"Nobody is going to die, sweetie," Rose said.

"Mam died," Caitlin said softly to Rose. "I don't want her to be a fossil."

Rose opened her arms, and Caitlin climbed up on her lap.

"I miss her," Caitlin said.

Rose gently rocked her. "I miss her, too, honey. But you know she's looking out for you right now from heaven."

"Auntie Vivian said I should pray for Mam," Caitlin said.

"That's a good idea. As long as you remember your mom and how much you love her, she'll always be here for you and Donal. And me and Aunt Vivian." Rose looked up at Meghan. "And Meghan."

"And Da?" Caitlin asked. "I don't remember much about him."

Rose fought through the tears by taking a quivering breath. "He remembers both of you. And he's with your mom, taking care of her and watching over you and Donal." She glanced at Donal, who frowned deeply as he looked at the fire.

Vivian stood and said, "All right now, enough. It's time for bed. Say good night."

Caitlin kissed Rose on the cheek. "Good night, Rose."

"Good night, sweetie. I love you," Rose said.

Caitlin slipped off her lap and walked over to Meghan. "Sleep tight, lass," Meghan said, kissing her forehead.

Donal stood and took Caitlin by the hand. "Good night, Meghan. Will we see you tomorrow?"

Meghan grinned. "Sure enough. Have a good sleep, Donal."

He kissed Rose on the cheek, said good night, and pulled Caitlin along with him, following Vivian upstairs.

"Those poor kids," Rose said.

"They'll make it through with your help and Vivian. I think I should be goin', as well. It's getting late."

They both stood facing each other in an awkward silence.

"Well," Rose said and walked to the door with Meghan following. As she opened it, she turned to Meghan. "What are you doing tomorrow?"

"Nothing important for now. Why?" She smiled curiously and waited.

"I need to go into Donegal. I have nothing to wear. I left in such a hurry, I just threw a few things in my suitcase. I was wondering if you'd like to join me. Maybe have lunch. I mean if you're not too busy."

Meghan cocked her head. "Well, that sounds grand. What time shall I fetch ya?"

Rose hid her grin. "Fetch me? How about ten?"

"Fine. Maybe we can have a pint afterward and a good chat."

"That's a great idea. We need to have a very good chat. See you at ten. Thanks for the wine."

"My pleasure," Meghan said, once again searching her face. "Good night, Rose." She hesitated for a moment, then leaned in and softly kissed her on the cheek. "It was a grand night."

Rose's heart raced as Meghan pulled back. "Why did you do that?"

"Seemed like the right thing to do," Meghan said. "Was I wrong?"

"No. It was nice."

"Yes, it was." Meghan backed up.

Rose gently started to close the door. "Good night, Meghan. Drive safe."

She smiled and leaned against the door after closing it. It was then she noticed Vivian standing on the landing, her arms folded across her chest, sporting an auntly glare.

Auntly?

"Hello," Rose said weakly.

"Hello to you," Vivian said. "Are ya sure you should be makin' plans with her?"

"It's just shopping and lunch. And we do need to talk." Rose turned off the lights and met her on the landing.

"I know you," Vivian said as she mounted the stairs.

"I should hope so." Rose laughed, then cleared her throat. "Aunt Vivian, I'm a grown woman."

"That I know. I'm not tryin' to tell you how to live. You've always been a free spirit." She stopped at the top of the stairs. "I like Meghan. I think she suits you. And I think it's grand to find a little happiness with all this sadness. Just be careful, that's all I'm sayin'. Now off to bed with ya." She kissed Rose on the cheek and walked away.

"Good night." Rose smiled and headed to her room.

"And try not to be as wild as the rest of the Culhanes," Vivian called out quietly, then closed her bedroom door.

Chapter 8

Promptly at ten the next morning, Meghan came to fetch Rose.

"Meghan's here." Caitlin ran into her room and knelt on the chair to watch Rose.

Rose glanced at her reflection in the mirror while hearing Meghan talk to Vivian downstairs. Her hands were shaking. "Why are my hands shaking?"

"Are ya cold?" Caitlin picked up the hairbrush. "I love my hair."

"Yes, you have beautiful hair." Rose laughed. "And no, I'm not cold. It's…" She looked down at Caitlin's inquisitive look. "I'll explain when you're older. Though if you're anything like your brother, you're old enough now. You be good for Aunt Vivian. And don't chase the peacocks. I love you."

"Love you, too," Caitlin said absently, looking in the mirror and brushing her hair.

She gave Caitlin's red head a kiss, then ran her fingers through her hair and grabbed a sweater.

As she bounded down the stairs, Vivian looked up. "For the love of Mary, you sound like the children."

Rose stopped and took the final steps quietly and slowly. "Good morning, Meghan."

Meghan grinned; Rose could almost see her smiling eyes behind the sunglasses. "And a good mornin' to ya, Miss Culhane. It's a fine day for a drive."

And it was. It was sunny and clear, and a soft breeze blew the white sheer curtains in the living room windows.

"Well, you two have a good time. Don't worry about anything. Will ya be back for supper?" Vivian asked.

Rose was still looking at Meghan. Vivian sighed and gently pushed them toward the door. "I'll take that as a no. But, God forbid, if you find yourselves with nothin' to do, supper is at the same time. Now go enjoy the day."

Rose kissed Vivian on the cheek. "You have my cell if you need to call."

"Which I won't. I've been takin' care of things long before you were born. Go on now." She pushed them out the door.

"You washed it," Rose said, looking at the sparkling clean Land Rover.

"Consider yourself properly flattered. I don't wash this often. I spend too much time off road. It hardly seems worth it."

Rose slipped into the passenger seat and buckled up.

"So Donegal. On a shopping spree," Meghan said, pulling around the circular drive.

"I'm not sure how much of a spree, but I need something for the wake," she said quietly.

Meghan only nodded and shifted gears. "Can I make a suggestion?"

"Certainly."

"Donegal hasn't many clothing shops in it for all its tourism. I might suggest Letterkenny. It's nearby and has more to choose from."

"Okay, that sounds fine. And I noticed a picnic basket in the backseat. Care to explain?"

Meghan laughed as she watched the road. "I thought it'd be nice to enjoy the weather while we have it. It's not usually this warm. If you'd rather not…"

"Oh, no. I think a picnic is a great idea."

In no time, they were strolling down the main street in Letterkenny. Rose felt at ease for the first time since she arrived in Ireland. She glanced at Meghan, who looked in store windows as they walked, and knew Meghan was one of the reasons. After their first meeting, Rose felt very comfortable around Meghan Quigley. Though she wanted to know more of what brought her to Peacock Walk, Rose liked and trusted Meghan with each new encounter with her. Like this one. It was a warm, sunny day, and she enjoyed Meghan's company.

As she daydreamed, the inevitable happened. Meghan had stopped at a storefront window, and Rose ran right into her.

"I'm so sorry," she said with a laugh.

"Ya nearly knocked the sunglasses off me head," Meghan said, pulling her into the store.

"Honestly, I hate shopping," Rose said, looking at the clothes on the rack.

"We have much in common then. My mother used to have such a difficult time with me. I despised wearin' a dress or gettin' dressed up for anything."

"I'm not averse to wearing a dress, just shopping for them. How about this?" Rose picked up a simple black dress made of light wool with a subtle hint of gray fabric woven in the bodice.

Meghan stepped back and nodded. "It will do for its purpose. But in the future, ya must get something that makes your eyes sparkle." She looked over her sunglasses. "I'm not sure if they're green or hazel in color."

"Depends on what I'm wearing," Rose said almost shyly and avoided Meghan's grin. "Well, I need shoes…" She scooted out of the way and found what she needed.

After paying for her new wardrobe, Rose and Meghan walked along the street, dodging tourists.

"That was painless." Meghan took the shopping bags from Rose. "Ya might need your hands free. I don't want ya runnin' me over again. So what else do ya need?"

"Nothing right now. I'll come back later in the week."

"I can join ya, if you like."

Rose shrugged. "That would be nice. But then I buy lunch."

"Ya have yourself a deal."

They took in the rest of the shops on their way back to the Land Rover.

"Where to now?" Rose said. "And I hope you have enough food in there. I'm starving."

"A little beach in Killybegs. There are bigger beaches where the tourists love to go, but I have a little spot I go to sometimes." She looked at Rose and smiled. "And ya can only get there in this thing." She affectionately ran her fingers across the dashboard.

"You two need to be alone?"

Meghan laughed and started the engine. "Ah, Rosie. Do ya mind if I call ya Rosie from time to time?"

"No, I suppose not, and I suppose I'll leave where we go to you. I'm all yours." When she realized what she said, she quickly looked out the window and enjoyed the scenery; she was extremely grateful Meghan said nothing.

They drove the next few minutes in silence, Rose stealing a glance at Meghan every now and then.

"Take a look."

Rose followed where she pointed. At the bottom of the road, the Atlantic Ocean burst into view, surrounded by rolling green hills.

"It's breathtaking," Rose said and immediately held on to her seat belt when Meghan took a sharp left turn. "Um, there's no road here."

Meghan laughed. "It's here somewhere. Hold on."

Rose did as they bounced around on the rocky path. "Is this legal?"

"I assure you, it is. Not many people know of this. Only the locals."

"Of which you're one?"

"Well…"

Rose shot her a worried look. "You scare me."

Meghan just laughed as the Land Rover rolled over the craggy rocks and high grass. She stopped at another breathtaking view of the Atlantic. They were in a small inlet, and because of the location and swirling winds, sand dunes had formed on one side. With the sporadic high sea grass springing up, they could have been on any beach on the East Coast of America. It was the rolling gray stone hills behind them that signified this could be nowhere else but the rugged west coast of Ireland.

"We can walk from here." Meghan shut off the car.

Rose, still stunned by the beauty, slowly got out of the Land Rover. Meghan had already retrieved the picnic basket and blanket.

"Rose, are ya comin'? I can't carry ya."

She laughed and followed Meghan down the narrow sandy path to the beach.

"Just on the other side of these rocks is the largest portion of the beach. That's where the tourists go. How about here?" she asked, looking around. "Yes, I think this'll do us."

Rose took the large blanket and set it on the sand. Meghan got to work on the picnic basket. Suddenly, Rose was ravenous as she watched Meghan pull out several containers.

"I hope ya like seafood," she said absently.

"Love it."

"I've got some boiled prawns, brown bread, butter, and a little crab salad. I just grabbed whatever fruit and cheese was within reach at the market." She set the containers on the blanket along with two plates and silverware. "Oh, and this." She pulled out a bottle of white wine. "Be right back." She took the bottle and ran down to the rocks, near the beach. She came back without the bottle. "The water is too cold to swim in, especially for you Americans, but perfect to chill the wine. We'll give it a few minutes while we set up."

"You seem to have everything under control," Rose said, watching the production.

"Simple but efficient." She looked at Rose over her sunglasses. "Just wanted it to be fun for ya."

Rose smiled. "So far, it's been a wonderful day."

"Has it?" Meghan asked in her soft brogue. "Then I'm happy. Try some cheese." She sliced off a hunk and set the grapes and apples on the plate.

Rose stretched her legs out in front of her. "This is beautiful. Do you come here often?"

"Not as much as I'd like to," Meghan said, gazing at the ocean.

"Do all the women you bring here love it?" Rose took a bite of cheese and avoided looking at Meghan.

"I don't know. I haven't had another woman here."

Rose looked up as the broad grin spread across her face. Meghan leaned in. "Are ya satisfied with that answer?"

Rose tried not to laugh; it was a losing battle. "Yes," she said simply.

Meghan nodded and took a deep breath. "I do love the smell of sea air. Don't suppose ya get that in Chicago."

"No," Rose said, popping a grape in her mouth. "Just the smell of the occasional dead fish." She grinned when Meghan laughed. "We have nice clean beaches, though, and it gets warm in the summer. Lake Michigan warms up about July, and it's beautiful, as well. But nothing like this."

"I'm partial to the west of Ireland. Probably because I was born in this area." She stretched out on her side, propped up on her arm.

They sat for a few minutes in silence, listening to the waves lap up on the shore and the wind whistle through the tall sea grass. In another moment, Rose could have fallen asleep right there. Meghan jumped to her feet.

"The wine should be cool enough now." She ran down to the rocks and returned smiling, waving the bottle overhead.

"The nut," Rose said, shielding her eyes against the sun.

"Good and cool. Didn't take long." She uncorked the wine and poured it into two small glasses, handing one to Rose. She held her glass toward Rose. "To new friends."

"New friends," Rose said, touching her glass to Meghan's. The wine was cool and crisp and went well with the huge prawns and crab salad. "Did you make this?"

"I did not, though I can cook. I haven't had time lately. Thank God for the little store in Sligo that caters to the tourists' palate. I did make the brown bread, however. That stuff keeps forever."

As Rose watched Meghan take a drink of wine, she could tell her mind was elsewhere.

"What's going on?" Rose asked quietly. "I think we should talk now."

"I'm not sure where to start," Meghan said.

"Try the beginning." Rose knew she sounded sarcastic,

and that was not at all what she wanted. When she saw the sad, almost resigned look on Meghan's face, she felt horrible. "Look, I'm sorry. Kathleen said you were a trustworthy person, and my cousin was not one to be taken in. I trust you. So please, just level with me. From the beginning."

"The beginning…" Meghan sighed deeply as she sat up. She absently pulled at her earlobe; it was almost like a nervous habit, as one would pull at her eyebrow when deep in thought.

"And please don't start with where you were born," Rose said with a wary grin.

Meghan chuckled softly. "Right. Well, ya know I'm a geologist."

"Yes. You study rocks."

Meghan laughed again. "Like I said, I'd like to think it's a little more complicated than that. But essentially, that's it."

"That can't be all," Rose said when Meghan did not continue.

"It's not. I'm just tryin' to figure out how to make sense of this." She stopped and gently pulled at her earlobe once again. "All right. I work for a government-funded task force that monitors companies and corporations. We make sure they adhere to environmental and ecological standards that have been set by the government."

"So you're like Greenpeace?" Rose took a sip of wine.

"Not exactly. Though we have the same goals, it's just our methods are different. My concern, as a geologist, is to make sure no one is strafing the land and causing any adverse effects from whatever business they have with the land and the environment. Take waste management, for example."

Rose smiled at the eager tone in her voice; she realized Meghan Quigley loved her work.

"A friend of mind is a microbiologist. He's very intelligent. He and others in his field make sure the waste companies aren't just dumping everything without the proper chemicals and procedures. I have another friend who's an environmental lawyer. She could spend every minute of every day and still not have enough time to legally get at some of these corporations. I suppose that's where

Greenpeace comes in. Some can't wait for the wheels of justice to get goin' after they grind to a halt."

"That's very interesting and a noble endeavor. And I admire you for that. But what does this have to do with Kathleen?"

Meghan hesitated for a moment while she took a bite of cheese. "She was indirectly involved, I think…"

"Involved in what? You're sounding suspicious again."

Meghan looked out at the ocean; she tossed back what was left in her wineglass and started to close the containers.

"What are you doing? Are we leaving?" Rose hated to sound so disappointed.

"Yes." Meghan gathered the containers and repacked the basket.

"I'm sorry if I offended you. I didn't mean…"

Meghan looked up, once again searching Rose's face. "Do ya trust me, Rosie?" she asked in a pleading voice.

"Yes, I do. I—"

Meghan quickly leaned over and kissed her lightly on the lips. This, Rose was not expecting. She nearly jumped out of her skin when Meghan's soft lips met hers. Unfortunately, just as quickly, Meghan pulled back.

"Ya didn't offend me. You've been kind and patient with me, and ya barely know me, but I'm not apologizing for that kiss."

"I don't want you to," Rose said.

Meghan smiled. "And you have every right to sound suspicious. I'm not explaining this well at all. I've got a PhD and an MB and a BA, and all of it is bollocks if I can't explain it to ya."

"Bollocks?" Rose grinned and finished her wine.

Meghan chuckled. "Well, that's more of a British term. I spent a good deal of time at Cambridge. Yes, by the stunned look, I went to Cambridge, as well. I'm well traveled." She slammed the basket lid. "How would you like to see my home?"

"Wha..?" Rose was stunned when Meghan snatched the empty wineglass from her. "Do I have a choice?"

"Ya do not."

"Then I'd love to see your home."

Chapter 9

Meghan took the coast road as long as she could before heading inland to Sligo. Rose watched the ocean and the countryside fly by her window; she absently licked her lips, which still tingled from their brief, unexpected kiss.

"So ya didn't mind that I kissed ya?" Meghan asked, as if reading her mind.

Rose grinned and looked at her. "No, I didn't mind at all."

"Good." Meghan shifted gears and watched the road as she drove.

"Why did you?" Rose asked.

"I've wanted to do that since you opened the door. I was taken by surprise how it affected me." She chuckled. "I suppose I wasn't expectin' ya to be so attractive."

Rose took a couple of shallow breaths. "I will admit, I thought the same."

"Ya did? That's good to know."

They drove in silence for a few minutes; Rose stole a glance at Meghan, who smiled as she concentrated on the road.

"I don't think there's a spot in Ireland that's not breathtaking." Rose looked at the Atlantic Ocean just before Meghan turned inland.

"It is. We're almost there."

For some reason, Rose shivered; the thought of seeing Meghan's home seemed somehow exciting to her. Calm down, she told herself. It's just her home. She gave Meghan a quick glance. As she drove, she looked somewhat pensive now. Rose noticed her fingers lightly tapping the steering wheel, almost giving her an anxious posture.

"I live right outside of Drumcliffe."

"Where Yeats is buried."

"Yes. If ya look over there, you'll see Ben Bulben off in the distance."

Rose saw the mountain so associated with the poet W.B. Yeats. With its near flat top and sloping ridge, from a distance, it almost looked like part of the Grand Canyon.

"It was formed during the Ice Age," Meghan said.

"Really?" Rose watched Meghan, who now seemed almost animated as she spoke. "Am I about to get a geology lesson?"

"You are indeed. So listen carefully, there'll be a test later."

"Yes, Professor."

Meghan laughed as if enjoying the playful exchange. Rose was enjoying herself; she hoped Meghan was, as well.

"During the Ice Age, all of Ireland was under several glaciers. When the glaciers moved over time, they formed the shape we see now. It has many layers, but mostly limestone and mud rock. Great fossils, too. Mostly seashells and such, but ancient nonetheless."

"So you really did go to college?" Rose gazed out the window. She glanced at Meghan, who shot her a look that had Rose laughing.

"I'll have ya know, I was accepted at Cambridge when I was only seventeen."

"I'm impressed. Must have had low enrollment that year."

"Ah, your cousin told me to watch out for your biting sarcasm. She just never said how bad it was." She turned off the main road. "Lucky for you, we're almost there."

"Did Kathleen want us to meet?" Rose asked.

"Yes, she did. We spoke of it often, which is why I probably feel so comfortable with you. I feel as if I know you."

Rose looked at her when Meghan laughed. "What? What did she tell you?"

"Nothin', nothin'. Well, just that ya have a scar on the back of your thigh."

Rose's jaw dropped. She hid her face in her hands. "I can't believe she told you about that."

Meghan let out a genuine laugh. "Got yourself stuck on a fence, did ya? I hope the apples were worth it."

"As I remember, they were. I'm at a disadvantage. You seem to know more about me than I do of you."

"Well now, we can't have that."

Rose truly wished she'd stop shivering every time Meghan spoke.

"Here 'tis." Meghan turned onto a dirt hilly road toward a whitewashed stone cottage surrounded by a stone fence.

"It's like something out of a movie," Rose said. "Do you own all the land?"

"Not all, just a couple acres. The owner parceled off some land when the economy went belly up a few years ago. I got the land and this cottage at a good price." She parked in the gravel drive on the side of the cottage. "This is it."

"It's lovely and charming," Rose said, slipping out of the Land Rover. The afternoon turned cloudy and cooler; she followed Meghan up the cobblestone walk. "All it needs is a thatched roof."

"That's what everyone says. But I truly don't have the strength or the money to put on a new roof. Keepin' it whitewashed is work enough."

Rose followed her in; it was very typical for an Irish cottage. Hardwood floors, low-beamed ceiling, and a stone fireplace with a leather couch set in front of it. A couple of deep-cushioned chairs had the living room area feeling cozy and inviting. In the far corner was an old desk, strewn with books and rolled-up sheets of paper, which looked like floor plans to Rose.

"Two bedrooms are right off the living room, bathroom at the end of the hall. Kitchen right over here." Meghan led her through a swinging door to the kitchen. "Nothin' formal."

"But definitely charming," Rose said, looking around. An old white enamel stove, a small refrigerator, a heavy wooden kitchen table with four old unmatched chairs. And in the back of the kitchen was the back door with two windows on each side giving a spectacular view of the rolling hills. "Just beautiful."

"Thanks. The bank in Sligo adores me," Meghan said dryly. She opened the refrigerator. "I've got Guinness and Guinness. Oh..." She snapped her fingers as if remembering and opened two separate thin cabinet doors under the countertop.

Rose laughed when she saw a wine refrigerator, and the other housed a rack for red wine. "Came with the cottage?"

Meghan laughed along with her. "No, I had this installed myself. When I lived in France..."

"You lived in France?" Rose didn't mean to sound so shocked.

"Only for six months. I was asked to speak at a conference, then took over for the professor when he took ill. But I got hooked on their love of wine. Mind ya, I love our Guinness."

"I understand completely."

"What'll it be?" Meghan swept her hand in front of the little refrigerator.

"Red. You choose what kind."

Meghan chose a bottle. "Make yourself at home."

"I'll use the bathroom, if you don't mind."

"End of the hall."

Rose walked down the hall and peeked into each room. One was sparsely decorated; she hoped that was the spare. But the other had an enormous four-poster bed situated between two windows. With the thickness of the quilt, Rose knew it had to be a feather bed. She fought the childish urge to jump on it.

"Did ya fall in then?" Meghan's voice called out.

Rose jumped and put a hand to her heart. "Don't do that."

"Are ya snoopin'?" Meghan asked.

"Of course not. I..." She stopped when Meghan raised an eyebrow. "Yes."

"Good. I want ya to feel at home." She looked in the bedroom. "That bed is Spanish—"

"Don't tell me you lived in Spain, as well?"

"No, no. But I have been around," Meghan said with a wisp of a smile.

"I can imagine," Rose said. "I'll be right out."

Rose washed her hands and looked around the bathroom. "Even the bathroom is cozy." Once again, she quelled the urge to be childish and open the medicine cabinet.

She found Meghan in the living room lighting a fire. She looked up when Rose stood beside her.

"It's turning cloudy and chilly. We might be in for some rain." She stood and dusted off her hands before picking up two glasses of wine on the mantel; she handed one to Rose. "So I think we should get back to our conversation."

A wave of disappointment hit Rose as she sipped her wine. She was enjoying getting to know Meghan, but she realized the situation, and now she felt guilty for enjoying herself while Kathleen…

"Rose," Meghan said softly. She reached out and held her hand. "It's all right."

"What?" Rose hated that she felt like crying.

Meghan pulled her into her arms. If felt natural for Rose to cling to her. "It's a horrible thing that's happened. But it's all right to take a break."

"I know. It's just still that raw feeling, you know?" Rose laid her head on Meghan's shoulder. "But this feels nice and comfortable."

"Yes," Meghan whispered, kissing her forehead. "Very nice."

Rose leaned back; she reached up and ran her fingertips along Meghan's jaw. "This is happening a little fast."

"The best things happen quickly."

Rose raised an eyebrow. "Where did you hear that?"

"It just came to me. I suppose I'm sayin' it because I want to believe it," Meghan whispered; she kissed her once again.

When Rose deepened the kiss, she pulled Meghan closer. And in that instance, nothing mattered but kissing Meghan.

"God, Rose." Meghan kissed her with more urgency now, her hands running up and down Rose's back.

Rose's heart raced and pounded in her chest. Suddenly, she realized the reason she was here with Meghan. She reluctantly pulled back; she saw the lust in Meghan's eyes so intense, she actually felt weak.

Meghan breathed as though she'd just run a race. "I…" she whispered, then licked her lips. "That was…" She shook her head. "Are you all right?"

"I'm fine." Rose reached up and cupped her face.

"But somethin's botherin' ya." Meghan took her hand, kissing her palm. "And I think I know."

"Just because we've kissed doesn't mean you can read my mind," Rose said. "And if you don't stop kissing my hand…"

When Meghan let her hand go, the disappointment was palpable.

"What?" Meghan asked. "You told me to stop."

"And you listened to me. You'll have to get over that."

Meghan laughed and took a step back. "Well, we'll get back to this. But for now, let me tell you what's going on. Come here." Meghan guided her to the desk in the corner of the room under the window.

"What is all this? Your work?"

Meghan pulled at her earlobe and nodded. "Are you at all familiar with the Tellus Project?"

"No. Never heard of it. But I feel another lesson coming on."

"It's a project that Northern Ireland started years ago, about 2004. They said it was a geological mapping project. The short of it, they surveyed samples of the streams, rocks, and soil with the intent to make new maps that are better than the existing geological and geophysical maps so they have a better knowledge of the natural resources, the environment, and geology." She stopped for a moment. "Are ya with me so far?"

"Yes, so far. And I hope it's leading somewhere. Go on."

"They used state-of-the-art equipment. It was amazing."

"You were a part of it?"

"No, not then." Meghan grinned. "Don't get ahead of me."

"Sorry. I'm a little impatient. You might as well know that now."

"Point well noted. Now the project lasted from 2004 to 2007. And it was a huge success. As a geologist, I can tell you, it's exciting to know that although there's too much going on with this planet—we're killing it—we can have projects like this to aid us in better knowin' Ireland, and well, it's worth it."

"Okay, so Northern Ireland has this project and it's a success, but you weren't involved in it. So where do you come in? I'm assuming you are involved somehow."

Rose watched Meghan as she set her glass down. She looked under the pages and books as if looking for something. "There they are," she said absently. She picked up a pair of black horned-rimmed glasses.

"I didn't know you wore glasses," Rose said. "It changes your appearance completely."

Meghan blushed as she adjusted the glasses. "That bad?"

"No," Rose said. "Quite the contrary."

Meghan seemed stunned, which had Rose smiling. "I've got the biggest urge to kiss ya again."

"Later," Rose said, feeling her heart skipping all over the place. "Continue."

"Well, I can't read a thing without them. So where were we? Ah, yes." She opened several of the rolled pages, stretching them out over the desk. She used a couple of books at the corners of the maps to keep them from rolling closed. "In 2011, the Republic of Ireland started Tellus Border. It's the same thing Northern Ireland did, but we did it with the six counties that border Northern Ireland. Donegal, Sligo, Leitrim, Cavan, Monaghan, and Louth. These are survey maps."

Rose stood next to her. The map was of Ireland, anyone could see that. But after that, it was anyone's guess.

"Each map shows the data collected, from soil, bedrock, and streams and where they were collected. And all these data produced the same result as up north. We have better maps now than our older geological and physical maps. The project was finished in 2013. There was a conference with all the results and all of it open to the public. The technology was just amazing. And there were so many people and organizations on board. And there was also nothing political about it. No one had a hidden agenda. It was all for science and the future of Ireland as a whole." She laughed quietly and pulled at her earlobe. "Not very sexy, I know."

Rose continued looking at the map. "Oh, I don't know about that." She looked up to see Meghan grinning.

"Are ya flirtin' with me?"

"I believe I am. Do you mind?"

"I insist."

Rose grinned and looked at the map once again. "It seems very worthwhile and important. And you figured in how? The suspense is killing me, and if you don't tell me—"

"All right. When the project was completed, the government offered funded research to a limited number. I was asked along with many associates from geology to ecology and environmental scientists to assist in the field of one study of geology. To help those who were gathering the samples. I assisted in talkin' with the landowners and explainin' what we were doin'. And just to make sure nothing was contaminated and they took only what was necessary and left the area as untouched as possible."

Meghan rolled out another map, presenting it to Rose. "Take a look."

Rose examined the map. "It's very colorful."

Meghan laughed. "Yes, it's very colorful. And pretty."

"Don't be condescending. I just said the first thing I noticed."

In the highlighted border counties on the map, the colors ran the spectrum from dark blue to pale yellow all over the areas. The study was listed in the corner of the map. Rose blinked several times as she read *Sediment and Bedrock Geochemistry—Gold*. The map showed the highest and lowest range according to color.

She looked up at Meghan. "Gold? Are you serious?"

Meghan nodded and took out another map and unrolled it. Rose eagerly examined this map. This one showed where gold was found in certain streams and water.

"Meghan, there really is gold here?" Rose took a long drink of wine.

"As far back as two thousand years ago. You've seen the museum pieces, I'm sure. The Celtic artifacts made of gold and bronze. It's been in the streams and hills since before Ireland was formed."

"Why didn't anyone try and mine for gold?"

"Back in the eighteenth century, they mined for antimony. It's a metal used to make bullets. They had no thought of the gold, which they thought was lead, but they didn't know. But antimony, in conjunction with lead and tin, manufactured bullets. They mined right past the gold veins and discarded what they found as waste because it wasn't what they were lookin' for." Meghan waved it off then. "That's not important. The point is, when the conference showed these results, everyone had to consider the possible ramifications. I mean, there were already licensed mining companies in Ireland. But what they worried about was—"

"Those who want to do it without a license," Rose offered.

"Exactly." Meghan pushed her glasses up the bridge of her nose.

"And that's where you come in?"

Meghan frowned deeply as she watched the map. "That's where Desmond Flaherty comes in."

Rose hung her head. "I had a feeling you were going to say something like that."

Chapter 10

"You're going to explain this, right?" Rose asked. "And I did hear you correctly?"

"Unfortunately, ya did."

Rose held up her wineglass. "I think I'll need a refill for the explanation you're about to give me." She jumped when a clap of thunder shook the cottage.

"And here comes the rain," Meghan said, heading for the kitchen.

Rose listened to the rolling thunder while looking at the maps. Desmond? Gold? As absurd as it might sound, Rose couldn't help but think this was something Desmond would do. Don't find a real job, just illegally mine for the pot of gold. She looked up when Meghan stood beside her; she took the glass of wine from her. "Thanks."

"So here's exactly what happened. Where I figure in." Meghan took off her glasses and cleaned them on her shirt. "When they asked me to help, I was already workin', as I said, for the task force. So it seemed logical to lend my assistance. And for almost a year, it was very boring. I'd go wherever they were surveying and stand guard, for lack of a better word. Then one night, I was sittin' in a pub with a couple of colleagues. I overheard a few fellas talkin' at the bar. They were goin' on and on about pannin' for gold in the streams in Donegal. Everyone thought they were crazy, but I knew finding alluvial gold had been done for centuries."

"Alluvial? Please explain, Dr. Quigley."

Meghan winced. "That sounds so formal. Alluvial is the river deposits of soil and sediment. Like the old prospectors, ya pan for it, and ya find it in the form of dust or flakes, and sometimes nuggets."

"And it's illegal?"

"Not if you own the property. You just have to declare it to the government, that's all, like anything. But getting back to this fella. What struck me odd was where he found the ore. It was on private land, and after some detecting I did on my own, I found out he didn't own any property, and it was more than likely illegal. And it was then I found out it was Desmond Flaherty."

Rose shook her head in disbelief. "When was this?"

"A few months before he died," Meghan said. "Ya see, Rose, I don't begrudge a man for trying to make some money or support his family. But after I found out exactly where this was happening, me and a couple associates went to the area. It was trashed. They weren't just pannin', they didn't know how or what they were doin'. It was obvious. Our concern was the exploitation of the land and the resources. And if he's stealin', then there were other things probably involved. And the sooner someone put an end to it, the better."

"So what did you do?"

"We told our superiors, and that was it. We were told it would be taken care of."

"And was it?"

"Just in that particular area. We went back there several times, and the stream was cleaned up and no one was there. But then I got a call from a fellow geologist in Northern Ireland. He was with me when we found Flaherty. And he found a similar thing going on just over the border, from Donegal to County Tyrone, which as ya know is in Northern Ireland."

"Was it Desmond?"

"We don't know, but when my friend went to report it, someone slashed the tires in his car. And then he got a phone call that he said sounded right out of the movies. How he'd better back off and all that. They threatened his family." Meghan frowned deeply as she stared at the maps.

"Meghan, this is scaring me. What did he do?"

Meghan shrugged. "He backed off. He was only in Ireland to help with the project. He lives in Scotland. I don't blame him. So he told me everything he knew, then went back home."

"What did you do?"

Meghan looked at Rose then. "I didn't have time to do anything because the next day, I found out from my superiors that Desmond Flaherty was killed in that car accident and the incident was considered closed." She absently pulled at her earlobe as her gaze darted around the maps strewn all over the desk.

"Okay. I'm getting to know you. I've noticed when you pull at your earlobe like that, you're thinking about something. If this is done with, why do I get the feeling it really isn't over?"

"I don't know. It's just naggin' at me. There were reports comin' in..." She stopped. "There have been licenses given for mining along the border counties and in Northern Ireland. When they mine for gold, it's not like they take a pickax and suddenly the nuggets fall out of the rocks."

"How is it done?" Rose held up her hand. "The short version, please."

Meghan laughed. "Okay. The short of it is, when they drill, they come out with long cylindrical samples of rock, like thick stone rods. The gold vein lies within that rock cylinder, along with other minerals. The mining company does their process to extract the gold. And that's the other part of this. I got word that in certain mining facilities, some of the cylinders were missing."

"As in stolen?"

"They're not sure. There's such a vast amount of them mined, they just can't be sure. But my friend said there's enough missing to cause talk. Companies have their own security and such, but somehow..."

"And you think Desmond did this, as well?"

"His name came up too often not to think of it. Then after all this comes out, he's dead."

"So Desmond found his pot of gold and died for it? Are you saying Desmond was..."

"I don't know exactly what I'm sayin'. It's all odd and now with Kathleen. I don't know, Rose."

73

"Do you think he did this, whatever it is, on his own?"

Just then, the flash of lightning and the clap of thunder had them both jumping. They heard the torrential rain start. Meghan looked at her watch. "Good Lord, we've been talking for nearly two hours. We'll get back to this, but it's almost suppertime. You'd better call Vivian."

"I hate to have you drive in this..." Rose said, pulling out her phone.

"You could tell her that you're spending the night," Meghan suggested.

Rose nearly dropped her phone. As it slipped out of her hands, they both reached for it before it hit the floor.

"Because you're more than welcome." Meghan quickly continued, "I'd like you to stay."

"I'd hate to have you drive in this."

"Ya said that already."

"I did?" Rose then let out a nervous laugh. "Well, let me call her." She quickly dialed the number. "Aunt Vivian? Hi."

"I'm glad you're callin'. It's been stormin' here for an hour. Where are ya?"

"I...um...I'm at Meghan's. We've been talking, and the time got away from us. How's everything there?"

"We're fine. Now I don't want Meghan drivin' in this weather. God forbid, we have another accident..."

Rose winced when Vivian's voice trailed off. "Meghan invited me to stay the night. I don't want her driving in this, either. Are you sure you'll be all right?"

"Of course we will."

Her voice started breaking up. "Damn cell. Aunt Vivian? Are you there?"

"Yes. You'd better stay right there, Rose. This phone connection is horrid."

"I will. We'll be home in the morning." She held the phone close to her ear as the static started again.

"All right. Goodbye, Rose. See you in the..."

"Aunt Vivian?" Rose waited for a moment. "The rain must be worse there. We lost the connection. So I guess I'm staying."

Meghan grinned. "Excellent. Now enough talk of gold and stealin' for now. You must be hungry. I don't have much. But I think I can whip up an omelet."

Rose stopped her as she started to walk away. "All the sudden, I'm not hungry for an omelet."

Meghan cocked her head. "You're not? Then what are ya hungry for?"

Rose took her by the hand. "Show me your bedroom."

Meghan led her down the hall, stopping by the doorway. "Are ya sure?"

Rose leaned against the doorjamb; she reached up to caress Meghan's cheek. "I'm sure of one thing right now. I want to feel something other than sadness and doubt. I want to feel your body against mine. I—"

Meghan placed a bruising kiss against her lips. "I want to feel that, as well."

"I need you," she whispered in a ragged voice. She took Meghan's hand, pushing it down her own body.

"God, Rose." She sighed deeply.

Meghan's hand roughly parted her legs and massaged through the heavy fabric of the denim.

Rose sagged against the door and parted her legs farther. "Yes," she hissed. She frantically unbuttoned her own blouse.

Meghan pushed her hands away and opened her blouse, then unhooked the front clasp of her bra with ease. She immediately ran her hands over Rose's exposed breasts.

"Oh, God!" Rose cried out, arching her back. She jumped when she felt Meghan's hands unbutton, then unzip her jeans.

Meghan slipped her fingers past the waistband of her panties.

"Touch me, please," she begged and raised her hips.

Gasping at the warmth that engulfed her fingers, Meghan easily slid her fingers between her legs.

Rose could barely breathe when Meghan's fingers teased her and her tongue bathed her nipples, first one, then the other. The anticipation was unbearable. This was no time for teasing.

"Bed, please." Rose groaned deeply; she desperately tried to control herself. The way Meghan was touching her, it wasn't easy.

Meghan nodded frantically; both women tore at each other's clothes. Jeans, bras, and panties flew in every direction. And in the next moment, they crashed onto the bed, each trying to gain dominance.

Rose finally relented; she was breathless as Meghan lay over her, and with one quick erotic move, she entered Rose with one finger, pulled back, and added another.

"Yes, Meghan," Rose cried out, arching her back. Clawing now at her back, Rose felt her orgasm rise; when Meghan thrust deeper and faster, that did it. Rose cried out as she writhed beneath her. Meghan continued to love her until Rose fell limp, her hands falling from her back.

Meghan gently stroked her, sliding her fingers through her wetness. She gazed down into Rose's flushed face and kissed her trembling lips lightly. Rose's eyes fluttered opened, and she grinned. Meghan chuckled at the impish grin.

"It's too bad," Rose said in a ragged voice, "that you're not a medical doctor because I think I'm about to have a heart attack."

Meghan actually blushed deeply and shrugged. Rose reached up and caressed the crimson cheek. She swallowed convulsively as she reached up and palmed Meghan's smaller breasts. Meghan whimpered as Rose continued. She grinned at the helpless woman above her. "Don't move. Please, stay just as you are."

Meghan, breathing heavily through her nose, just nodded in compliance.

Rose teased her hard nipples, sending a shudder through Meghan as a deep groan escaped her. One hand wandered down Meghan's flat abdomen, and Rose grinned as the muscles involuntarily fluttered from her touch. She deftly slipped her fingers between Meghan's legs, touching and teasing her. Each movement caused Meghan to jerk and tremble. "Straddle me," Rose ordered. Meghan did so quickly.

Meghan balanced on her outstretched hands, placing them on either side of Rose's head. She was panting uncontrollably now.

Rose looked up; she could see the perspiration bead on Meghan's forehead. "You look so beautiful," Rose whispered. Meghan could only nod; Rose's fingers easily slid through her wetness. "And you're so ready."

She caressed her hips and ran her fingers up Meghan's back. "You want me now, don't you?" Meghan just nodded furiously once again. Rose slipped her hand back between her legs, amazed at the moisture she found there. Meghan groaned deeply and rocked slightly back and forth, her breasts swaying freely.

"Oh, God." Meghan moaned, her eyes shut tight in almost a grimace. Rose watched her as she flicked her fingers around her hard clit. Meghan jerked against her hand and moaned. Rose then moved her fingers farther through her wetness and teased her opening.

Seeing this woman above her close to orgasm brought out the erotic side of Rose. "Tell me what you want," she said in a low commanding voice.

Meghan's eyes opened and tried to focus. Rose saw the lust in her eyes and gave Meghan a challenging look. "Tell me."

"Oh, God, Rose. Fuck me," she whispered, looking into her eyes.

Rose felt her own arousal start again, and she did just that. She plunged two fingers deep, causing Meghan to arch and throw her head back. She let out a strangled cry as she rocked back and forth.

"A bit harder, please." Meghan gasped.

Rose smiled inwardly at the polite request. She wanted her to say, "Fuck me harder," but perhaps that would come later.

Soon, Meghan was sweating and panting through her impending orgasm. Rose reached up and grabbed her breast, and that was it. Meghan tensed as tight as a bow, suspended on the edge of her orgasm. Rose was in awe as she watched this woman above her, giving herself completely to her. It was a magnificent moment.

"Meghan, open your eyes," she pleaded. Blue eyes instantly popped open, clouded with desire. "I want to see it in your eyes. Now."

Meghan whimpered as her body broke into a thunderous orgasm. She jerked and trembled through it, never losing eye contact with Rose. Finally, her arms gave out as she collapsed on Rose's body. She was quivering and shaking as Rose held on to her.

"Geezus," Meghan mumbled into her neck. "Please, don't touch me right now. I need a minute," she begged helplessly.

Rose gently rolled the limp woman onto her back. She now loomed over her and kissed her deeply.

"That was tremendous." Meghan sighed in an exhausted voice. She looked at Rose and grinned. "And very erotic."

Rose chuckled and wiped the damp hair off her brow. "I'm not sure where that came from. You just looked so beautiful."

The thunder rolled, and the lightning flashed. Meghan shifted and now lay next to her. Rose pulled her close to her and sighed when Meghan placed a delicate kiss on top of her breast.

"That was truly wonderful, Rosie," Meghan mumbled.

"I want to show you again how wonderful, but…" Rose yawned. "I'm getting old."

Meghan laughed; she reached down and pulled the quilt over them. "We have all the time in the world."

Rose nodded and absently ran her fingers through Meghan's hair. She hoped Meghan was right.

Chapter 11

Rose felt a mixed bag of emotions as they drove back to Peacock Walk in the morning. She glanced at Meghan as she concentrated on the road. With the rain pelting the windshield and the rhythmic sound of the wipers, Rose nearly fell asleep. After the previous night's sexual gymnastics, she was exhausted—maybe she was getting old. She smiled now, remembering how Meghan could be gentle one moment and lustful the next. It certainly was a roller-coaster ride for both of them.

"What are ya thinkin'?" Meghan asked softly.

Rose reached over and caressed her hand. "I'm thinking, even with the maps and the gold and all of whatever this is…I'm thinking how wonderful last night was. And this morning."

"No regrets?"

"Not in the least. I enjoyed every minute."

"Good. I did, as well. I admit I was a little nervous. I haven't been with a beautiful woman in a while. I spend too much time in the mud rock."

Rose gazed at her profile. "Ditto. Well, about the beautiful woman part, not the mud." She reached over and brushed the back of her hand against Meghan's soft cheek.

"None of that. We'll be in a ditch. Keep your hands to yourself. For now," Meghan added with a wink.

"You look too sexy for a wake," Rose said; she then realized what she said and grew silent.

Meghan reached over and cupped her cheek while glancing at the road. "We'll get through this, Rose. And the children and Vivian."

"And you'd better watch the road." Rose kissed her fingertips before letting her hand go. "I'm glad you're here, Meghan. And not just because of last night."

"I'm glad to be here. Can't think of anyplace I'd rather be."

Rose's heart melted at the soft, sincere tone in Meghan's voice. "I feel the same." She watched the countryside through the rain. "I thought it would have stopped by now."

"We're in Ireland. Give it a minute, it'll stop."

"Do you think Kathleen knew anything more than what you and she discussed?"

Meghan shifted gears before she answered. "I think so. But I can't be certain. She was just too excited when she called that morning. As if she had something new. I just wish she would have told me, but the weather was so bad while she was driving."

Rose saw the anger and frustration play out on Meghan's face. "You did all you could. Don't blame yourself."

"I know. When I first told her what I knew about her husband, she was shocked, yet she took it in stride."

"I know exactly how she took it. Because after the initial shock, I thought it was just like Desmond to do something like this. I just wish I knew if he was in deep, and that's why he died. Or was it just an accident?"

"I feel the same way about Kathleen. Did she know something that could have…?"

"Are you thinking of what the inspector said about the brake line?"

"Yes. But I'll be honest with ya. A friend of mine had that problem with his Land Rover. He would take it off road all the time, driving over craggy rocks and in shallow streams. I know they're built for rough drivin', but I suppose it happens."

When Meghan's voice trailed off, Rose knew she didn't believe it. Somehow, Rose didn't believe it, either. What did Kathleen know?

By the time they returned to the house, the rain had stopped and the sun tried to peek through the cloudy sky. It was early; the children were still sleeping. They found Vivian in the kitchen making tea.

"Good morning," she said with a tired smile. "That was some storm."

"Good morning," Rose said and kissed her cheek. "It certainly was."

"Meghan, you look happy," Vivian said, offering her cheek.

"I am. Thank you." Meghan kissed the offered cheek. "Kids still sleepin'. That's good."

"Well, they fell asleep in front of the fire. The lights went out for a while. Have a seat."

Vivian brought the teapot to the table while Rose gathered the teacups from the cupboard.

"So did you have a nice evening?" Vivian asked as she poured the tea.

Meghan and Rose exchanged quick glances; Meghan hid her grin as she drank.

Vivian regarded both women. "I don't want the details. A simple yes or no will do."

"Yes," Rose and Meghan answered at the same time.

Vivian nodded, offering a knowing smile. "Hmm. Oh, by the way, Brendan Flaherty called. He won't be able to come for the wake, but he'll be here later tonight. Said he had some business in London. He was all apologetic, but I assured him it was considerate of him to come whenever he could."

"It is nice of him." Rose took a drink of tea, watching Meghan butter a piece of brown bread.

Meghan looked up. "I'm hungry. We didn't eat dinner last night," she said with a grin.

"You didn't?" Vivian asked. "What were you doin'?"

Meghan had the bread in her mouth; her blue eyes grew wide as she stared at Rose. "Well, we'd better get a move on. It's going to be a long day."

And it was a long day. They stayed out of the living room when the funeral director arrived. Rose was grateful that Kathleen's expressed wishes were a closed casket and a short wake with the funeral the following day. Aunt Vivian knew this and adhered to Kathleen's wishes, although she would have preferred the old

Irish way and had the wake for at least two days. With all the kids had been through, even Vivian had to agree this was the best way for them.

The wake was subdued, but at times, like all Irish wakes, there was laughter and storytelling. However, Rose noticed her distant cousin Sorcha in the far corner of the living room, chatting away with a few women from the village. For a moment, Rose regarded her, suddenly realizing how old she looked. Rose knew she was near Aunt Vivian's age, but she looked older somehow. Maybe it was the way she wore her white hair pulled back too tight that gave her the perpetual painful wince, like someone was sticking her with needles. Or perhaps it was just that Sorcha Culhane was a nasty woman; as far back as Rose could remember, she always had a snippy attitude. A lonely old woman, Rose thought.

"She's like a viper waitin' to strike," Vivian whispered in her ear.

Rose stifled a laugh and turned around. "That's not very nice on this solemn day, Aunt Vivian."

Vivian snorted. "Kathleen would say the same if she were here."

"I have to agree with that. As I remember, Kathleen had no use for Sorcha, either. And if I recall, she got along with Des."

"And isn't that tellin'," Vivian said. "Och, she's comin' over here."

"What are you two whisperin' about?" Meghan said from behind them.

Vivian and Rose laughed quietly. "We're tryin' to get to the kitchen before Sorcha... Too late," Vivian mumbled. "Sorcha. Are ya leavin' then?"

Sorcha narrowed her blue eyes. "I am not. I haven't seen Rose in so long. How are ya, dear?"

"Fine, Sorcha." She raised an eyebrow before she kissed the offered cheek. "It's been years. How have you been?"

"I'm gettin' old and tired. I'm nearly through with this life," she said almost angrily.

Vivian mumbled something under her breath.

"It's a horrible thing that happened," Sorcha said.

"Kathleen was a good mistress of this house. No offense to you, Vivian."

"None taken," Vivian said dryly.

Sorcha smiled slightly. "And, Vivian, who is this woman?" She looked Meghan up and down.

Meghan stepped up and offered her hand. "I'm Meghan Quigley. A friend of the family. And you are?"

Rose and Vivian took a step back and watched.

"I'm Sorcha Culhane, Vivian's cousin. My mother and her mother—"

"Were both mothers?" Meghan interjected, still holding her hand.

Sorcha's nostrils flared with anger; she slipped her hand away from Meghan. "And how did you know Kathleen?"

"Fate brought us together. I haven't seen you in the village. Are you from Trahern?" Meghan asked.

"I was born in the village, yes, but I live in Buncrana now. It's farther north."

"I know the area. Ya can't get much farther north than that," Meghan said with a wide grin, "and keep your feet dry."

Rose laughed along with Vivian, but Sorcha merely smiled.

"So I understand you were in the village with a gentleman at the pub. And you're here alone? You're not his girl?"

"I'm my mother's girl. Are you here alone? Or is your gentleman about?" Meghan looked around the living room.

Rose was getting a migraine from the effort not to laugh out loud at this exchange.

"Where are ya from?"

"Sligo," Meghan said with pride. "Yeats's country."

"And you're a poet?"

"Sadly, no. I'm a geologist." She looked at Rose and smiled. "I study rocks."

"Hmm. Seems like a childish endeavor."

"Yes," Meghan said sadly. "It is."

"I understand you've been in the village askin' questions," Sorcha said.

"But I was with a gentleman. Surely, that makes it acceptable."

Meghan cocked her head and smiled. "I have been in Trahern. It's a quaint little place." She looked at Rose. "I think I like it here. Seems friendly enough."

Rose grinned reluctantly. She then caught Sorcha looking from her to Meghan. When the light bulb went on, Sorcha nodded. She had found out years ago that Rose was gay and made it very clear she didn't approve, as if Rose actually cared. Here we go, Rose thought.

"Tell me, Rose," Sorcha said, tearing her gaze from Meghan.

"Oh, brother," she mumbled. "Tell you what?"

"Are ya married yet?"

"Sorcha, really," Rose said, sounding shocked. "Meghan and I hardly—"

Vivian wedged her way in between them. "Rose, help me with the sandwiches."

"Why? What are they going to do?" Rose allowed Vivian to pull her away to the kitchen.

When Rose returned to the living room, and after she and Vivian had a good belly laugh in the kitchen, poor Meghan was still chatting with Sorcha. Rose felt guilty leaving her, but if Vivian hadn't pulled her away, Rose was sure she'd say something she'd regret, and it was Kathleen's wake after all. She looked over to find Donal and Caitlin sitting together on the couch. She smiled when Meghan excused herself from Sorcha and made her way over to them. She took Caitlin by the hand.

"Let's go bother the peacocks, Cait," Meghan said. "Donal?"

Poor Donal looked so uncomfortable in his suit and tie; he nearly jumped at the chance to escape. He took Caitlin's other hand. "C'mon then, Caitlin. We'll chase 'em away from the house."

"Thank you," Rose whispered to her. She wanted so much to kiss her and hold her, but with a room full of Trahern villagers and under Sorcha's judgmental glare, it was hardly the time or the place. Though Rose really, really wanted to, she opted for a caress across Meghan's back as she walked out with the children.

"It's a tragic thing," Mr. Murphy said behind her.

Rose turned around. "Yes, it is. So much sadness for those kids."

"Mrs. Dunne's apple cake is good, though," he said with a slight grin. "She only makes it for this occasion."

Rose chuckled in spite of the situation, knowing Kathleen would have gotten a good laugh out of it. "Everyone has been so gracious. We'll have food for a week."

"It's the Irish way," he said, holding a pint of Guinness. "Though not like the old days. They'd be laid out for days. With the old women keening and wailing outside like a bunch of hags, which is why there was probably much more of this flowin'," he said, raising his glass. "I remember when old Jerry passed."

Rose raised an eyebrow and sat down, knowing this was going to be a good story.

Mr. Murphy took a drink, wiping the side of his finger against his lips. "He had relatives comin' from every county and some from America. The wake could've gone on for a week." He laughed loudly, and that did it.

Suddenly, several men and women were at his side. Rose shook her head. She glanced past them to see Vivian rolling her eyes.

"God bless his soul," one man said. "Jerry was a kind man."

"That he was." Still laughing, Mr. Murphy continued. "At his wake, this one fella, a youngster, had never been to a wake if ya can imagine that. So he says to me, 'Sean, I've never met Mr. Sullivan.'" Mr. Murphy chuckled and took a drink from the pint. "I tell him, not to worry, boyo. He's the one laid out under the window. Ya can't miss him."

Rose laughed along with the rest of the villagers. She realized how much she missed the art of Irish storytelling and laughter.

"So then the young lad asks me what he should say. I tell him, stand in line, and when it's your turn, ya tell them you're sorry for their loss and move on."

This emitted a few chuckles, a couple of winks, and rib jabs between the men. Mr. Murphy took another drink. "So he walks up to the widow Sullivan and says, very solemnly now, he says, 'Ma'am, I'm so sorry for your loss. Move on.'"

Well, that caused a cackle of laughter and slaps on the back.

Rose raised an eyebrow. "Did that really happen?"

Mr. Murphy looked indignant. He then put the pint to his lips. "Not a word of it," he said, which started the laughter all over again. "I think I saw it in one of your American movies."

Thus was the way of the Irish wake. And truth be known, the levity was a welcome relief to the sadness and grief in Rose's heart. Soon, all the mourners had left, including Sorcha, who promised to be back in the morning for the funeral—hooray.

The women from Trahern helped Vivian in the kitchen; it was spotless when they left. The funeral director came to take Kathleen's body. The next day would be the funeral. And now the house was quiet, and a heavy feeling of loss seemed to permeate every room.

In the back of Rose's mind, she thought about Kathleen's will and what that would mean. But for now, she sat in the living room with Caitlin on her lap, sound asleep. Donal sat by the fire, his suit coat discarded, along with his tie. He looked far too old in his dress slacks, his starched white shirt with the sleeves pushed up to his elbows and his black hair disheveled. He stared at the fire while Meghan spoke to him in a voice so soft Rose could barely hear her. From time to time, Donal would nod in agreement. Then Meghan reached over and ran her fingers through his thick hair. It broke Rose's heart when she saw the tears in Meghan's eyes as she kissed the top of his head.

"I miss Mam," Caitlin whispered.

Rose looked down at her sleepy face. "I do, too, honey." She picked up Bunny and wriggled it back and forth.

Caitlin smiled and took the stuffed animal and held it close; she instantly fell back to sleep.

"I think we should get her to bed," Rose whispered.

Meghan walked over and picked up Caitlin, allowing Rose to stand.

"Do I have to go to bed, too?" Donal asked.

"Aren't you tired?" Vivian asked. "You look exhausted."

"I just want to sit and watch the fire for a bit," he said.

"I think that's fine," Rose said. "I can take her."

"I've got her," Meghan said, motioning to the stairs.

Together they got Caitlin into her pajamas and under the covers. Meghan gently put Bunny under the quilt. "She's so tiny in this bed."

"I know," Rose said, smoothing back her red hair. "She looks so much like Kathleen."

"She does." Meghan smiled. "Right down to the blue eyes."

"This is so hard for them," Rose said. "Two parents within a year." She looked up at Meghan. "What am I going to do?"

"Things have a way of workin' out. We'll figure it out." She put her arm across her shoulders.

"Meghan," Rose said. "I don't want you to think, because of last night, that you are responsible for us. You've done so much already."

Meghan smiled sadly. "Let's get out of here before we wake her up."

They partially closed the bedroom door and stood in the hallway. Meghan turned Rose to face her and held her at arm's length. "I'm goin' to say this only once. Last night was remarkable and fun and sexy and any other adjective I can think of. But it's not the only thing happenin' between us. We both know that. Let's just take a day at a time. We'll help the children through this, and in the process, maybe help ourselves, as well." She held out her hand. "Do we have a deal?"

Rose chuckled quietly and took her hand. "We have a deal."

As they walked downstairs, they heard Donal talking with Vivian. They stood on the landing, not wanting to interrupt.

"You're the man of the family now, Donal. You've been since your father died. Even before if the truth be known."

"I know, Auntie. Why do ya think Da never wanted to be around us?" he asked; he sounded more curious to Rose than sad or angry.

"You and I have never talked about your father," Vivian said. "And I don't want to speak ill of the dead. But your father was a restless soul. It's not that he didn't love his family. He did, I believe. In his own way."

"He could never be normal. Just get a job and be a father."

Rose glanced at Meghan, who frowned deeply as she listened. Rose knew she was thinking of what Desmond had done, and because of it, he might have been killed. Rose reached over and held her hand while they listened. She also realized she had to tell Vivian what she found out.

"I want to tell ya something, Donal. Just because you can bring a child into this world does not mean you'll be a good mother or father. It takes time and love and patience. Your father lacked a great many things, but I think deep down he loved all of you. He just didn't show it very well."

"I miss Mam," he said in a soft voice that broke Rose's heart. She felt Meghan tighten her hold on her hand.

"I miss her, too. More than ya know. But there was a reason God took her now. And it's not for us to know. Just remember all she taught ya. And all the memories you have. If you love your sister and be the good, kind person ya are already, her memory will live forever."

Rose choked back the tears; she took a quick breath and almost sobbed openly. Meghan pulled her into her arms. "It'll be all right," she whispered against her hair. "I'm right here."

Rose nodded and pulled back. "Thank God for that." She took Meghan by the hand and walked into the living room.

"Is she asleep?" Vivian asked.

"Sound asleep. I think you can sleep in your own bed tonight, Donal," Rose said.

He nodded and stared at the fire once again.

"Looks like it could use another brick or two of peat," Meghan said.

Donal quickly grabbed two earthen bricks and tossed them on the fire, then sat back again and watched the flames. His thick hair flopped across his brow; he swiped it away with his hand. Rose couldn't help but think how much he looked like his father. Black hair, blue eyes, even his profile.

He turned back and looked at all three women. "What will happen now?"

"Well, after the funeral, we have to go see Mr. Downey and

see what's in your mom's will." Rose looked at Meghan, who smiled. "Then we'll take it one day at a time, kiddo. And we'll all get through this."

Donal nodded; he looked as if that was an acceptable answer. And he looked far too old for his fourteen years.

"I just thought of something," Vivian said tiredly. "Brendan Flaherty isn't here."

"That's right. Something must have come up," Rose said.

Vivian sighed, put her head back, and closed her eyes. "Perhaps he'll be here for the funeral. I gave him the time."

After a few minutes of silence with all of them staring at the fire, Rose saw Vivian's head nod forward. "I think it's time for bed," Rose whispered.

Donal walked over to Vivian and placed a hand on her shoulder. She immediately woke.

"Is it time for Mass?" she asked, quickly looking around.

Donal stifled a laugh along with Rose and Meghan.

"You missed it completely," Rose said.

"I must have dozed off." Vivian laughed as she stood. "You young fools. I'm going to bed. Good night," she said to Donal and kissed his cheek. "And you two behave yourselves. Meghan, it's late. Why don't you spend the night? And you can stay in the spare room. I've already made it up for Brendan, but it doesn't look like he'll be here tonight." She looked at Rose. "I'm sure you'll make do."

Rose knew her mouth was open, and she was blushing. She glanced at Meghan, who grinned as she kissed Vivian on the cheek. "Thank you, Vivian. I'll be fine wherever I lay my tired arse down."

Donal laughed along with Meghan.

"Don't be vulgar. Good night."

"You're next," Rose said to Donal after Vivian walked up the stairs.

"Good night, Rose," Donal said, hugging the life out of her.

Rose kissed the top of his head. "G'night, honey."

He turned to Meghan. "Good night, Meghan. Thanks for taking care of my mom when ya did. And thanks for being here now."

Meghan swallowed and nodded. "I'll be here for ya whenever ya need me, Donal. Any time."

He reached out for her then, and Meghan pulled him into a fierce hug. She then slapped him on the back. "Off to bed with ya now."

Donal said one last good night and ran up the stairs.

"Well, that young man will have me cryin' like a baby," Meghan said, wiping her finger under her nose.

Rose grabbed her by the hand and pulled her down next to her on the couch. Meghan shifted, so Rose could lie down, resting her head on Meghan's lap. Meghan absently ran her fingers through Rose's hair.

"That feels so good," Rose whispered, looking up at her. "Thank you for being here. You made this day easier."

"No need to thank me," Meghan said. "I'm glad to do it."

Rose reached up and gently traced her fingers along Meghan's jaw and down her neck. "You should have packed a bag. Will you spend the night?"

"As much as I'd love to, I need a change of clothes." She looked at the clock on the mantel. "It's not such a long drive. But I'd better be goin' soon." Meghan grinned and kissed the offered fingertips.

Rose snaked her arm behind Meghan's neck; in the next instant, she was in Meghan's arms.

"I'll never get out of here," Meghan whispered against her lips. You're a shameful woman, Rose Culhane. You're gonna have to kiss me now."

"Gladly," Rose said and did just that.

Somewhere in the ether, Rose heard a small voice. She sighed, still locked in a tender kiss.

"Rose?"

Rose nearly jumped out of her skin; she jumped off the couch when she heard Caitlin's quiet voice.

"What's wrong, sweetie?" Rose asked, scrambling over to her.

"I can't sleep." She rubbed her eyes with one hand while holding Bunny in the other.

"Oh, sweetie."

"Can I sleep with you?" Caitlin asked.

"Sure." Rose looked at Meghan, who raised an eyebrow in disappointment.

Rose took her hand, and Caitlin reached for Meghan, as well. "Meghan, can I sleep with you, too?"

Meghan's back straightened. "Uh, I think I should go home, darlin'."

Rose lifted Caitlin into her arms. She looked disappointed, as well. Meghan laughed and kissed Caitlin's head. "Let me lock up for ya."

Rose waited until Meghan checked the doors and met them at the front door. By now, Caitlin was sleeping in Rose's arms.

Meghan raised an eyebrow. "Now she falls asleep."

Rose stifled a laugh as Meghan opened the door. "Good night, Meghan."

Meghan leaned in and softly kissed her on the lips. "Good night, Rose. My Rose," she added and kissed her again.

"I am?" Rose grinned, and she gently rocked back and forth.

"I'm beginnin' to think so." Meghan laughed nervously and absently pulled on her earlobe. "Now off with ya before I start recitin' poetry or some such nonsense. I'll be back around eight."

Rose laughed and watched her walk down the steps.

"Did you hear that, Caitlin? I'm her Rose," she whispered with a smile.

She closed the door and walked upstairs with Caitlin still sleeping.

Chapter 12

Rose sat on the edge of the bed, looking out at the gray, damp morning. Unfortunately, it was typical Irish weather for a funeral. She stretched and stood with a groan, careful not to wake Caitlin, who slept soundly. Rose pulled the thick quilt over her and kissed her head. In her sleep, she pulled the stuffed bunny close to her.

It was only six thirty, but she couldn't sleep. Dreams of Kathleen invaded her sleep all night. And when she wasn't being kicked by Caitlin in her sleep, she thought about Meghan; a much happier scenario galloped through her mind. When all this was over, she hoped they could have some time to really get to know each other.

She dragged herself down the hall and into the shower, allowing the hot water to hit her in the face. Feeling much better and at least awake afterward, she dressed, then checked in on Donal.

Just as she was about to open his door, he opened it.

"Shit," Rose said, putting a hand to her heart.

Donal giggled, rubbing his eyes. "We say shite here."

"You don't say it at all. You scared the life out of me."

"Sorry. Good morning."

"I guess so," Rose said, laughing, as well. "How did you sleep?"

"Fine. Um, Rose…" he said, bouncing from one foot to the other.

"Oh, sorry." She backed out of his way as he ran down the hall.

From the aroma of bacon and coffee, Rose knew Vivian was in the kitchen. When Rose walked in, she noticed how tired Vivian looked.

"Good morning, Rose," she said quietly. "I made coffee and tea. A rasher of bacon and some sausages. And..." She stopped and placed her hands on the back of the chair.

Rose quickly walked over to her and put her arm around her shoulders. "You didn't have to cook all this."

Vivian patted her hand and straightened. "Keeps my mind occupied. Are the children up?"

"Donal is. I think I'll let Caitlin sleep a while longer. She slept with me last night."

"And Meghan?" Vivian asked, getting the plates from the cupboard.

"She went home. I worried about her driving, but she had no change of clothes." She glanced at Vivian, who smiled as she set the table. "Aunt Vivian..."

Vivian looked up. "You don't have to explain a thing to me. I understand." She chuckled quietly. "I'm an evolved Irishwoman. That's not to say I agree with ya, mind you. But I do love you. And Meghan seems to be a very nice woman."

Rose cocked her head. "Have I told you lately how lucky I am to have you and the kids?"

"Yes. But I never tire of hearing it."

They looked up when Caitlin and Donal walked into the kitchen. Still in their pajamas and barefooted, they looked like two lost waifs standing by the table. The sight of them broke Rose's heart.

"Well, look what the cat dragged in," Vivian said to Caitlin's giggle. "Breakfast is ready, darlin'."

Just as Rose sat down, she heard a knock at the back door. Through the small windowpanes, she saw Meghan's smiling face.

"Why is she comin' to the back door?" Vivian asked.

Rose jumped up. "I'll get it." She ran around the table to the door.

Vivian rolled her eyes at the children. "Your cousin is as

bad as the both of you. Stop runnin', Rose. Meghan's not goin' anywhere."

Rose laughed as she opened the door. "Good morning." She knew she sounded breathless.

"Good morning, Rose. I hope I'm not too early."

"Oh, no, no." Rose stepped back as she reached for her hand.

Meghan took her hand, giving it a reassuring squeeze. When Rose saw the smile and the want in her blue eyes, she nearly leapt into her arms.

"Let the poor woman in, Rose," Vivian said, standing by the stove. "So we can at least close the door."

"Oh, sorry."

"Good morning, Vivian," Meghan said. "I hope ya don't mind I'm here a little early, but I smelled the bacon and sausages all the way from Sligo."

Vivian laughed. "You're always welcome here anytime, Meghan. Ya know that. Sit down."

Meghan sat next to Caitlin. "Good morning, Cait. How did ya sleep, lass?"

Caitlin nodded, still holding Bunny, which she held up to Meghan.

"Oh, my apologies, Bunny. Good morning to you, as well. I hope ya slept as well as Cait." Meghan leaned in. "What was that ya said? Ya slept fine?"

Caitlin tried not to smile as she regarded Meghan. "Bunny misses Mam, too."

Rose watched the tender scene and said nothing; she glanced at Vivian, who had tears welling in her eyes as she held the heavy frying pan doling out the bacon and sausage.

Meghan reached over and gently ran her fingers through Caitlin's red curls. "I know she does. But your mam would be so proud of ya. You're being such a good girl to take care of your brother and Bunny. Now eat your breakfast. But don't let Bunny eat everything."

Caitlin raised an eyebrow. "Bunny doesn't like sausage. She eats grass and flowers."

"Ahh, right. Maybe we can take her out with Mr. Murphy's sheep. There's plenty of grass there."

Breakfast was quiet and subdued with everyone thinking about what the day would bring. Well, maybe not Caitlin; she happily ate her sausage and brown bread. Rose glanced at Donal, who ate in silence, his brow furrowed as if deep in thought. Rose worried about him. While he promised to talk to her, Rose knew he would keep things inside, and she couldn't help but think there was something else bothering him—as if the death of both parents wouldn't be enough.

And too soon, breakfast was finished, and the sad day had to continue. Rose wished with all her heart she could take the pain and sadness away. She looked at Meghan, who looked out the window, her mind seemingly miles away. It was then Rose thought of what they had discussed at her house. Between preparing for the wake and now with the funeral, Rose hadn't thought of all the talk of maps and gold and Desmond's death. Well, after today, they'd have plenty of time to talk. But first, she'd have to sit with Kathleen's lawyer and see just what changes Kathleen made before she died.

"Come along now," Vivian said to the children. "It's time to get dressed."

Donal and Caitlin dutifully walked out with Vivian, leaving Meghan and Rose to clean up the breakfast dishes.

Meghan reached out and pulled Rose into her arms. "How are ya holdin' up?"

Rose laid her head on Meghan's shoulder, reveling in her warm embrace. "I'm fine, I guess. Just everything is rolling around in my head. I can't keep a straight thought."

"I know what ya mean." Meghan tightened her embrace. "I've been goin' over all this in my head. From Desmond's death to Kathleen's." She held Rose at arm's length. "I was thinking we'd have time in the days to come to discuss this. But then I realized you have a job and a life in Chicago."

"I know," Rose said sadly. "I told them I'd call after I saw Kathleen's lawyer. I hope to have a better handle on what to do after that." She looked at Meghan and smiled. "Whatever happens, I…"

Meghan gently placed her fingertips against Rose's lips. "Let's not make any decisions or say anything until, like you say, we get a better handle on this. But I will tell ya, Rose Culhane, I've become very fond of you."

Rose grinned. "You have?"

"I have." Meghan pulled her back into her arms, kissing her tenderly on the lips. "I can't get you out of my mind."

"I feel the same." Rose glanced at the clock on the wall. "And I wish that's all we had to think about. Unfortunately, we'll have to talk about us later." She stepped back and licked her lips. "And we will discuss this."

"We will. I agree. Now go get dressed. I'll clean up here. Off with ya," Meghan said, playfully swatting her on the ass.

The Mass at St. Michael's was reverent and quiet. Rose sat on the end of the pew next to Caitlin, then Donal. Vivian sat at the other end with Meghan in the pew right behind Rose. Rose made a mental note to give Meghan a big kiss—as if she needed a mental note—when Meghan offered to sit with Sorcha. Rose smiled when Meghan whispered that she'd do it for the poor souls in purgatory.

It was a small gathering because it was a small church, but it seemed everyone from the village of Trahern was there. The priest gave a beautiful sermon; he spoke so warmly and serenely about Kathleen and the Culhane family. Rose was grateful, she knew she'd never be able to get up there for the eulogy.

When the service was concluded and they filed out, Rose noticed Brendan Flaherty at the back of the church. He looked so much like Desmond, for an instant, Rose caught her breath. He was as tall as Desmond but didn't have his brother's charismatic presence. You knew when Desmond walked into a room; with Brendan, he seemed to just be there. No gregarious laughter, no back slapping and camaraderie like his older brother. Though she only met him a few times, Brendan Flaherty always seemed subdued. Must be that creative, almost brooding posture some writers had. Now he caught Rose's eye; he smiled sadly and nodded.

Rose did the same; she put her arms around Donal and Meghan as they walked out of the church. Meghan drove, as they followed the hearse to the cemetery just on the outskirts of Trahern. Vivian sat in the back with the children talking quietly to them. And of course, the light drizzle of rain made the entire situation that much more sad and depressing.

Once again, the parish priest said kind words as they stood under the umbrellas. Rose had her arm around Caitlin, who, while clinging to Rose, just stared at the casket. Donal stood next to her while Vivian held the other umbrella over them. He placed his hand on Caitlin's shoulder.

And just when it couldn't get any sadder, Mr. Murphy appeared holding a set of bagpipes. When he played *Nearer My God to Thee*, that did it. Rose felt her chest tighten; the tears that flooded her eyes made it impossible to see. Meghan quickly stood behind her, placing both hands on her shoulders.

Then it was over. Rose took a deep quivering breath and felt Meghan usher them back to the Land Rover. Caitlin cried and held on to Rose and Donal. Vivian held a hanky to her nose while Meghan put her arm around her shoulders. The rest of the afternoon was a blur for Rose. They went to the only restaurant in the village for the luncheon. She remembered Vivian talking to Brendan for a time. Rose barely recalled what, if anything, she ate, but she made sure Donal and Caitlin had eaten.

Once back at the house, Rose saw the assortments of breads, cookies, and pastries set out on the kitchen table. In the refrigerator were two big pots, which Rose was sure contained enough food for several days. A few women from the village had set it all up for them. Once again, Rose was overwhelmed by the graciousness of the people from Trahern.

She put the kettle on for tea while Vivian entertained Brendan and Sorcha in the living room.

Meghan walked in and snagged a cookie. "Sorcha is not a likable woman."

Rose laughed as she took the teacups out of the cupboard. "Well, you have your place in heaven. You were very sweet to her at the church."

"I couldn't let her sit alone. And for a moment, I thought she was goin' to sit next to Vivian." She walked up behind Rose and kissed the back of her head. "How are ya?"

Rose turned to her and kissed her on the lips. "I'm fine. You're here."

Meghan sighed. "Ah, you've got to stop talkin' like that, Rose. You'll have me thinkin' ya like havin' me around."

"I do like having you around," Rose said, kissing her once again.

When the kitchen door swung open, they both jumped. It was Sorcha. "Am I interrupting?" she asked.

"Yes," Rose said. "But don't let that stop you."

"As sarcastic as I remember, Rose. You're like your father."

"And I'll take that as the compliment I'm sure it was meant to be," she added very sarcastically.

Meghan cleared her throat. "Well, let's make that pot of tea."

"I want to talk to you first," Sorcha said.

"About what?" Rose asked as the teakettle started to boil—she knew exactly how it felt.

"What will happen with the children now?" Sorcha asked.

"I-I don't know," Rose said; she hadn't thought of this. She assumed Vivian would take care of them. She regarded Sorcha warily. "Why?"

Sorcha looked at Meghan. "This is a private matter."

As Meghan made a move to leave, Rose held on to her arm to stop her; she continued to watch Sorcha. "She stays. Now why are you concerned about the children?"

"Because they have no parents. Who'll take care of them?"

"I appreciate your concern, Sorcha, but tomorrow, we're meeting with Kathleen's lawyer. We'll see what happens after that."

"You'll be goin' back to America. Vivian is getting old and—"

"Surely, you're not suggesting you'll take them? This is their home. What…" Rose shook her head. "This is not open for discussion."

"Someone has to look after them," Sorcha said almost angrily.

Rose nearly laughed out loud. "Don't worry. Have a cookie." She offered her the plate. "We'll be out in a minute."

Sorcha huffed angrily and marched out of the kitchen.

"What nerve," Rose said, tossing the towel on the counter. "The old biddy."

Meghan quietly made the pot of tea and placed the cups on the tray, then set up the pastry and small plates on another, while Rose went on.

"I mean, really. Who does she think she is? Barging in here, making plans for Donal and Caitlin as if they'd want to live with her. They don't even know her. Over my dead body…" She stopped and watched Meghan pour the water in the teapot. "Don't you agree?"

Meghan looked up. "I do. I do."

"What are you doing?"

"I'm learnin' to stay out of your way when ya get your Irish up." She grinned and picked up the tray. "Grab the teacups, Culhane, before ya have a stroke."

Rose grumbled as she picked up the tray and obediently followed Meghan. "She's not getting those kids," she whispered angrily. "Over my dead body."

Chapter 13

Brendan Flaherty stood when they walked into the living room and took the tray from Rose.

"Thank you," she said. "And thank you for coming, Brendan."

"It's the least I could do. Kathleen was a good woman. I was just talking to Vivian and the children about that." He looked at Meghan then. "I'm sorry. We haven't met."

"Oh, Brendan. This is Meghan Quigley, a friend of the family. This is Brendan Flaherty, Kathleen's brother-in-law."

"It's nice to meet you," Meghan said.

"Would that it was under better circumstances," he said kindly.

"I would have to agree there," Vivian said, pouring the tea. She handed one to Sorcha, then Brendan.

"Some nice person put a few bottles of fizzy drinks in the fridge," Meghan said to Donal and Caitlin.

They looked at Vivian, who nodded. "Only one each for now."

"Why don't you go and chase the peacocks before it rains again?" Rose offered.

"Sure." Donal ran to the kitchen with Caitlin right on his heels.

"They're good kids," Brendan said. "It's got to be hard for them. For all of you."

"It is, but we'll get through it," Rose said, staring at the plate of pastries. All of the sudden, she was ravenous. "How have you been?"

"Oh, fine. I'm working on a few stories for a local paper in London right now. Freelancing for the time being." He laughed and drank his tea. "Have to pay the rent before I think about writing the great novel."

"Why London? If you don't mind my askin'," Meghan said. "One would think Ireland had plenty of inspiration."

Brendan shrugged. "I suppose I needed to get away. Someplace for myself. And Desmond, God rest him, wasn't the best influence."

"He was a hard one to figure," Vivian said thoughtfully. She reached over and placed several cookies and a small piece of cake on a plate and handed it to Rose. "You've been starin' at it."

Rose blushed and took the plate. She noticed Meghan watching Brendan with a curious eye.

"Des was a lucky man," he said, almost to himself. He absently looked around the living room.

Rose exchanged glances with Vivian but said nothing.

"How so?" Meghan asked.

Brendan smiled then. "He had a perfect life. A wonderful wife, children, a home, and property."

Rose continued to watch Meghan, who still looked cautious and tentative. She remembered all she found out about Desmond; maybe Brendan knew something. Perhaps that was the reason for the curious expression on Meghan's face.

"Des had a wild wanderin' soul," Vivian said. "I know he loved Kathleen and the children."

"Then he should have taken better care of them," Brendan blurted out. When he realized what he said, he quickly took a drink of tea.

"Would ya like something a little stronger?" Vivian asked. She looked at Meghan, who nodded.

"I know I would. How about a whiskey?" Meghan asked him.

Brendan nodded. "That would be grand."

"Rose? Vivian?" Meghan asked.

Though Rose really wanted something, she knew she'd be out like a light if she did. She and Vivian declined. Brendan watched Meghan as she walked into the kitchen.

"I apologize for that outburst. Des was as good a father and husband as he could be, I suppose."

"Kathleen fell head over heels when she first met him," Vivian said, smiling at the memory. "And oh, did Desmond Flaherty fall for her. He was a charmer."

Rose saw the dark look transform Brendan's face as he stared at his empty teacup. Vivian was oblivious as she continued.

"And Donal certainly got your family genes, Brendan. And little Caitlin is the picture of her mother. With that fiery red head of hers."

Meghan walked into the living room. "Vivian, you've got a good bottle of Irish." She handed Brendan a tumbler with a good amount of whiskey in it.

Brendan raised his glass. "To Kathleen's memory. I'm sorrier than I can say."

They all took a drink and sat in silence for a moment. Rose smiled when she heard Donal and Caitlin laughing outside. She envisioned Caitlin's red hair blowing in the wind as she chased the peacocks.

"Brendan, you'll stay here while you're in Ireland," Vivian said.

"I don't want to be in the way. I can easily stay in Donegal."

"I won't hear of it. I have the guest room all made up for you."

"All right then, thank you. I appreciate the kindness." He tossed back the rest of his whiskey and stood. "If ya don't mind, I think I'll go into Trahern. I haven't been there in years."

"Not at all," Vivian said. "Let me show you up to your room first. You can get settled in."

Brendan went out to his car and returned with his luggage, then followed Vivian up the stairs. Rose turned to Meghan.

"Okay, you look very suspicious. What are you thinking?"

"Nothin', really." Meghan looked down at her glass. "Do ya know how close Brendan was to his brother?"

"No, actually. Like I've said, I've only met him a few times. I do remember Kathleen saying he moved to London to get away from the family, well, probably Desmond. He just said as much."

Meghan nodded and sipped her whiskey. Rose could see by her expression, Meghan's mind must be racing. With everything that had happened, Rose hadn't had time to concentrate on what Meghan told her the other night. The unknown had her feeling anxious and troubled. And speaking of troubled, Rose watched Meghan as she now gazed out the window. There was much she and Meghan needed to discuss about Desmond and Kathleen.

And now, with the meeting with Kathleen's lawyer in the morning looming over her head, she only wanted to concentrate on what was in Kathleen's will.

Chapter 14

"I don't know what to expect," Vivian said as Rose pulled in a small lot across from the lawyer's office in Donegal.

"I don't, either. But he was specific. You and I are the only ones required to be here." Rose shut off the engine. "Well, let's go."

As Rose opened her door, Vivian stopped her. "Rose, whatever happens in there, I—"

Rose patted her hand. "Kathleen knew what she was doing. It'll be fine. We'll get through it."

They casually walked to Mr. Downey's office. "It was nice of Meghan to offer to stay with the children."

"Yes, it was. She's a good woman."

"I know she is." Vivian smiled and slipped her hand in the crook of Rose's arm. "And I can tell ya like her and she you. It's a shame she had to drive all the way home last night."

"Well, given the circumstances and our house guest, we thought it was best…for now."

"I understand." She playfully bumped her shoulder into Rose. "At least Sorcha went home."

They both laughed as they walked up to the door and stopped. "Well, this is it."

The office smelled of pipe tobacco and the heady aroma of a peat fire. A young woman looked up when they walked in.

"Good morning, Miss Culhane," she said quietly.

"Good morning," Vivian and Rose said simultaneously.

Rose felt the heat rise to her face when Vivian raised an

eyebrow. "Oh, she meant you." She looked at the woman. "Sorry, I'm a little nervous."

The woman laughed. "I understand. Let me tell Mr. Downey you're here. Please have a seat."

They sat in the comfortable chairs by her desk. "I am nervous," Rose whispered.

"It'll be fine," Vivian said, fidgeting with her purse.

In a moment, Mr. Downey appeared. He held out his hand to Vivian. "Vivian, I'm so sorry. Kathleen was a lovely woman." He then looked at Rose. "And you must be the cousin from America. Kathleen talked of you often. Please, come in, and we'll get started."

They followed Mr. Downey into his office and sat in front of his desk, waiting patiently as he opened the manila folder and put on his reading glasses. "I'm sorry I couldn't attend the services. I was in Dublin," he said solemnly as he leafed through the pages.

"That's all right, Michael. It was a lovely service," Vivian said. "Did Kathleen change much?"

He looked up over his glasses from Vivian to Rose. "A few things, yes. But we'll get to it. Let me read the preliminaries and get that out of the way."

He cleared his throat and started with the usual, "I, Kathleen Culhane Flaherty…" Rose listened, trying to concentrate on what he was saying and not allowing her mind to jump all over the place.

She was embarrassed when he stopped and said, "So that's just the legal mumbo jumbo I'm required to tell you. Here is what concerns both of you." He handed them copies of Kathleen's will. "You can read along."

Rose and Vivian took them. Rose glanced at the legal paper, trying to stop her hand from shaking.

"As you can see, Rose, Kathleen appointed you the executrix of her will."

"Why not Aunt Vivian?" Rose asked.

"Because this was her wish," he said simply. He looked at Vivian. "It was no offense to you, Vivian."

"Oh, I know. Rose," Vivian said, looking at her, "whatever is in here is Kathleen's wish. I'm not offended in the least."

"Okay," Rose said. "I just wasn't expecting this."

"Well, then hold on to your hat," Mr. Downey mumbled.

Rose and Vivian exchanged curious glances as he continued, "You'll see in the first paragraph, Kathleen put all stocks and investment holdings in the children's names and in a trust fund until they reach twenty-one. She wanted to transfer any cash accounts to you and Vivian, which will require both signatures. We'll do that when we're finished here."

"That seems only right." Rose read along and nodded.

"I agree," Vivian said. "They should be provided for, absolutely. The children are the most important issue."

"That's exactly what Kathleen said. I have the paperwork all ready, as well. Once we get everything agreed upon, as I said, I'll just need signatures to get it all in order to get it filed. Now here's the main codicil to her will," Mr. Downey said. "Kathleen appointed you, Rose, as Donal and Caitlin's legal guardian. I had all the paperwork drawn up. Kathleen was to tell you about this, but unfortunately... Now all it needs is your signature, if you agree."

Rose was stunned. She read the passage again. "I... Why me?" She looked at Vivian. "Why not you? You should be their guardian. You live with them."

Vivian seemed just as stunned. "She must have had her reasons, Rose." She looked at Mr. Downey to elaborate.

"If you read further..."

Rose and Vivian did as he instructed. It was Vivian who spoke first when they were finished.

"It does make sense," she said softly. "The children love both of us, I know. But you have a special bond with them, and that's the way it should be. Kathleen left it very clear, if you don't want to do this, then I will be their guardian."

"And if you read even further..." Mr. Downey said. "If you agree and accept legal guardianship, then it naturally will be your responsibility to make provisions should something happen to you and Vivian. But that will be another matter for the future.

Although," he said, scratching his head, "Kathleen mentioned you might consider a Meghan Quigley. She seemed to think you would have a special relationship with her." He laughed quietly. "She told me she only hoped you would. Do you know what she meant?"

Rose glanced at Vivian, who smiled, but concentrated on the pages she read. Rose laughed quietly then. "Yes, Mr. Downey, I know what she meant."

Poor Mr. Downey looked confused and a little befuddled. "Well, I'm glad someone does. Kathleen was adamant about not having any member of Desmond Flaherty's family having a say in the children's upbringing. Though she said his parents were deceased and the only living relative was a brother in London."

"Brendan Flaherty," Rose said. "He's here for the funeral. Staying at the house now. But he does live in London. He's a writer."

"He shouldn't have anything to say in this," Vivian said. "He's only met the children once or twice." Vivian set the pages on Mr. Downey's desk. "I have no problem with this, Michael. I think Kathleen was right to make Rose their legal guardian."

Rose read it once again. "Why didn't she want Desmond's family to have any claim on the children?" But she answered her question when she thought of Desmond and what Meghan had told her. Kathleen must have known what Des had done. She looked up to see Vivian and Mr. Downey watching her.

"That was curious to me, as well," he said, sitting back. He took out his pipe. "Do ya mind?" He lit the pipe and blew a puff of smoke into the air. "She never told me why. All she said was she didn't want anyone tryin' to lay claim to her children or Peacock Walk, which brings us to the last part of her will."

Rose read further. "She wanted to make sure the property stays in the family. No one is ever to sell it or divide it up. It goes to Aunt Vivian, then to me, then the children. That seems logical."

Vivian agreed once gain. "It is. I think this is the best. Nothing changes really."

Mr. Downey handed Rose another few pages. "This is the

107

paperwork for the bank accounts to be signed. And these are for the guardianship. Kathleen expressed her wish that you stay here in Ireland, Miss Culhane. But she also realized, as you read on, that you have a life in America. She told me she knew you'd do the right thing for the children."

Rose listened as she read. Vivian reached over and placed her hand on Rose's forearm. "This is a big decision."

"It is," Mr. Downey said, puffing his pipe. "You can certainly take time to think about it."

"I don't need to think about it," Rose said, smiling at Vivian; she reached over and took her hand. "The transition for the children has to be as painless as possible. This is what Kathleen wanted for Donal and Caitlin. We stay a family, and we stay here."

Rose looked at Mr. Downey. "Got a pen?"

Chapter 15

When they pulled up the gravel driveway, they saw Donal and Caitlin running toward the car. Behind them was Meghan. When Rose saw her, her heart skipped a beat. She just sat there and watched her as she waved to them.

Vivian cleared her throat. "Yes, she's a handsome woman. Now quit moonin' over her."

Rose laughed. "I can't help it." As Vivian opened her door, Rose put her hand on her arm. "You don't mind?"

Vivian smiled and patted her hand. "This world is changin'. It was never a thought in my day. But as I watch the news and see what's goin' on in America and even here in Ireland, I can't help but think it's time for all of you. I'm not sayin' I understand it, but no, darlin', I don't mind. You seem happy together, and I'm not sure much else matters in this world."

Rose reached over and hugged her. "Thanks, Aunt Vivian. I love you."

"I love you, too."

"Rose!" Caitlin opened her car door. "Donal chased Mr. Murphy's sheep up the hill. And Salty barked at him."

"He did?" Rose said, slipping out of the car.

"But Bunny saved him," she said, holding up the savior.

"I needed no savin'," Donal said, shaking his head.

"You almost got stuck in the briar," Meghan said to him. She laughed along with him when he took a playful swat in her direction. "Did ya get everything settled?" she asked, helping Vivian out of the Land Rover.

"We did," Vivian said. "Let's go inside. We'll tell you everything."

Caitlin launched herself at Vivian, who grunted and laughed as she hugged her. "Where's your Uncle Brendan?"

"His car is gone." Rose noticed Donal's grin fade.

"He said he wanted to take a drive, revisit some places, I suppose," Meghan said.

As they walked up to the house, a few peacocks squawked and ran toward the trees.

"They seem a little more skittish than usual," Vivian said.

Rose put her arm around Caitlin. "Were you chasing them again?"

Caitlin giggled and hugged Rose. "No, but I don't think they like Uncle Brendan."

"Why is that?" Rose asked as they walked into the living room. "Nice fire. It's chilly today."

She sat in the chair by the fire, pulling Caitlin onto her lap. "Now tell me why the peacocks don't like your uncle."

Caitlin shrugged. "They put up a big fuss when he walked by them."

Vivian let out a groan when she sat in her chair by the window. "Those birds always squawk."

"Uncle Brendan was mean to them," Caitlin said.

"Mean how?" Rose asked.

Caitlin looked up with her big blue eyes. "He tried to hit one."

"He did not, Cait," Donal said. "He was just tryin' to walk through them. Ya know how they are with people."

"Donal, take Caitlin into the kitchen. There are some cookies left on the counter," Rose said. "Eat at the table."

Caitlin jumped off Rose's lap and ran to the kitchen with Donal. They waited until the children disappeared through the kitchen door.

"All right, Rose, tell Meghan what happened before the children come back," Vivian said eagerly.

Meghan sat opposite Rose by the fire and waited. Rose took a moment, then explained everything that transpired at Mr. Downey's office. She watched Meghan's expression change from curious to surprised to almost incredulous when Rose told her about Kathleen's wish for her to be the children's legal guardian. When she finished, Meghan sat back and shook her head.

"I'm not sure what I was expectin', but I didn't think of that," Meghan said. "What are ya goin' to do?"

"I signed the legal papers to start the process of guardianship. Mr. Downey said there's nothing that can stop it, and it's just a matter of filing the forms with the courts," Rose said.

"I, for one, think it's the best thing for the children," Vivian said. "Kathleen was right on this."

Meghan nodded thoughtfully; she glanced at Rose. "So you have a decision to make."

"To stay here or take the children to America," Rose said. "I can't imagine taking them from their home. This is all they know." She looked around the living room. "Someday, they'll inherit all this."

"Yes, they'll own Peacock Walk and the squawking peacocks," she added sarcastically.

"Then are ya sayin' you'll stay on here in Ireland?" Meghan asked.

Rose saw the tentative expression and smiled. "I suppose that's what I'm saying." She scratched her head. "I have a lot to do."

"You do whatever you need. You're on no timetable here. Take the time you need." Vivian walked over to her and kissed the top of her head. "I need to make sure they haven't eaten every cookie in the kitchen. I'll leave you two to discuss things."

Rose looked up. "I love you, Aunt Vivian."

"I love ya, too, darlin'."

When Vivian walked out, Meghan sat on the hearth next to Rose. She took her hands and kissed them. "This is a great deal to think about. What about your job?"

"Do you know what I do all day?"

Meghan grinned. "I haven't a clue."

"I examine spreadsheets. I'm on the bottom rung of the managerial ladder. I'm sure they can find someone to replace me without too much trouble."

"But your home? Your friends?" Meghan gently prodded; she ran her thumb over the back of Rose's hand.

"I rent an apartment. I can easily get out of the lease. And I have a few friends who will adjust." Rose stopped and cocked her head. "I sound like I have a pathetic life, don't I?"

Meghan laughed along with her. "Seriously," Meghan said finally. "It's a big change."

"It is a big change," Rose said. "But a change I'm willing and wanting to make." She stared at the fire. "And not just for the kids." She looked at Meghan then.

"That's good to hear," Meghan said. "So what will ya do next?"

Rose took a thoughtful breath and let it out slowly. "I suppose I'll call work and talk to my boss. Then I'll talk to Sharon, she's a friend, and fill her in. I'll have to fly back there and make all the arrangements. I honestly don't have that much. The only thing I own is my car." She laughed at the idea. "I never realized how much I don't have."

Meghan leaned over and took her hands. "You do now."

Rose smiled, holding on to Meghan's hands. "Yes, I do. It's amazing how everything has changed in such a short time. Though the reason is very tragic."

"It 'tis, Rose." She stopped and looked down at their hands.

Rose gently tightened her grip. "What's on your mind, Doc?"

Meghan chuckled. "I was just thinking about us."

"Good."

Meghan looked up then; the smile on her face had Rose smiling in return. "We don't know each other well—"

"I thought we got to know each other pretty well back at your house."

"Ya know what I mean."

"I do. I'm teasing. I know we have a lot to learn about each other. But we're on the same page, right?"

"I believe we are. I've no regrets about the other night. I loved every minute of it. Can't get it out of my mind, actually."

Rose loved how she blushed when she laughed nervously. "I

can't, either. It makes it very hard to concentrate on all that's been happening. Why don't we do this…?"

Meghan cocked her head and grinned. "I'm all ears, as you Americans say."

"Let's take each day as it comes. We both have a lot to think about and talk about, for that matter, because at some point we have to discuss this business with Desmond and gold."

"Yes, we do. I have to tell you what Kathleen and I discussed, which to tell the truth, wasn't much more than I told you, and I haven't heard anything more from anyone."

"But you think there's something going on, don't you?"

"I don't know. With Desmond and now Kathleen…" She shook her head. "We'll get to that later. There's enough ya have to contend with for now."

"You're right. I need to tell the children. It's important that they get back some semblance of normalcy in their lives. Then when we talk more about Desmond, we'll tell Aunt Vivian." She held on to Meghan's hands. "The future is wide open, and I want you to be part of it."

Meghan stood and pulled Rose up with her, wrapping her arms around her waist as she did. "I think that's a grand idea, Rose Culhane," she whispered against her lips. "I want so much to be part of your future."

It was a tender, brief kiss but one filled with promise and anticipation of what would come.

Chapter 16

Rose was nervous, and there was no wondering why. She was on the verge of completely changing her life. Filled with excitement, anticipation, and trepidation—oh, and nausea—she dialed Sharon's number at work. And after a few minutes of explanation, there was silence on the other end.

"Sharon? Did you fall off your chair?"

"I-I'm here," she said. "At least I think I am."

Rose laughed. "I know it's a lot to take in."

"It is. But you know I'm not really surprised. Somehow, I had a feeling this would happen."

"You did?" Rose sat on the edge of her bed and looked out the window at the foggy day.

"When you called about your cousin's death, my first thought was of the children and what would happen. I guess it's the way you've always talked about your relationship with her and the kids. You've always been happy when you went there for a visit and always a little depressed when you came back. This might sound crazy, but I think you belong there."

Rose listened as she watched the fog roll by her window. Suddenly, she felt a sense of loss for the first time. "This is a big decision. What if I'm not the best thing for the children? What if I can't do this? And what if it doesn't work out with Meghan? Oh, my God. I think I'm going to throw up."

Sharon laughed quietly. "Shut up. You're not going to vomit, and your cousin would never have made you their guardian if she wasn't sure. And as far as Meghan? Holy shit, woman. You tell me about an attractive woman with a PhD, who probably adores you, and from the way you've been talking, you feel the same. It's like something out of a gothic romance novel. No one is telling you you're madly in love right now. But hell, give it a chance. You haven't had a serious relationship as long as I've known you. And I've known you for five years."

"That's pathetic."

Sharon laughed again. "Was pathetic. That's in the past. And you tell me the kids like Meghan and so does your aunt."

"Yes, they do." Rose let out a deep sigh. "It's such a big responsibility. I mean with Donal and Cait."

"But you'll have your aunt there, as well. I think your cousin wanted to make sure someone was there for them, to help them, and guide them, and hell, just love them. And that's you."

"I feel like crying," Rose said, sniffing back the tears.

"Nothing wrong with that. A good crying jag is good for the soul, just wait till we get off the phone. So enough of that. What's next?"

"Well, I have to tell Bob. He is my boss after all."

"Oh, right." Sharon laughed. "I suppose he should know. Then what?"

"I'll need to come back there."

"Why?"

"Why?" Rose was stumped by that. "Well..."

"What do you need? I can send it to you. I can pack any clothes you want, and by the way, your wardrobe is atrocious, and I can have anything you want shipped there. You realize you're a minimalist in the strictest sense of the word."

"I am not. I have things I want. Though I can't think of anything right at this moment."

"You big liar. I bet I can go to your apartment right now and go through your closets and find nothing you would want to pack and send to Ireland. And as far as furniture, what would you want?"

"Well, my...well, there's the..." She sat in a chair by the window. "Wow. There's nothing I really need or want. Oh, pictures, all the pictures on the walls and in the box under my bed."

"Under your bed? Good grief. All of which I can pack and send to you. What else?"

"I… Well, I have to think. I'd have a better handle on it if I was actually there."

"I have an idea."

"Oh, God, I really am going to throw up. What?"

"You know I've been looking for a new apartment. Why don't you sublet your apartment to me? I want something in the city. Yours is perfect."

"That's actually a great idea. I hadn't thought of that. But what about—"

Sharon let out an impatient groan. "Do you want your bedroom set?"

"No. It's not really a set."

"Your living room or kitchen?"

"Well, no. But my car. I—"

"That old POS?"

"Hey."

"Rose, really. I'm sure your landlady will have no problem with this. I can move in and take care of everything with no rush. I can sell the car and send you the money if the guy doesn't laugh in my face first, of course. I can pack your pictures and any other knicker-knackers," she added sarcastically.

"I have no real knicker-knackers," Rose said with a sigh. "This truly is pathetic."

"Not pathetic. I think deep down you never wanted to put down any real roots, even though you've lived here all your life. You never bought anything new. You never bought a house or a condo. Never spent any money on anything. In the back of your mind, I think you always knew you'd someday be living in Ireland. You talked about it more than once, you know. I remember one night after you got back from a visit. We sat at a bar, and you went on and on about living there so much, I wanted to buy you a one-way ticket just to shut you up."

"You're probably right. This is very strange."

"I know. It's happening fast. But the kids need you there with them. If you want to do it later and come back, fine. But I don't see the need. I can take care of all this for you. You have enough to think about."

"But I can't ask you to do all this."

"All what? This is my idea. I want to move into your apartment. Call your landlady. She's a nice old gal. I'll move in, and you can take your time if you want anything. And as far as your banking, hell, everything is done online or by fax. Now call Bob, tell him adios. Maybe I'll get your job, too."

Rose laughed along with her. "If anyone deserves it, you do. I'll suggest it. You'll be sorry, though."

"So you're going to do it?" Sharon asked.

Rose took a deep confident breath. "Yes. This is a good idea. Thanks, Sharon. You've made this decision so much easier for me. And when all this is over, you can come here for a visit. I'll buy your ticket."

"Deal. I'm gonna miss you," Sharon said.

Rose felt her pain in her chest, even though she was relieved and happy. "Me too. I never realized just how much until this moment. But we'll be talking to each other practically every day until this is settled."

"Right. Now I'll connect you with Bob, then you call your landlady. Love you."

"Love you, too."

Rose told her boss everything that had happened; well, she left out the part regarding Desmond and the gold. He wasn't thrilled, but he understood. And he liked the idea of Sharon taking her job, which Rose knew he would. Bob hated the hiring process, including the interviews.

After that was all settled, she called Mrs. Wallace, her landlady, who was tearful and sad, until Rose mentioned she had someone to move in right away who had a steady job and was eager and mature. Then all was right, and she agreed completely. Next was her banking. She would take care of that later in the week.

So for now, it seemed all was set. Again, things were happening with lightning quickness. Rose barely had time to breathe. Her mind was still reeling when she heard a soft knock at her bedroom door.

"C'mon in," she called out.

Meghan poked her head in. "May I?"

"Of course." Rose laughed when Meghan walked in and looked around.

"Nice room. I was just a little worried. Ya've been up here for a while."

"I've been on the phone with Sharon, my boss, and my landlady," she said and flounced on the bed and stretched out.

Meghan sat beside her. "And what's the verdict?"

"Well, let's see," Rose said, scratching the back of her neck. "Sharon is going to sublet my apartment. My boss was not thrilled about my quitting, but he understood and was grateful for the call. I think Sharon will get my job, which she deserves. This way, I can take my time, and Sharon can send whatever I want, which isn't much."

"It's all okay then?" Meghan asked quietly.

"Seems so. Oh, maybe sometime this week, I'll need to go into Donegal and open an account at Aunt Vivian's bank. Or whichever bank Kathleen used. Would you come with me?"

"Of course I will." Meghan reached over and ran her hand over Rose's abdomen. "I'll be there whenever ya need me."

"Thank you," Rose said. "That means a lot to me."

"So you're stayin'?" Meghan grinned and slipped her hand under Rose's sweater.

Rose let out a deep sigh when she felt the warmth of Meghan's hand on her bare skin. "Yes, and if you don't stop, I'll be coming, as well."

Meghan laughed and playfully slapped her stomach. "At some point, we'll have to discuss when we can be together again, Rosie. I miss lying next to ya. I miss makin' love to ya." She leaned over and lightly kissed Rose on the lips. "I miss these lips, as well."

Rose threw her arms around Meghan's neck, pulling her down. Meghan deepened her kiss and slipped her hand farther up to cup Rose's breast. "So what are you saying? You miss me?"

"Rose," she whispered in a warning, coarse voice.

The throbbing started when Rose heard her quiet plea.

"Meghan," she whispered while kissing her, "we can't do this here. At least not now."

Meghan, nearly breathless, pulled back. "I'm so sorry. I—"

"Don't you dare apologize." She reached up and caressed Meghan's cheek. "We'll make time."

Meghan nodded and stood, offering her hand, which Rose took. "We will. And you need to talk to the children."

"I know. I've been thinking about how I'll tell them." She slipped her arm around Meghan's waist as they walked to the door.

"It'll be fine. They love you, and I think they'll be happy with you bein' their guardian."

"I hope so." As Meghan reached for the door, Rose stopped her. She kissed her deeply before pulling back. "Thank you again."

"Ya never need to thank me, Rosie. I'm always here."

Donal and Caitlin were lying on the living room floor and looked up from their board game when Rose and Meghan walked in. Vivian sat in her chair, her reading glasses perched on the end of her nose while she read.

"Hey, kids, can we talk for a minute?" Rose asked.

Vivian looked up with a curious look, then put down the book.

Meghan cleared her throat. "Perhaps I should go and—"

"No, please stay," Rose said. Meghan sat on the couch and remained silent.

"What's wrong, Rose?" Donal immediately sat up.

"Oh, honey. Nothing is wrong." Rose sat in the chair by the fire. Caitlin quickly scrambled up onto her lap. "You know Aunt Vivian and I went to see the lawyer earlier today to read your mom's will."

"What's a will?" Caitlin asked.

"Let's see. How do I explain this?" Rose said, cuddling her close. "Your mom wanted to make sure you and Donal, Aunt Vivian, and I were taken care of. So she wrote some things down for us."

"Because she's not here to take care of us?" Caitlin asked.

"Yes, sweetie, that's right. But she loved all of us so much she wanted to make sure we were all right."

"What did it say, Rose?" Donal asked, inching his way toward her.

Rose glanced at Vivian, who smiled and nodded reassuringly. "Your mom wanted me to be your legal guardian." She winced and waited for their reaction.

"What does that mean?" Caitlin asked.

"It means I'll be staying here with you, and between me and Aunt Vivian, we'll take care of you."

"Are you my mam now?" Caitlin asked.

"Oh, honey, no. I could never take your mother's place. It's just because you're children, and by law, you need someone who will step in and take care of you, like a parent."

"So you're still cousin Rose?" Caitlin looked up with big blue eyes.

"Yes, sweetie, that will never change."

"I get it," Donal said; he smiled then. "So you're staying here in Ireland? And we're not moving to America?"

"Is that all right?" Rose asked.

"It's grand," Donal said; he knelt in front of Rose. "We're a family, right?" He looked back at Vivian, who had tears in her eyes as she nodded. "All of us?"

"All of us." Rose fought back the tears as Donal hugged her around the neck, then ran over to Vivian and hugged her, as well.

"Rose?" Caitlin said.

"Yes, sweetie?"

Caitlin leaned into her. "Is Meghan going to live with us, too?"

Rose felt the heat rise from her toes; Vivian's eyes grew wide, and Meghan's jaw hit the floor.

"Your face is all red, Rose. What's the matter?" Caitlin said.

Donal grabbed Caitlin by the hand, yanking her off Rose's lap. "Don't ask such silly questions."

"Why is it silly?" Caitlin asked as Donal dragged her out

of the living room. "Stop pullin' me. And don't call me silly. Ya *amadan*."

"Caitlin Mary!" Vivian called out to them. "Don't call your brother an idiot!"

Meghan laughed. "Things might be gettin' back to normal quicker than ya thought. God love them."

As the children ran out the front door, they ran into Brendan coming in.

"Whoa," he said with a laugh. "Where are ya off to?" He walked into the living room. "They're in a big hurry."

Vivian laughed. "They're children. They're always in a hurry. How are you, Brendan?"

"I'm grand, thank you. How are you ladies doin'?" He sat back in the chair by the fireplace. "Oh, did ya go into Donegal and see the lawyer?"

Rose quickly looked up. "How did you know?"

Brendan seemed confused. "Ya told me at the funeral. Don't ya remember?"

Rose couldn't honestly say she did. "I'm sorry. The day—"

"I know. It was a hard day for everyone. Don't apologize. So did you get everything settled?"

Rose saw Meghan's curious expression as she regarded Brendan. Rose knew she would have to tell Brendan about the children. And in addition, she had to tell Aunt Vivian all of what Meghan had told her about Desmond. But what did it have to do with Kathleen, if anything?

All settled? Rose laughed inwardly—hardly.

Chapter 17

"Brendan, have a seat, please." Rose offered the chair by the fire.

Brendan obediently sat without a word. He smiled as he looked around the room. "All right, I'm sitting. It can't be that bad."

Rose was about to answer when she saw Meghan's curious expression toward Brendan. Rose wondered what was going through her mind, but she tore her gaze away and regarded Brendan.

"I don't think it's bad at all. And yes, we did get everything settled. I know you're Donal and Cait's uncle, and I know you care for them. So being a relative, I figure you have a right to know. Kathleen made me legal guardian over the children." She left out the part that Kathleen didn't want Desmond's family to have any claim over her children. "I hope you understand."

For a moment, Brendan looked at her, then Vivian; he looked as though he was gauging his response. He then smiled and nodded. "Of course I do. I've barely spent any time with them. And with no grandparents and only you and Vivian, I can completely understand why she'd do this. And I agree with it. Anyone can see how they love you and Vivian. And that's as it should be."

He sounded sincere enough, but the doubtful look was still present on Meghan's face; it unnerved Rose as she wanted to know why Meghan looked so skeptical.

"I'm glad you understand," Vivian said, pulling Rose back into the conversation.

"I do." Brendan put his head back. "It's such a sad thing all the way round. First Des, and now Kathleen." He lifted his head and regarded them. "Seems so fantastic in a way, doesn't it? I mean, what are the odds of them dyin' in almost the same way?"

"It does seem odd," Vivian said absently.

"Yes." Meghan spoke for the first time. "It does seem coincidental."

"Ya don't seem convinced," he said.

Meghan shrugged. "I suppose I'm not one for coincidences."

Brendan looked surprised. "You think their deaths are connected?"

"I don't know. I suppose it's possible, just..."

"Improbable," Rose interjected. She wasn't sure if Brendan should be included on what she knew about his brother, but then again, Desmond was his brother; perhaps he had a right to know.

Brendan seemed lost in his thoughts; Rose took the time to give Meghan a look of "should we tell him?" Meghan responded by pulling at her earlobe, a gesture that Rose had no idea how to interpret.

"Now that you have me thinking about this, the last time I talked to Des, he seemed...I don't know, preoccupied I suppose is a good word," Brendan said, looking from Meghan to Rose. "Ladies, is there something I should know about?"

Rose wanted to reach over and slap Meghan's hand away from her ear and start talking.

"Was there something wrong?" Brendan continued. "Look, I know my brother was a dreamer and not one to hold down a job, but if you're implying that his death was something other than a horrible accident, I'd like to know how you came to that conclusion. I think I have a right to know."

"I must agree with Brendan," Vivian said with a curious smile. "Is there something we should know?"

"Yes, Vivian, and I'll get to it." Meghan turned to Brendan. "When you say Desmond seemed preoccupied, what exactly do ya mean?"

Brendan seemed to be getting irritated; he took a long breath. "He came to London for a visit. I noticed he looked like something was on his mind. I asked him as much. He said he was on to something, but he couldn't say. I figured it was one of his wild schemes." He laughed quietly and looked at Rose. "You met him, Rose. He always had something goin' on. If he only spent all that energy to just get a job…"

"I know. He meant well, I think," Rose said. "Did he say what he was into?"

Brendan shook his head. "No. Only that he'd fill me in when he could."

"When was this?" Meghan asked.

"About three months before he died."

"Brendan," Meghan stopped momentarily, "I'm tryin' to figure how to tell you what I know and have it make sense."

Brendan smiled sadly. "Well, if it involves Des, it would be easy."

They all agreed with that assessment when they laughed quietly. Meghan then told Brendan and Vivian all she knew. Rose sat back and listened as Meghan told them about the Tellus Border project and what its purpose was. When Meghan got to the mining of gold, Rose watched Brendan's reaction. He seemed curious while he listened to what Meghan knew.

"Gold?" he said cautiously. "Des?"

"Meghan, are you sure?" Vivian asked.

"Yes, that's what I think. Soon after I overheard him talking at the pub in Trahern about finding the pot of gold, I told my supervisors. They took care of it from there. But weeks later, a friend of mine who was working in Donegal doin' primarily the same thing I was doin' heard about a mining company that was missing quite a bit of what it mined."

"Explain how the gold is mined. I found it fascinating," Rose said.

"Yes. I'd love to know." Vivian sounded eager.

So Meghan explained the basics of how they mined for gold, the same way she explained it to Rose. When she finished, Vivian seemed astounded.

"I had no idea. It's quite amazing, actually," she said.

"And you think Des stole the rods?" Brendan asked.

Meghan shrugged. "I think so because since he died, we've heard nothing further about it."

"And the mining company got them back?" Vivian asked hopefully.

"No. The rods are still missing." Meghan glanced at Rose. "So I have no idea what to make of it."

"This is a little fantastic." Brendan sighed and sat back. "I mean, you're telling me my brother illegally mined for gold, then stole it from a mining company in Tyrone. And now he's dead. And no one knows where the rods are. It sounds like something out of a novel." He laughed softly. "I wish I thought of this storyline."

"Is this why you came here and talked with Kathleen?" Vivian asked Meghan. "That makes sense."

"You told Kathleen about this?" Brendan asked. "Did she tell you if she knew what Des did with the gold rods?"

"No," Meghan said, watching him. "She was shocked when I told her."

"Do you think Kathleen's death is connected?"

"We don't know."

"Well, wasn't it investigated?" Brendan asked.

Meghan still watched Brendan. "As much as Desmond's accident was."

"An inspector did come by and asked a few questions," Rose said. "He just wanted to keep us updated, he said. He told us the mechanic said it looked like the brake line of Kathleen's Land Rover was damaged. But he couldn't know for sure if it was intentional because it was an older model, and if she took it off road, it was very possible that it could have happened anytime. So…"

"And they've said nothing more to you?" Brendan looked from Rose to Meghan.

"No," Rose said.

"And Kathleen said nothing to you?"

Before Rose could speak, Meghan said quickly, "No, she said nothing to any of us."

Well, that was a big fat lie, Rose thought. She tried not to look surprised, but she did not have a good poker face. Vivian on the other hand, looked unaffected—she'd make a good spy.

"Brendan, did the police ever question you about Desmond's death?" Meghan continued to watch him.

Brendan shook his head. "No. I came for the funeral, then went back to London."

Rose remembered the time and had to agree, Brendan didn't stay for very long before he returned to London.

"If the authorities aren't looking into any of this, then what's your point?" Brendan asked. "I mean, if Desmond was under investigation, surely Kathleen or I would be questioned. And I know I've never been." He sat forward. "Do you think they talked to Kathleen? Maybe she knew something?"

"I think she would have said something to me if she did," Vivian said. "And she didn't."

"Maybe she didn't want to worry you?" Brendan offered. "Or the children."

At the mention of Donal and Cait, Rose's heart skipped a beat. All this talk of stealing gold and the possibility of their parents' deaths not being accidental had her stomach churning.

"Perhaps," Meghan went on coolly. "It's a moot point, I'm afraid. I suppose whatever Desmond was into will stay a mystery." She shrugged and stood. "If there's something there, I'm sure the authorities will figure it out, or at the least, they'll ask more questions. Vivian, would ya mind if I took a wee bit of your whiskey?"

Rose knew her mouth dropped at the abrupt change in topic. But again, Secret Agent Vivian seemed unfazed.

"Not at all. I may join you this time. Brendan?"

He grinned. "I'd never say no to a drop of Irish."

"It's almost suppertime. Why don't I reheat the food that's left?" Rose followed Meghan to the kitchen.

Once she got through the kitchen door, she pulled at Meghan's arm. "What's the big idea? What are you doing?"

"I'm being a gracious host." Meghan smiled while she poured three glasses of whiskey. "Would ya like one?"

"Yes. A small one. I don't want to pass out on the living room floor."

"That's always a good idea," Meghan said. "I'd hate to have to hurt my back liftin' ya."

Rose grunted sarcastically as she took out the leftovers. She turned on the oven and shoved the pots in. "Now tell me why you lied to Brendan. You and Kathleen did talk to each other about this."

Meghan put the glasses on a tray and turned to Rose. "Because he said the mining company was in Tyrone."

"So? It was in Tyrone. You told me."

"I never mentioned that to Brendan. It might have been a lucky guess, but I don't believe in luck."

"What about us?" Rose asked.

Meghan winked. "No luck there. It's fate, Rosie. Now the question is, how did he know the mining company is in Tyrone?"

"I don't like that look in your eyes."

Rose felt her jaw drop when she saw the serious, challenging look in Meghan's blue eyes. She picked up a glass of whiskey and tossed it back, then shivered violently. She poured more into the glass. "Okay. What do we do now?"

"Now we find out what Brendan knows." Meghan leaned over and gave her a quick kiss. "And I need ya coherent. So go easy on the Irish."

Meghan juggled the tray of drinks as Rose playfully slapped the back of her head.

They laughed as they walked into the living room but quickly stopped when they found Vivian alone.

"Where's Brendan?" Rose asked.

"He got a call and said he was sorry, but he needed to go. Something about a friend needing a ride somewhere. Are one of those whiskeys for me?"

Meghan laughed and offered the tray and waited while Vivian examined the glasses. "They're all the same, Vivian."

Vivian took a glass. "You can never be too sure."

"Well, so much for finding out what Brendan knows." Rose took a glass and sat on the couch. She looked at Meghan. "Which one is yours?" She motioned to the two glasses on the tray.

Meghan picked one up and tossed it back. She cocked her head. "Nope. That wasn't mine. Must be this one."

Vivian laughed and sipped her whiskey. "So now that we're

alone, you have to elaborate and tell me what you think is going on. All this talk of gold and stealing. Are you sure of all this?"

"Yes, I'm afraid we are," Meghan said.

"So let me understand. Desmond was illegally mining for gold, then stole those—what did you call them?" Vivian looked at Meghan.

"Rods of ore. That's how they mine for elements. Within the rods are veins of gold and other minerals. After they mine them, they do their process and extract the gold. That's what went missing from the mining company's inventory. It was about six months after the first incident with Desmond and pannin' for gold in that stream."

"So Desmond pans for gold, then six months later, some mining company is robbed, and when they discovered them missing, Desmond is killed in a car accident," Rose said.

"And nothing is ever mentioned again," Meghan said. "That's why I came here and met Kathleen."

"I remember when you showed up," Vivian said. "I have to admit, I had my suspicions about you."

Meghan blushed and took a drink. "And I can't blame you. After Desmond died, my supervisors never said anything to me. And when I asked, they said they gave all the information to the authorities." Meghan pulled at her earlobe. "But when I spoke with my colleague, he told me the rods were never recovered. So that's when I came here to meet Kathleen. I thought perhaps she knew something. But she had no clue. She did say, though, that Desmond seemed withdrawn or preoccupied. So I went into Trahern and asked a few questions but got nowhere."

"But evidently, Kathleen must have found out something," Rose said. "Aunt Vivian, did Kathleen seem different to you somehow? She never said anything to you?"

"No. This is all new to me. I had no idea what you two were into," Vivian said to Meghan, "but I knew there was something."

"She must have talked to someone," Meghan said. "That's where she had to be that morning. She said she needed to talk to me but didn't want to talk on the phone, especially since it was stormin'."

"And how ironic that she died in that storm on her way home," Vivian said sadly. She sipped her drink and put her head back. "Such a tragedy."

They all sat in silence for a moment or two before Rose spoke. "So what happens now?"

"I don't know," Meghan said. "I'm not even sure if there is anything to do."

"If the authorities know about the stolen rods, they know about Desmond. If they needed anything from us, we surely would have been contacted by now. Don't you think?"

"Yes, I agree. And if they thought Kathleen's accident was not in fact an accident, they would have called us. And they haven't." Rose ran her fingers through her hair. "So maybe it's all over with Desmond, and Kathleen's death was truly a tragic accident."

"Unless something else happens, I think that's our best assumption," Meghan said.

"And what of Brendan?" Vivian asked.

Meghan and Rose exchanged confounded looks.

"Any suggestions?" Rose asked.

Meghan shook her head. "Not a one."

Vivian stood. "I suggest we stop all this mysterious talk and put it all behind us. Now I smell something heavenly coming from the kitchen. Go get the children, Rose. Meghan, you'll stay for dinner?"

"Of course. Thank you, Vivian."

"So that's it?" Rose asked, holding out her hands. "There's no mystery?"

"Be careful what you ask for, darlin'," Vivian said over her shoulder.

Chapter 18

Rose stood in the kitchen, gazing out the window while she drank her tea. She thought of the last week and how things did seem to be leveling out since they last discussed Desmond, gold, and Kathleen. Perhaps Aunt Vivian was correct, and they should just forget all that talk. One thing Rose was sure of, she was glad she never mentioned anything to the children. They needed to get back to some semblance of normalcy.

Caitlin, with the resilience of a seven-year-old, was eager to get back to her violin and step dancing lessons—Rose wasn't sure if she was looking forward to that; she was told by Vivian that Caitlin's practicing could get quite irritating; she sadly remembered back in Chicago when she and Kathleen joked about Cait's dancing skills. And Donal, though still somewhat withdrawn, spent the day with his friends playing football, which to Rose was just soccer. It was almost July, and both had until the end of August before they had to go back to school. Rose was happy to see the education schedule in Ireland was almost the same as in the States. So they had two months of fun.

It was Brendan who had all of them curious. He didn't go back to London, saying he needed to get away from the city and wanted to stay in Trahern for another week and visit old friends there and in Donegal. Of course, Vivian insisted he stay at Peacock Walk, and of course, Brendan accepted.

Back in Chicago, Sharon was in the process of moving into Rose's apartment; they would take their time, as planned, and decide what if anything other than family pictures Sharon would send to her.

All in all, although everyone missed Kathleen horribly, life at Peacock Walk was getting back to normal. Rose was not under any illusions that this would happen overnight; everyone was going through his or her own grieving process. The recent nights were very sad for all of them; the children would stay up late, not going to bed until they were dead on their feet. Even Rose had difficulty sleeping, crying herself to sleep on several nights. Being alone didn't help, which brought up the final situation—Meghan.

Both agreed that for now, Meghan would not spend the nights. They figured the children didn't need any more to contend with right now. But Rose didn't feel right staying overnight at Meghan's and leaving the children alone. She knew Aunt Vivian was there, but the first couple of nights, Caitlin wandered into her room and climbed into bed. It was then Rose realized she was sleeping in Kathleen's room, and Caitlin was used to getting into bed with her mother when she couldn't sleep. Rose couldn't deny Caitlin now and not be there for her at night.

So—Rose was frustrated. And so was Meghan. Only Meghan was more patient. Rose brooded.

She did this now, frowning deeply as she watched Mr. Murphy's sheep wandering the green hills. She ached for Meghan, and if something…

"There you are. What's the big idea not greetin' me at the door with a kiss?"

She grinned when she felt Meghan's hands on her shoulders; she sighed when she felt the warm lips on the back of her neck. "I have to warn you. I have a girlfriend, and I think she's the jealous type."

"Is she now?" Meghan whispered against her ear. "Sounds like a bore. Ditch her and come away with me."

Rose laughed and turned to face her. "Good idea. Let's go right now. We'll just get in that tank of yours—"

"Land Rover."

"Who cares? And we'll just take a drive and get away."

"I'm glad you said that. I had a nice talk with Vivian last night."

131

"How did you talk to Vivian?"

"It's called a cellphone. We have them here in Ireland, too. We're not a backward people. Now she's offered to watch the children next weekend."

Rose grinned. "Really?"

Meghan nodded. "Yes. I thought we'd go into Donegal on Friday and get your bank situation settled. We'll have lunch at a nice little place, then go into Letterkenny and get you some clothes. Ya need more than two pair of jeans."

"And then?" Rose asked, feeling like a little kid.

"I took the liberty of makin' a reservation at a B&B in Donegal for the weekend. Just a little getaway."

"That sounds heavenly." Rose let out a dejected sigh. "And I feel guilty."

"I know ya do. But—"

"Rose!"

They both turned around when Caitlin ran into the kitchen, her cheeks flushed and her red curls bouncing. "Aunt Vivian told me you're goin' into Donegal next weekend."

"Well," Rose said, glancing at Meghan. "I thought I would, but—"

"There's a candy store there. I can't remember the name, but Mam used to go there and bring us chocolates. Can ya bring us somethin'? Can ya?"

Meghan ran her hand across her mouth to hide her grin while Caitlin patiently waited.

"Well, sure, honey. What do you want?"

"Don't care. Thanks, Rose. I have to get back to my violin. And I have to practice step dancing. You want to watch me?" Before Rose could answer, Caitlin dashed out. "I'll be right down. You go in the living room. Oh, hi, Meghan."

"Hi, Cait," Meghan called after her.

"I'll miss you, too," Rose said in a weak voice.

Meghan laughed and pulled her into her arms. "Looks like we're not going anywhere right now. I think it's a command performance."

Vivian walked into the kitchen. "What command performance?"

"Cait wants to practice her step dancing for us in the living room. We're all invited," Rose said.

Vivian rubbed her temples. "I feel a headache comin' on."

"Where's Donal?" Rose asked. "If we have to do this, so does he."

Meghan laughed. "I think he's outside roamin' the hills with Mr. Murphy."

"Oh, no. He was with Brendan. I wish he'd leave," Vivian said.

"Aunt Vivian, quit inviting him to stay then," Rose said, kissing her cheek as she passed.

Meghan was looking out the window. "Donal's coming back with Brendan."

They all watched as they walked back to the house. Brendan had his arm around Donal's shoulders, but somehow, Donal didn't look very comfortable walking with him. Rose watched as Donal nodded at something, then quickly ran ahead of him. She lost sight of Donal as he ran to the back door. But she saw the deep frown on Brendan's face as he watched Donal. Rose wondered what he had said to Donal and made a mental note to ask him later.

"Stop runnin'!" Vivian called out to Donal, who had raced in.

"Sorry, Aunt Vivian," he said breathlessly. "Hi, Meghan."

"Hi, Donal. Having a good time with your uncle?"

Donal pulled a face and shrugged, but he said nothing. Rose pulled him into a hug. "You're all sweaty. Go wash up. Cait has to practice her step dancing, and she wants us to watch."

Donal groaned and held on to Rose. "Please don't make me. I'll be good, I promise," he said dramatically, looking up with pleading eyes.

For a moment, Rose thought of relenting. She then shook her head. "Not a chance. Nice try, though. If we have to go through this, so do you."

"Go on now, wash up." Vivian pushed him out of the kitchen just as Brendan walked in.

"Well, good afternoon," he said, wiping his feet on the mat. "I just had a nice talk with Donal, ya know, man to man."

Rose nodded and glanced at Vivian, who raised an eyebrow.

"And now I'm off. I won't be home for supper," he said, walking past them. "Have a good night."

"Brendan, before you leave," Rose said, stopping him. "It's not that we don't love your company, and you're welcome here, you know that…"

Brendan held up his hand. "I know what you're going to ask. And I don't have to get back to London anytime soon, but I might be stayin' with a friend in Donegal. So I'll be out of your hair by week's end." He smiled nicely. "I appreciate the hospitality, truly I do."

"Not at all," Vivian said. "You can stay as long as you like."

Rose gaped at her, as Brendan smiled and walked out. Vivian turned to Rose. "What?"

"You just got finished saying you wish he'd leave, then you give him an open invitation," Rose said to Meghan's laugh. "What are you laughing at?"

"Nothin'. Nothin'." Meghan held her hands up. "I'm going to get a seat for the performance."

Rose and Vivian followed Meghan to the living room. Cait was already there with her iPod sitting on the ottoman. "Meghan, will you help me move this rug?" Cait asked with a groan.

"Sure," Meghan said. She rolled up the oval rug so Cait had plenty of wooden floor to dance. "How's that?"

"Perfect. Thanks," Cait said with enthusiasm.

Rose again realized how much she looked like Kathleen with her wild red head, flushed cheeks, and big blue eyes.

"Okay. Aunt Vivian, you sit there, and, Rose, there, and, Meghan, right there."

"Yes, Your Royal Highness," Rose said with a sweeping bow as Cait giggled.

They dutifully took their assigned seating on the couch. Cait ran to the staircase, her dance shoes clattering on the wooden floor. "Donal! Are ya comin' anytime soon?"

"Cait, please stop yellin'," Vivian yelled at her.

Meghan held on to Rose's hand and laughed as Donal slowly walked down the staircase; he looked as if he were walking to the gallows as he shuffled into the living room.

"You sit there," Cait said, roughly pushing him onto the floor in front of the couch.

"This is silly," he said.

Cait put her hands on her hips. "It is not! I have to practice in front of people."

"Right now, I wish I was a goat!" Donal said defiantly.

"And right now, ya smell like one. Did ya wash?" Vivian asked him.

"Donal's a goat." Cait laughed and swirled around and picked up her iPod. "This is what I've learned so far."

She pressed the button, and the lively Celtic music started. Cait quickly took her place in the middle of the room and waited for the right beat, then started.

Rose winced as she watched her young cousin flail about. She glanced at her companions on the couch—Meghan cocked her head as she watched; Vivian looked as though she had witnessed Cait murder step dancing before. Vivian reached down and lightly slapped Donal's head as he giggled.

Poor Cait looked as though she was having some kind of episode. Her arms flew about, and her cheeks grew rosy red as she tried desperately to remember her steps and dance to the music. The noise on the hardwood floor was deafening; it sounded like there were ten people dancing. Vivian rubbed her temple while she smiled and nodded her encouragement.

Rose leaned into her. "I'm not sure, but isn't your body supposed to be perfectly still and only your feet move?"

Vivian nodded sadly while she continued to watch Cait, who looked more like she was tap dancing than the Irish step dance. She stopped several times when she forgot her place and ran into the ottoman; it was a nice respite, as quick as it was. Then, God love her, she'd go right back at it. When it came time for her to do a high kick, poor Cait's shoe slid on the floor and right out from under her. She landed with a thud and a groan on her backside.

Rose pulled Donal's hair in case he started laughing.

"I'm all right," Cait said, quickly standing. She continued on like a trouper.

And thankfully, the music stopped. With flushed cheeks and breathless puffing, Cait smiled and waited for the applause. When it didn't come, she swiped a red curl off her forehead and gave them an incredulous look.

"Oh," Vivian said and started applauding. She nudged Rose, who nudged Meghan.

"Magnificent," Meghan said proudly while applauding vigorously. "Brava!"

Rose kicked at Donal, who grudgingly joined in. He lazily clapped his hands.

Cait bowed. "Now I'll play my violin!"

Donal groaned as Cait ran up the stairs, tripping on the second step. "I'm okay!"

"Stop run…" Vivian sighed and sat back. "I give up."

"Do I have to listen?" Donal turned around to them. "Do I?"

"Yes," Vivian said. "She needs your support, Donal. Especially now."

Donal opened his mouth and looked at Rose, who nodded in agreement with Vivian.

Meghan lightly ruffled his hair. "It'll be quick. Then we'll go out and kick the ball around. How's that?"

"I'm ready!" Cait ran into the room and took her place. She had her sheet music with her and placed it on the ottoman.

The small violin was adorable; Rose had no idea such a horrible screeching sound could come out of such a beautiful instrument. It sounded like a cat caught in a dryer. Just when they thought it was over, Cait reached down and flipped the sheet over. "This one is better."

Rose gently kicked Donal when he snorted sarcastically while Meghan whispered in her ear, "If she could play that thing and dance at the same time, we could take her on the road. Maybe make some money."

Rose tried not to laugh as she watched Cait, her brow furrowed in concentration. Rose wasn't sure, but she thought it was *Three*

Blind Mice that Cait was trying to play, but again, she wouldn't put money on it.

Again, they applauded when Cait finished. She bowed in adult fashion to each of them. "What do you think?"

"Ya need more practice," Donal said seriously, then scooted out of the way of Rose's foot.

Cait frowned deeply, but Donal walked up to her. "Ya sounded grand, Cait. Better than I could ever do."

"Really?" she asked, looking up at him.

"Really. Mam would be proud. Go upstairs and put those dancin' shoes in the trash—"

"That's not funny!"

Donal laughed. "Go on, and we'll kick the ball around with Meghan."

Cait gathered her sheet music and clambered up the stairs.

Rose pulled Donal into a hug. "You're a good brother. Now beat it, and go have fun. Don't hurt Meghan."

After playing with Donal and Cait, Meghan look exhausted. The least Rose could do was make a nice dinner for all of them.

And after cleaning up the dinner dishes and putting the children in bed, Vivian let out a tired groan. "I'm off to bed. I know it's early, but this has been an exhausting day. Good night," she said, kissing Rose and Meghan on the cheek.

They both laughed as Vivian hummed *Three Blind Mice* as she slowly mounted the stairs.

Meghan struck a thoughtful pose. "What's that?"

"What?" Rose asked, looking around.

"It's quiet and we're alone."

"Imagine that." Rose laughed when Meghan pulled her down onto the couch with her. She settled in and stretched out, laying her head on Meghan's lap. "I can't wait for this weekend when we really have time alone."

Meghan absently ran her fingers through Rose's hair. "Me too," she whispered. "Are ya as amazed as I am how things have turned out, Rosie?"

Rose nestled her head into her lap and smiled. "I'm happily

amazed. And I'll admit, when Kathleen first told me about you, I was skeptical."

"Ya were?"

Rose rolled over on her back and looked up at Meghan's smiling face. "I was protective of Kathleen and the children, and she sounded so mysterious about you."

"And now?"

"And now…" She stopped and thought for a moment. "Now I think I might be falling in love with you."

Meghan's stunned look had her laughing. "Too much?" she asked softly, reaching up to caress Meghan's cheek.

"Not at all." Meghan kissed the palm of her hand. "I might be feelin' the same thing, as well."

Rose scooted up to sit on her lap; she wrapped her arms around Meghan's neck. "Who knew this would happen?"

Meghan frowned deeply. "I certainly didn't. But when I first saw you, when you opened the front door…" She stopped and shook her head.

"What?" Rose whispered; she was shocked to see tears welling in Meghan's blue eyes. "Tell me?"

"Kathleen had talked about you so much, I felt as though I knew you. I had an image of you in my mind's eye. But it was nothin' compared to actually seein' you. You're beautiful, Rosie."

Rose lowered her eyes. "I'm not, but I thank you for thinking so."

Meghan reached in, placing her fingertips under her chin. "You are. Don't even think otherwise." She tenderly kissed her lips.

Rose sighed and rested her head against Meghan's shoulder. "This is so comfortable."

"Maybe for you. You're sitting on me bladder," Meghan said playfully.

Rose laughed. "Want me to move?"

"Not right now, but I'll let ya know."

They sat in silence for a few moments. Rose absently ran her fingers up and down the side of Meghan's neck.

"You know we've never talked about the gold and Desmond," Rose said. "It seems so long ago, I nearly forgot about it."

"I know what you mean. Sometimes I think it never really happened. I've heard nothing from my company since I told them all those months ago."

"And the police have never called again about Kathleen's accident. Remember the inspector mentioned the brake line in her Land Rover?"

"Yes. Perhaps it was just an accident. And maybe the same for Desmond. Could that be possible?"

"I don't know. It just seems so odd they both died the same way."

"And nothing's been mentioned about the gold since." Meghan shook her head. "Maybe there is nothing to this at all."

Rose let out a contented sigh. "Wouldn't that be great? Like we said. We can get on with our lives." When Meghan didn't answer, Rose lifted her head to see Meghan looking deep in thought. "What's wrong?"

"Oh, nothin'. Just thinkin', that's all." She smiled then and kissed Rose on the forehead. "No more talk of gold."

"Good," Rose said, sidling closer. "I can think of other things to talk about. Like how much I want to—"

"Rose?"

Rose quickly sat up when she heard Cait's voice. "What's wrong, honey?"

Cait stood in the doorway; she rubbed her eyes with one hand, and in the other, she clutched Bunny close to her. "I had a bad dream."

"Come here, sweetie," Rose said, opening her arms.

Cait ran to her and jumped up on Rose, causing her to fall back against Meghan, who let out a painful grunt as she moved to allow Rose to sit next to her.

"Hi, Meghan," Cait said, settling against Rose.

"Hello." Meghan let out a wheeze as Rose laughed.

"Rose, did you have a bad dream, too?" Cait lay her head on Rose's lap. "Is that why Meghan was holding you?"

Rose ignored Meghan's muffled laugh. "Yes, Cait. I had a bad dream. Now you try to go back to sleep. Okay?"

"Okay," Cait said through her yawns. "Say g'night to Bunny." She held up the stuffed animal.

"Good night, Bunny," Rose whispered.

"You too, Meghan." Cait waited patiently for Meghan.

"Good night, Bunny. Good night, Cait," she said.

"Kiss her," Cait said with a tired grin, pushing Bunny at Meghan.

Meghan raised an eyebrow but obediently kissed Bunny on the top of its head.

Completely satisfied, Cait once again settled against Rose, and in a few quiet minutes, she was sound asleep. Rose ran her fingers through Cait's red curls, then looked back at Meghan, who watched Cait.

"One day, we'll be alone. It won't always be like this," Rose whispered.

"Yes, it will," Meghan said. "Thank God."

"Well, you're not going anywhere for a while. I don't want to wake her up just yet. You might as well get some sleep."

They settled back; Meghan held on to Rose, who held Cait, who cuddled Bunny in her sleep.

Yes, Rose thought as she drifted off, she hoped it would always be like this.

Chapter 19

Finally, it was Friday. Rose was so excited about their weekend she barely slept the night before. Meghan arrived early, which Rose hoped was a sign of her eagerness to get the weekend underway, as well.

"Have ya packed?" Meghan asked.

Rose gulped down her coffee. "Not yet."

"Well, it shouldn't take too long. Ya don't have much. Get a move on, woman."

Vivian laughed along as she sipped her tea. "Go pack before Meghan explodes."

Rose laughed. "I'll be right down."

She ran up to her room, packed whatever she had, then ran downstairs to find Vivian at the door.

"Rose! Good Lord. I'm tryin' to get the children to stop runnin' down those stairs and now you…" Vivian threw up her hands in defeat.

"Sorry," Rose said breathlessly. "Are you sure you don't mind?" She looked out the window to see Meghan with Donal and Caitlin.

"Not at all. It will be good for you to get away for a couple days. And we'll be fine. Don't worry."

"Where's Brendan?"

"He went into Trahern again. Said he'd be back by suppertime. And I don't mind sayin' he's getting on my nerves. I wish I never told him…Oh, well."

"Is he ever going back to London?"

"He'd better and soon. Now enough of him. Don't keep her waitin'. Oh, would ya mind? There's a wool shop in Letterkenny." She handed Rose a slip of paper. "Just tell the woman it's for me. She'll know."

"Sure, I'd be glad to, Aunt Vivian. Do you need anything else? I've already been asked to bring chocolates back."

Vivian laughed. "Cait no doubt. No, darlin'. This is all I need. Have a good time. We'll see you Sunday. If we're not here, we're at church."

Rose kissed her on the cheek. "See you Sunday. Thanks."

Donal opened the passenger door for her. "Have fun, Rose."

Rose ruffled his hair. "Thanks. Take care of everything while we're gone."

He puffed out his chest. "Of course I will. Ya have nothin' to worry about."

Meghan picked up Cait, who squealed with laughter. "Behave yourself."

"I will. Put me down. I'm not a baby."

"Sorry," Meghan said, setting her down. "Goodbye, Donal. Mind your aunt."

"We will," Donal said, stepping back. He grabbed Caitlin's hand and pulled her away.

As they pulled away, Caitlin struggled against her brother's grasp. "Leave me be, ya *amadan*."

"Cait!" Rose stuck her head out the window as Meghan drove down the gravel drive. "Don't call your brother an idiot." She sat back and looked at Meghan. "Too much like a mom?"

"No, darlin'. You've got the screeching part down perfect. I think me ears are bleedin'."

The clouds broke, and by midmorning, it was sunny and warm, perfect weather for Rose and Meghan while they lazily wandered the shops of Letterkenny.

"You don't have to carry all the bags," Rose said, bumping shoulders with Meghan.

"I was wonderin' when you'd say that," she said, handing over several shopping bags. "I need a drink. How about we go back to Donegal and get everything settled at your bank, then stop for a bite to eat? We can't check in until later this afternoon. We've plenty of time."

"You're the boss, Dr. Quigley. I'm in your hands."

Meghan winked. "Yes, you will be."

"I'm sure I will." She slipped her hand in the crook of Meghan's arm. "I just want to be alone with you."

"I want the same thing. Now let me go before I do something right here."

The back of Meghan's Land Rover was filled with boxes and shopping bags. Rose made a mental checklist, satisfied she remembered the most important thing: chocolates.

The conversation was light and happy as they headed to Donegal and the bank. There the gaiety ended; it took far longer than Rose wanted. By the time she had opened an account and presented all the paperwork from Kathleen's will, Rose was frazzled. She walked out of the bank manager's office to find Meghan in a chair, legs stretched out in front of her.

Meghan greeted her with a compassionate smile. "Ya look done in."

"I hate red tape. My mind is fried."

Meghan laughed and steered her out of the bank. "Let's stop at the closest pub. I'm exhausted from carrying all your parcels, madam. I need sustenance."

They sat next to each other at the quiet table by the window and ordered a lunch of fish and chips.

Meghan eagerly rubbed her hands together when the waitress placed the plates in front of them.

"I must say, it wasn't very gallant of you to make me carry most of the bags," Rose said, eating her fries.

"Now, now. If we're to be workin' on a partnership, we have to be fifty-fifty. No time like the present, and speakin' of presents."

Rose raised an eyebrow and watched while Meghan wiped her hands on the napkin, then fished a small box out of her jeans pocket. Meghan grinned and handed Rose the white box.

"When did you have time to do this?" Rose asked, opening the box.

"While you were bantering with the saleslady."

Rose saw the silver triquetra charm on a delicate silver chain.

"Do ya like it?"

"It's beautiful." She took it out and held it up to examine it.

"I'm sure ya know the meaning of a triquetra, or trinity knot, as they call it here sometimes." She reached over and took Rose's hand. "Three promises. To love, honor, and protect ya."

Rose held her hand tightly. "Thank you, Meghan. Help me."

Meghan took the necklace and waited for Rose to turn around and lift her hair off her neck. After fastening the clasp, Meghan ran her thumb over the back of her neck for just a second.

"I love it," Rose said, caressing the charm. "I'll never take it off."

Meghan chuckled and continued eating. "I'm glad ya like it. Now eat up. You're going to be quite busy tonight."

Rose smiled shyly but said nothing. All sorts of erotic visions flashed through her mind. She was about to impart the scenario on Meghan when she heard a man call out Meghan's name.

"What are the odds?" He smiled as he walked up to the table.

He was a tall, thin man, about forty or so, Rose thought. He wore glasses that looked too small for his face. As Rose looked closer, she noticed the tape on the side, holding them together. He wore a tweed sport coat and a rumpled denim shirt underneath.

"Angus!" Meghan quickly stood and pulled him into a fierce hug. "What in the devil are ya doin' here?"

Angus grinned and adjusted his glasses. "I was called back from Edinburgh." He glanced down at Rose. "Oh. Hello."

"Oh, I'm sorry. This is Rose Culhane. Rose, this fool is Angus Campbell. A friend and colleague."

Angus held out his hand. "It's a pleasure. Are you a geologist?"

"Good grief, no," Rose said, realizing what she said. "I mean…"

Meghan and Angus laughed. "Not to worry. I feel the same sometimes."

"Sit down, Angus."

"I don't want to intrude."

"No, please, do join us," Rose said, offering him a chair. Angus sat down, setting his leather briefcase on the other chair. "Thank you. It's very kind of you."

When Meghan looked for the waitress, Angus reached over and snagged a french fry off her plate. Rose imagined they were close enough friends for the playful gesture.

"So what are ya doing in Donegal?" he asked, after telling the waitress what he wanted.

"We're on holiday," Meghan said. "For the weekend."

"Are you now?" He looked from Rose to Meghan. "Then I am interrupting."

Rose laughed. "Not now, but you will be…"

Angus threw his head back and laughed. "Ya got yourself a wild one, Quigley."

"I have," Meghan said, smiling at Rose. "So why did they call ya back?"

Angus waited until the waitress set the pint of ale in front of him. He glanced at Rose first.

"It's all right," Meghan said, "she knows."

Angus seemed surprised; he adjusted his glasses. "She does?"

"Desmond Flaherty was married to her cousin."

"Really?" His smile faded as he regarded Rose. "I heard what happened to your cousin, and I'm dreadfully sorry."

"Thank you. But if you're from Scotland, how in the world did you hear about Kathleen's death?"

"It's one of the reasons I was called back." He looked at Meghan then. "The authorities here in Ireland contacted my company."

Meghan sat forward. "Something new about Flaherty?"

Angus nodded and took a long drink. "They haven't told me anything yet. Only they want me to answer a few questions. I'm not sure what else I can tell them. I'm supposed to meet with them tomorrow. I'm staying in Donegal at The Abbey Hotel." He laughed and took another drink. "I can't believe I ran into you. You haven't been contacted?"

"No," Meghan said thoughtfully. "Though I feel the same way you do. I don't know what else I'd tell them other than what we've already said."

"What does this have to do with Kathleen's death? If anything?" Rose looked from one to the other for an answer.

"I don't know." Angus looked at Meghan. "Any idea?"

"Rose and I haven't had much time to discuss too much. I showed her the geological maps from Tellus Border. And about Flaherty." Meghan absently pulled at her earlobe.

Angus exchanged a smile with Rose. "I see she still does that."

"I've noticed it from time to time." Rose leaned closer to him. "Usually when she's thinking. I can smell the rubber burning."

Angus laughed and drank his ale. "She's got your number, Meg."

Meghan hid her grin. "That she does."

"So what are you thinking?" he asked.

Meghan sat forward, leaning her elbows on the table. "I wouldn't give anything another thought. I'd forget this entire gold business if Kathleen hadn't died in that accident. It just nags at me. And Flaherty's brother is staying at the house. He came in from London for the funeral and hasn't left."

"Is that odd?" Angus asked them.

"Just annoying," Rose said. "But we talked to him, and he seemed stunned but not altogether surprised to find out about Desmond." She looked at Meghan, who picked at her plate of food.

"What's on your mind?" Angus asked her.

"I don't know. We were all set to forget this whole thing. We figured it was just coincidental, and if no one contacted us again, it was over." Meghan put down her fork and sat back. "But now they want to talk to you. Did they ever find out about the rods that were stolen?"

Angus shook his head. "My superiors think it might be connected to our man Flaherty. But I suppose they don't know how. I'll probably know more after I meet with the inspectors."

"I never met Flaherty. Only saw him in the pub. But from what I can gather, I can't imagine him pulling this off by himself."

"Well, I knew Desmond," Rose interjected, "and I have to agree. Desmond wasn't one who took the initiative. God forgive me, but he was the type to ride on someone's coattails."

"What do you mean?" Angus asked.

Meghan continued, "How would he know what to take? Seriously, Angus. The average person knows nothin' about mining for any type of minerals, let alone gold. Unless…"

"Unless you know someone who does." Angus sat back. "He could have read up on it. All ya have to do is search the Internet. The Tellus website is right there, showing everything."

Rose listened as she picked at her food. Thinking of all that had happened, she couldn't keep a clear thought. "You think all of this got Kathleen killed?" She looked up at both of them. "Isn't that what we're talking about?"

Meghan reached over and covered her hand. "I'm so sorry to be talkin' like this, Rosie."

"Yes, I apologize, as well. We got caught up in this."

"No, don't be sorry," Rose said. "We've discussed the possibility. It's just now, with them wanting to talk to you again. If it wasn't an accident, then it changes everything."

"Well, I'll know more after the meeting." Angus gave Meghan a curious look. "Would ya like me to ask if you can join us?"

Rose saw the excitement in her eyes. "What time?"

"I meet them tomorrow morning around ten."

Rose touched her arm. "If you're able, I think you should."

"I think you both should," Angus said. "They have no idea I ran into you. I think they'd like to meet you, Rose. Let me make the call."

Rose nodded along with Meghan. "Go ahead."

He jumped up, pulled out his cellphone, and walked away. Meghan turned toward Rose.

"Are ya sure, Rose?" she asked. "We're supposed to have some time alone this weekend."

"And we will. But I think this is important. I want this behind us. If they determine there's nothing to do with Kathleen, we can forget all the gold business and get on with our lives. But I think we need to do this."

Meghan took a deep breath and nodded. "Things happen for a reason. And there's a reason we ran into Angus like this."

"I'm going to call Aunt Vivian and let her know what's going on…"

Meghan stopped her. "Maybe you should wait and see what happens."

Rose thought for a moment. She didn't want to worry Vivian needlessly, especially if this turned out to be nothing. "You're right. I'll wait and—"

"You're in," Angus said, sitting at the table. "They told you to come along but not to talk to anyone in the meantime."

"I'm a little nervous," Rose admitted. She pushed her plate away and took a drink of water.

"Don't worry," Angus said. "It'll be fine. Now I'm going back to the hotel. You two enjoy the rest of the day and night," he added with a wriggle of his eyebrows. "Do you know where to go, or should we meet at my hotel?"

"Unfortunately, I know where the garda station is," Meghan said.

Angus realized what she meant and nodded. "I'm sorry. That was insensitive of me."

"Not at all," Rose said. "I'm very grateful Meghan was here to take care of everything after the accident."

"We'll meet ya there at ten," Meghan said.

"That sounds fine," Angus said and stood. "We'll see you in the morning." He shook Rose's hand. "Good to meet you, Rose. Take care of this woman. She needs it."

Rose laughed. "I will. See you in the morning." She watched as Angus walked out of the pub, then turned to Meghan. "So you need to be taken care of?"

Meghan smiled. "I do. And, God help me, you're the only woman who can."

"Good. Let's get out of here. I don't want any more interruptions until tomorrow morning."

Meghan sighed happily. "Ah, Rosie. What a lucky woman I am."

Rose stood and pulled her to her feet. "And you'll find out just how lucky."

Chapter 20

As they drove out of Donegal, the landscape was much of what the west of Ireland was known for—rolling green hills and the rugged, wild feeling that was unmistakable. Rose smiled as she watched the hills, dotted with sheep and horses, drift by her window.

"I do love this part of Ireland the best, I think."

"I agree," Meghan said, shifting gears. "Untamed and free. And the B&B is up ahead."

Up on a hill was a stone house with a green pasture in front of it with several horses. All surrounded by a wooden fence that seemed to go on forever. As they approached the paved road that led to the house, Rose saw the name on the sign and laughed along with Meghan.

"Don't even try. It's Gaelic. This place has its own restaurant, and I understand the rooms are very comfortable, and…" Meghan wriggled her eyebrows. "Private."

"I can't wait." Rose felt the wave of anticipation ripple through her.

After they checked in, the owner took them down the hall to their room.

"I hope you enjoy your stay," she said over her shoulder as she opened the door.

Rose looked around the cozy bedroom. The king-sized bed took up nearly the whole room, but it looked very inviting. She noticed a bottle of champagne in a bucket on the desk and glanced at Meghan, who grinned.

The woman opened the door to the bathroom. "I think you'll like this."

They both peeked in to see a Jacuzzi in one corner and a walk-in shower in the other. "The dining room is on the other side of this building. It's open until ten o'clock. Breakfast is from seven to nine thirty." She handed Meghan the key to the room. "Let me know if you need anything."

"Thanks," Meghan said, then grabbed Rose by the waist as soon as the woman left.

Rose let out a shriek of laughter. "What should we do first?"

Meghan raised an eyebrow and tossed the key on the desk. "You don't have to ask," she said. She cupped Rose's face and lightly kissed her on the lips. Her hand then wandered down to cup and caress her breast; the nipple immediately turned rock hard as her thumb brushed against it.

Rose then gently pushed her hands away and started to unbutton her blouse.

Meghan gazed into her eyes, then watched as Rose let the blouse slip to the floor. She was trembling as she set her breasts free. With the bra discarded, Meghan lowered her head and kissed the top of her breast, eliciting small gasps from Rose.

This was not the raucous night at Meghan's. Meghan was being very deliberate and romantic. Rose actually felt shy when Meghan stepped back and watched her.

"What are you thinking?" Meghan whispered.

"I'm thinking the way you're looking at me…" She stopped and laughed nervously.

Meghan closed the distance between them and reached in, cupping both breasts. "Perfection," she whispered. She reached down and unbuckled the belt to her slacks, which slid to the floor.

Rose stood on trembling legs as she stepped out of them. Then Meghan's touch felt warm and inviting as she caressed her breasts once again, then traveled down her stomach and her hips.

"God, you are soft." Meghan sighed seriously as she reached behind and stroked her back.

Rose was sighing and gasping and moaning, and all at once,

she felt weak in the knees. "Meghan," she whispered as she felt Meghan's hands pulling down the silk panties. Now she was completely naked.

Meghan's gaze raked over her body. Her hands traveled over Rose's hips, then she pulled Rose close and caressed the round soft mounds of her buttocks. "God, I love the feel of you," Meghan whispered against her hair, pulling her body against her.

"You. I want to see you, too." Rose's voice was a mere whisper, and as Meghan started to take off her shirt, Rose pushed her hands away and slowly unbuttoned her shirt. Meghan closed her eyes and took a deep breath, letting out a small groan as Rose deftly pushed back the shirt and pulled it off her shoulders. Rose had difficulty swallowing as she reached in and unhooked the bra, which fell to the floor.

Meghan gathered her into her arms, then threw back the covers and gently laid her against the pillows. Rose sighed, loving the feel of her naked body against the sheets. She watched in awe as Meghan unbuckled her own slacks and stepped out of them. She then stepped out of her panties and smiled.

"I love you, Rose, and I mean to make love to you all night."

Rose opened her arms, welcoming the only one she'd ever need. This realization shocked her; she was amazed at the sight of Meghan's strong yet soft body standing there waiting. It was a remarkable feeling for Rose when Meghan lay next to her, their bodies touching.

"It's like this is the first time," she said softly.

Meghan agreed. "You're so beautiful. I can't say that enough."

"I don't think I'll ever tire of hearing it."

Meghan pulled Rose close, her fingers exploring every inch of her body. Gliding back and forth, demanding a response from Rose and getting it. Rose cried out when she kissed her lightly on the lips.

"Meghan, love me, please."

"Whatever you need," she murmured against her lips, her hand once again cupping her breast.

Rose's back arched slightly as she felt Meghan's hand drawing her passion from her. Meghan lowered herself and tenderly took her aching hard nipple into her mouth. Rose entwined her fingers in Meghan's thick hair, holding her head in place. With her other hand, Rose caressed her bare back, her nails lightly scratching back and forth.

Meghan moaned and groaned into her breast, sending small shock waves through both of them. It was incredible. Meghan was becoming aroused too quickly. She had to take a moment before she rushed too fast. She tried and tried, but Rose's soft hand all over her back was driving her insane. She lifted her head and gently took Rose's hand and held it over her head.

"You're distracting me," she whispered.

Rose sighed happily. "You just wait."

Meghan chuckled, then returned to her heavenly torture on one breast, then the other. From the groan of approval and the twitching of Rose's hips, Meghan smiled inwardly.

"God, this is amazing." Rose sighed.

Meghan released Rose's hand and caressed her breast, her fingers taking over where her tongue left off. That, unfortunately, left Rose's hands free. They wandered down and once again electrified Meghan. She moaned and groaned again as Rose's soft hands did their magic.

"Woman. Stop." Meghan growled lowly against her breast.

"What's the matter? Can't concentrate?" Rose gasped as Meghan's tongue again administered the heavenly torture. She arched her back, and with each pass of Meghan's tongue, the ache between her legs grew stronger; she could not hold off for much longer. Rose's breathing was out of control as her legs clenched together, quivering.

Meghan smiled as she allowed her hand to roam south. Down the flat of Rose's abdomen to the soft curve of her full hips. Then she boldly went farther, her fingers teasing. "You're magnificent."

"I'm on fire, Meghan. Geezus," she exclaimed and held on to her.

Meghan quieted her by kissing her deeply, her satiny tongue dancing playfully with Rose's. Once again, she reached down.

This time, her hand traveled down the top of her thigh, caressing from her knee to the thigh and back down the other.

Rose purred into Meghan's mouth murmuring, "Yes, yes."

Just the sound of Rose's voice was driving her mad. She loved it, wanting only to please her even more. Meghan teased her unmercifully, her fingers once again swirling around but not entering.

Soon, Rose was a mass of quivering flesh. "Meghan, please touch me," she begged against her lips.

Meghan smiled, then kissed her deeply and lovingly. "My God, what you do to me," she whispered into her hair.

Rose only sighed and held her close. She then parted her legs, welcoming Meghan's caress. Meghan slowly entered her, rhythmically thrusting, bringing Rose to the brink.

"Oh, God," Rose cried out as every nerve in her body was awakened. Meghan's touch brought her to an unbelievable height. She was calling out Meghan's name over and over as Meghan continued to love her. Then she arched her back and held her breath as her orgasm rippled through her. Her body shook and trembled uncontrollably. Then Meghan slowed her caressing as Rose's breathing became normal once more. When Meghan took her hand away, Rose shot her hand down and held it in place. "Please, don't take it away yet."

Meghan kissed her damp forehead. "I love you."

"Well, if this isn't love, I give up."

Meghan was caught off guard at first. She laughed and kissed her again. "Oh, this is love, there is no mistakin' it." Meghan slowly took her hand away.

Rose groaned in protest but did not stop her this time. "You're pretty good there, Dr. Quigley. I thought I was going to faint for a minute."

Meghan snorted in disbelief. Rose looked up, then rolled her onto her back. "I'm serious. I felt like I was having a seizure or something. I want you to feel that way, too."

Meghan reached up to caress her cheek. "I don't want to have a seizure, but I'll take whatever else ya have in mind…"

Rose reached over and caressed her breast. Meghan caught

her breath for an instant and closed her eyes. Rose watched her face for a moment as she lightly touched her nipple, loving how it turned hard under her touch.

Meghan winced and groaned. "God, woman."

Rose gently kneaded her breasts, then she took the nipple between her thumb and forefinger and rolled it back and forth.

Within a few seconds, Meghan was twitching. Her hands were behind her head, and her breathing came out in short gasping pants.

"Is this all right? No episodes yet?" Rose asked, and Meghan only nodded.

Rose couldn't wait any longer. She slid down her body, kissing her way down, settling comfortably between Meghan's parted legs. She kissed her inner thighs, down to the top of her knees, then back up once again. Each time, she heard Meghan groan and felt her body twitch. When she placed a kiss on her clit, Meghan nearly flew off the bed. Rose wrapped her arm around Meghan's waist, holding her in place, and continued loving her.

Meghan appeared to be having a seizure as she bucked and writhed with each swipe of Rose's tongue against her.

"No more. God," Meghan cried out, trying to push Rose away. "I can't take…"

Rose pulled her clit into her mouth, and that did it. Meghan nearly screamed, then whimpered, and finally, Rose thought she passed out. So she relented and gently backed away, placing a kiss on the top of her thigh.

"You are beautiful, Meghan," she whispered and crawled up her body to lie next to her.

Meghan breathed so rapidly, Rose got worried. "Are you all right?"

Meghan tried to swallow and nodded. "Water…"

Rose laughed and hopped off the bed and came back with the bottle of champagne and two glasses.

Meghan, spread eagle, just lifted her head and smiled. "Good girl. Give me a minute, and I'll join ya."

Rose popped the cork and poured two glasses. By then, Meghan sat up, adjusting the pillows behind her head. Rose gazed at her body.

"I know I've said this, but you are beautiful," she said, handing the fluted glass to Meghan. "I've never had a woman respond like that before."

"I've never felt that before." Meghan took the glass and touched it with Rose's before she took a long drink.

"Seriously?" Rose asked, cuddling next to her.

"Seriously." Meghan moved to pull the covers up, and Rose stopped her.

"I just want to look at you for a while," Rose said. "I have a feeling we're not going to get too many moments like this in the near future. I want to make the most of this time together."

"You're probably right." Meghan sat back against the headboard. She swirled her glass of champagne.

Rose saw the thoughtful pose. "Okay, what are you thinking?"

"I'm thinkin' about a certain scar on the back of your thigh that I haven't seen yet."

"Well, we'll drive by there in a minute," Rose said, taking a long, long drink. Her stomach fluttered at the idea of what Meghan proposed.

Meghan set her glass on the nightstand. "No time like the present. Lie on your stomach, please."

"Meghan…" Rose said in a warning voice. However, she did as Meghan instructed. "I better get a backrub out of this." She groaned when she felt the weight of Meghan's naked body on top of her.

"Oh, you're gettin' more than that, luv," Meghan whispered in her ear.

Rose felt her arousal start when Meghan peppered kisses across her back, then farther down. She gasped when she felt Meghan's hand between her legs, urging them apart. She complied and got to her knees when Meghan lifted under her hips. "God, Meghan…"

"Shh," Meghan whispered as she kissed the small of her back.

Rose could barely breathe; the throbbing started deep inside her when she felt Meghan kneel between her legs, her hands roaming freely up and down her back, then around to cup her breasts.

"So perfect," Meghan whispered.

Rose moved her hips when Meghan's hand toyed with her from behind. She hadn't been in this position in...well, almost forever.

"Are ya ready, luv?" Meghan asked, running her hand over her buttocks and her hips.

"Yes, please." Rose nearly whimpered. She cried into the pillow when Meghan entered her, thrusting slowly back and forth at first. Rose moved her hips in rhythm, trying to keep up as Meghan moved faster, slipping in one, then another finger. She felt her inner walls clamping around Meghan's fingers; she was so close. When Meghan reached around and flicked her middle finger around her throbbing clit, Rose exploded into a glorious orgasm that wouldn't stop. Her heart pounded in her chest, her hips jerked with each strong thrust from Meghan.

She couldn't take any more; her body gave out, and she collapsed on the bed. "Ohgodohgod." She moaned into the pillow. She gasped when Meghan withdrew her hand, then sighed when she felt her warm lips on the small of her back. When she rolled over, Meghan smiled and pulled her into a warm embrace.

"Now that was good," Rose said in a coarse voice.

Meghan laughed and kissed her dry lips. "One problem, though."

Rose opened her eyes. "What?"

"I forgot to look at the scar." Meghan sat up then. "So why don't we...?"

Rose reached up and pulled her down. "When I said I wanted to make the most of our time here, I thought it was implied that I liked to make it home in one piece, as well."

"Oh," Meghan said. "My mistake. Well then, how about another glass of champagne? Then room service?"

"Now you're talking."

They had showered, made love once again, and showered again. Afterward, they both wore the wonderfully soft terrycloth robes provided by the B&B because, as Meghan so delicately put it, "Why bother gettin' dressed when I'm just goin' to disrobe ya later on?" Rose had a hard time arguing that logic.

But when room service showed up with dinner, Rose felt it necessary to hide in the bathroom. She sat on the toilet and waited…and waited. "Meghan? Are they gone?" She opened the door to see Meghan sitting at the small table, eating a shrimp. Rose put her hands on her hips. "Thanks for letting me know."

Meghan laughed and held up a glass of wine. "Oh, they're gone, luv. Ya can come out now."

Rose glared and sat at the table. "Wow. What did we order?"

"I have no idea. I was starvin'. Dig in."

Rose took a few boiled shrimp and whatever else was on the platter. She realized she too was ravenous. "Making love makes me hungry."

"Then if I have my way, and I think I will, you'll be constantly hungry."

Rose laughed and took a drink of wine. "So tell me more about yourself, your family."

"Hmm…" Meghan thought for a moment. "As I said, my father taught at Trinity. My mother worked in an office in Dublin. I had an older brother, Tom."

Rose looked up then. "Had?"

"Yes. He was a horse trainer, got kicked in the head." Meghan popped an olive into her mouth.

Rose gaped at her. "Are you kidding?"

"Why on earth would I kid about such a thing?" But Meghan did laugh. "I suppose it does sound odd. But it's true."

"I'm so sorry. When?"

"About ten years ago. It really devastated my parents. Took them a long time."

"What about you?" Rose sipped her wine.

"Tommy and I weren't very close, but we loved each other. It was rough. But he was doin' what he loved." She scratched her head. "Boy, this does sound like a bad joke."

Rose chuckled and shook her head. "You have an odd sense of humor."

"That you are stuck with," Meghan said, raising her glass.

"Thank God." Rose leaned over and met Meghan halfway, exchanging a few heavenly kisses.

"So how about you? No loves in your life?"

"Not recently, no. It's hard to meet women. At least it's hard for me. You meet one you like, and they don't like you. They like you, and you can't stand them…" Rose shrugged.

"But all that's changed now," Meghan said softly. "We don't have to look anymore, do we?"

"No, we don't." Rose cocked her head and regarded Meghan. "We're very lucky, you and I."

"Yes, we are. Since I met you, I thanked God every night."

"You have? That's so romantic."

"I have a romantic side."

"And a lustful side," Rose said, feeling the blush creep into her cheeks.

"Well, you have no one else to blame but yourself for that."

"I'll gladly take the blame." Rose reached over and picked up a piece of cheese. "I noticed no steak or potatoes on this plate."

"Nope." Meghan winked. "Don't want ya to get tired out on me tonight. I still haven't seen that scar."

Rose's heart skipped a beat…again, for the millionth time. She just smiled and sipped her wine.

Chapter 21

"I hope I can keep my mind on what we're doing and not think about last night," Rose said as Meghan pulled in front of the garda station.

Meghan laughed. "I was thinkin' the same thing." She turned off the engine and took Rose's hand. "Whatever happens in there, we'll get through it together." She kissed the palm of her hand, then let it go.

"I think I love you."

Meghan reached over and took her hand. "Say that again."

"I think I love you." Rose laughed nervously. "There. Are you happy?"

"Very much so. You said it last night and this mornin'…"

Rose laughed as she held on to her hand. "I did say it last night, didn't I?"

"Yes, but that was, well, we were…This is different. "You… ya know, I think I might love you, too," she said. "And I can't believe we're declaring this in front of the garda station in the middle of Donegal and not in a more romantic setting." She shook her head. "Let's go before you start plannin' the wedding."

The station was small, but in the back behind a glass wall was a small office. An older gentleman sat behind the desk, and Rose recognized the younger inspector who came to the house after Kathleen died; she couldn't remember his name to save her life. A couple of uniformed garda mingled around the doorway. Beyond them, they saw Angus, who sat in the office. When he turned and saw them, he smiled and waved.

"Miss Culhane? It's good to see you again. Inspector Russell."
He held out his hand.

"Yes, Inspector, I remember you," Rose said, taking his hand.
"I only wish I could say the same."

"Dr. Quigley," he said kindly. "C'mon in, please."

They followed him into the office and sat down. All the
while, Rose was very aware of the older inspector behind the
desk. He rose when they came in and seemed nice enough when
introduced.

"Inspector Burke is taking the lead here," Russell said.

"I hope we can help," Rose said, glancing at Angus, who
winked.

"I hope so, too." Burke leafed through the pages of a manila
folder. "I'm sorry to hear about your cousin."

"Thank you," Rose said cautiously. "It was quite a shock."

"I can only imagine," he said in a kinder voice. He looked up
over his glasses and looked at Meghan. "Dr. Quigley, you're the
one who started this whole ball rolling. In your statement here,
you said you were hired to assist in the field with the geological
study being done. And one night in a pub, you overheard Mr.
Flaherty talk about finding gold in a stream. You then found out
where and told your superiors. Is that correct?"

"Yes, that's correct."

He looked at the file again. "I know it's all in here, but I'd like
to hear it in your own words. If ya don't mind."

"Not at all," Meghan said. "When I was asked to help, I
thought it seemed logical to lend my assistance since that was my
field of expertise, so to speak."

"And they asked you to do what exactly?"

"I would go wherever they were doin' the surveying and
make sure the workers were bein' mindful of the environment
around them. Answer any questions if I could and just basically
stand guard, I suppose is the best way to put it. It was boring, for
the most part."

"Until?" Burke asked.

"Until that night when I was sittin' in a pub with a couple of
colleagues. I overheard some talk at the bar. Normally, I don't

eavesdrop, but when I heard the word gold, it got my attention. They were talkin' about pannin' for gold in the streams near Donegal. Everyone around him thought they were crazy, but Angus and I knew that pannin' for alluvial gold had been done for centuries in Ireland."

"Alluvial?"

Rose leaned in. "That's what I said." When Burke raised an eyebrow, Rose sat back. "Sorry."

"You pan for alluvial gold," Angus said, eagerly sitting forward. "It's the river deposits of soil and sediment. Ya pan for it. Like in the Old West, in America." He grinned and pushed his glasses up on the bridge of his nose. "Do you see?"

"Yes, Dr. Campbell, I'm not an idiot."

"Well, I wasn't suggesting…"Angus cleared his throat and sat back. Meghan shook her head at Angus, who shrugged.

They waited while Burke continued to read the file. "So it's not illegal if ya own the property, but it says here, Dr. Quigley, that the stream Mr. Flaherty was using was not his property."

"That's true, which is why I went to my superiors. What struck me odd was where he found the ore. It was on private land, and after some detecting of my own, I found out he didn't own any property, and it was more than likely illegal. And it was then I found out it was Desmond Flaherty." Meghan shifted in her seat. "Inspector Burke, as I've stated before, I don't begrudge a man for trying to make some money for his family. But I found out who he was married to and the Culhanes were a prominent family in Trahern. I found it curious why he was doin' this. I didn't imagine he needed the money. Then after I found out exactly where this was happenin', Angus, uh, Dr. Campbell, and I went to the stream and found it completely trashed. It was obvious they didn't know what they were doin'."

"Very obvious," Angus interjected.

"I get it," Burke said.

"Anyway, my main concern was the land and what he'd done to it. That's one of the reasons I went to my supervisors."

"And the other reason?" Burke looked over his glasses at Meghan.

Meghan glanced at Rose and Angus before continuing. "I thought if he was doin' this, then there might be other things he was doin'. I figured the sooner they put an end to this, the better."

"What else did you think was goin' on?"

Meghan looked at Angus, who continued. "I heard from a colleague—we're both from Edinburgh—who told me there'd been talk from some workers at a mining company in Tyrone about all the gold that had been mined recently."

"And I thought if Flaherty was illegally pannin' for gold in the streams," Meghan interjected, "then he might have bigger ideas. It was just a logical progression for me, I suppose."

"And you were right?" Burke asked.

"As it turns out, yes. We had told our superiors and were told it would be looked into and taken care of. Dr. Campbell and I went back to the stream several times. It was clean and no one was there."

"But then I heard again from my fellow geologist in Northern Ireland," Angus said. "He was with us when we were at the pub that night with Flaherty. He had similar happenings just over the border from Donegal to County Tyrone. But when we went to file a report, well, that's when I got very scared. I don't mind tellin' ya."

"I don't blame you," Burke said. "Someone slashed the tires on your car and made a threatening phone call."

"Yes, sir. That's when I told you all I knew and went back to Edinburgh. My work with the project was just about over anyway. And I had things to take care of there. I'll be honest."

"And subsequently, Mr. Flaherty is killed in an automobile accident not far from his home," Burke sat back and smiled kindly at Rose, "which is where you come in, Miss Culhane. Your cousin, Kathleen Flaherty, sadly had a similar accident."

"Yes, she did," Rose said. Meghan reached over and held her hand, giving it a reassuring squeeze before letting it go.

Inspector Russell spoke for the first time. "I know this is still very difficult for you."

"It is, but if there's any way I can help, I'd like to." She looked at Burke. "What can I tell you?"

"When was the last time you spoke with Mrs. Flaherty?"

"She and her children came to Chicago in the spring for a visit. I knew then there was something wrong."

"How so?"

"Well, this will seem silly, but we had sort of a schedule for our visits. And it was my turn to come here, but she decided she and the kids needed to get away. That in itself wasn't so odd, but Kathleen just seemed off or preoccupied. She said she wasn't settled with the way Desmond died. Certain things were brought to her attention, but at the time, she seemed overwhelmed, I suppose is a good way to put it. She said she had met Meghan, and now, she couldn't wrap her mind around all that she knew. As it turns out, it was everything that's come to light about Desmond and this gold business." Rose took a deep breath before continuing, "And that's the last time I saw her. I didn't speak with her for the next few weeks, but that wasn't so unheard of. Then I got the call from my aunt about the accident."

"So you knew nothing about this until Dr. Quigley told you?" Burke asked.

"No. I had no idea."

"And, Dr. Quigley, in your statement, you said Mrs. Flaherty called you while driving home that morning but didn't tell you what news she had?"

"That's correct. She called around six. Said she had news, but with drivin' through the storm, she didn't want to stay on the line. So we agreed to meet at her home. She wasn't there when I arrived. I waited, then got worried, so I tried to find her. Not knowin' where she was comin' from, I just took a chance, and that's when I found her car…"

Burke nodded. "And what made you go to Mrs. Flaherty in the first place, Doctor?"

All eyes were on Meghan now. Rose reached over and placed a hand on her knee.

It was a good question. One that Rose had never thought to ask.

Meghan and Angus exchanged glances before Meghan explained. Rose noticed she absently pulled at her earlobe—a clear sign of contemplation.

"When Dr. Campbell and I found out about the stone rods that were missing from the mining company in Tyrone, we both thought of Desmond Flaherty. When he died, it worried me. There could be quite a bit of gold in those rods, Inspector. And I had a feeling Flaherty, if he was involved, had no idea just how much. I had gone to Trahern, the village where they lived, and found out where he lived, that he was married to Kathleen, and they had a family. I don't know, I suppose I felt responsible in a way."

"In what way?" Burke sat back and rocked in his chair.

"I was the one who basically turned him in. At the time, I didn't know he had a wife and family. It wasn't until after I told my supervisors that I found this out. That's what made it so curious to me why he'd do such a thing."

"All right. So you went to Mrs. Flaherty..."

"Yes. I met with her, and after we got to know each other, I felt comfortable in telling her what I thought."

"Mr. Flaherty was never investigated. His death was determined an accident."

"I know. But our colleague was threatened, and the rods were stolen. Mr. Flaherty died, so I suppose I consequently figured Flaherty was involved. And maybe something could happen to his family. I just wanted to make sure, I guess."

"And was Mrs. Flaherty surprised when you told her your thoughts?"

"Yes and no. She seemed stunned, yet in her own words, it sounded like something Desmond would do. She said he was always chasing the pot of gold."

"I have to interject something, if I may," Rose said. Burke nodded in agreement. "I knew Desmond. And I knew he and Kathleen had their difficulties. Des was not one to hold a regular job. He was always scheming for the quick money. And at one point, he nearly squandered all the family money. I'm not sure if you know, but Kathleen lives in our family home in Trahern. It's been our home for generations."

"Yes, I know. Peacock Walk, I think it's called. Interesting name," Burke said, glancing at the file.

"Yes, peacocks squawking all over the place." She smiled

when Burke laughed. "Anyway, Kathleen told me what Desmond had done, and I reacted like everyone else when told of Desmond's exploits. I was stunned but not surprised. I made a call to a friend, who was a banking investor, and he guided her in the right direction, and luckily, she wisely invested what she had left. But from then on, she put all that in the children's name. A trust fund, so Des couldn't get at it. That's just the kind of guy he was, Inspector. He wasn't bad or evil, just..."

"A ne'er-do-well, as my mother used to say," Burke said. "I understand the type. Seen 'em more than I care to in my line of work." He tiredly rubbed his face. "So gettin' back to you, Dr. Quigley. I can understand where you're comin' from. And I appreciate your concern. But what, if anything, did Mrs. Flaherty find out? You have no idea? In all the time you spent with her?"

"I wish I knew. With all my heart, I do," Meghan said sadly.

"And what about you, Dr. Campbell?"

Angus looked baffled. He nervously adjusted his glasses. "Um...in regard to what, sir?"

"Do you have anything to add?" Burke asked. "No hypothesis?"

Again, he and Meghan exchanged glances. Meghan slowly shook her head, but Angus grinned. Now Rose was worried, especially when Angus eagerly sat forward, seemingly ignoring Meghan's warning look.

"Ya want to know what I think?" he asked, still smiling.

Burke frowned. "Now I'm not too sure, but let's give it a go."

"Meg, I mean Dr. Quigley, and I were talking about this while havin' a pint, and we think Desmond Flaherty was into somethin' bigger than he could handle. We think he was in cahoots with someone who had to have knowledge about how they mined for gold because we figure Flaherty wasn't the brains behind it." He leaned across Meghan. "No offense to your cousin's choice of a husband, Rose."

"None taken," Rose assured him.

"But he was the brawn. Ya follow?" he asked Burke.

Meghan closed her eyes; embarrassment splashed all over her face. "Inspector..."

Burke held up his hand stop her. "I follow. Go on," Burke said, rocking in his chair. "You were havin' a pint, and Flaherty was in cahoots with a mastermind."

Rose patted Meghan's arm as Angus continued.

"Exactly!" he said. "Now we figure whoever is behind this planned it all, had Flaherty steal the rods, and he must have gotten greedy and they bumped him off."

Meghan winced and rubbed her forehead; Rose hid her grin as she watched Angus, who looked very proud of himself as he sat back.

"Bumped him off, did they?" Burke said, nodding. "So where are the rods? Who's the mastermind, and what does Mrs. Flaherty have to do with it?"

Angus's gaze darted around the room. "That I don't know," he said quietly and sat back.

Meghan glared at Angus. "Inspector, my colleague and I were just thinking out loud. We have no proof at all as you probably know. It's all speculation."

"Perhaps not, Dr. Quigley. You and Dr. Campbell are closer to the truth than you know."

Meghan and Rose were stunned. Angus hit Meghan on the arm. "Ya see! I was right." He looked at Inspector Burke. "We were right?"

"Inspector Russell, I think you can take it from here," Burke said, closing his file.

An anxious feeling swept through Rose while she watched Inspector Russell walk up to Burke's desk. He had a similar manila folder he set on the desk and opened it.

"As Inspector Burke said, you may nearly be spot-on with your assessment," Russell said, leafing through the pages. "Have you ever heard the name Fergus Moore?"

After a collective no, Russell went on. "He's a crime boss, for lack of a better word, in Northern Ireland. We've been working with Scotland Yard for years tryin' to get him on numerous charges. Smugglin' contraband being one of them. We—"

"Scotland Yard? Smuggling?" Angus said eagerly. "Contraband? As illegally smuggling?"

"Let the man finish, Angus," Meghan said to him. "And if you're smugglin' something, it's usually something illegal, for god's sake."

Rose watched Burke, who smiled slightly as he watched the two geologists.

"I think I know where this is goin'," Angus argued.

"Then let him tell ya," Meghan said angrily.

"Mr. Holmes? Dr. Watson…?" Rose quietly warned both of them; she was aware of Burke's smirking expression as he silently rocked in his chair. Rose was sure one of them would be behind bars before the day was through.

"As I was sayin'," Russell said, watching them, "we've had Moore under surveillance for quite some time now. He's very good at what he does and has loyal men workin' for him, which is why we're confused about Desmond Flaherty. We did a background check on him. Before he married your cousin, he was a small-time criminal. Petty theft, gamblin', and such. He dabbled in almost everything but seemed for the most part to be a loner, never really associating with anyone for too long. And we don't believe he ever worked for Moore. At least not in his younger days." He looked at Rose then. "He seemed to stop all this once he married Kathleen Culhane. At least he was never arrested, which is why he never was a thought until Dr. Quigley. Then we started investigating. And when Kathleen Flaherty died, we knew it had to be connected with all this. We don't know what she found out, but we know it was something. And we're thinking that's what she wanted to tell Dr. Quigley."

Rose couldn't breathe. A realization hit her right between the eyes. "If she knew something, whatever it was…that means someone really did kill her," she said frantically, reaching for Meghan's hand.

"We're not sure," Russell said quickly. "We have no proof. But there has to be something ya know, both of ya." He looked from Rose to Meghan. "Something you're unaware of."

"I can't imagine what," Rose said, holding on to Meghan's hand. "She never hinted at anything like this."

"Dr. Quigley, please think. Try to retrace your time with Mrs. Flaherty. She had to have said something." Russell closed his file after regarding the blank stares. "I think we've exhausted all of you. Why don't you go home? Take some time to think about this. If ya come up with anything, even if it sounds fantastic, give me a call. Ya still have my card?"

Rose nodded numbly. "Where would we start? I have no idea."

"Perhaps Vivian?" Meghan suggested. "Rose's aunt. You met her, Inspector."

Both inspectors agreed. "Maybe I could have a word with her in the next day or two?" Russell asked.

"With all this happening, we're going home today," Rose said, glancing at Meghan. "I'll call you in the morning. How's that?"

"That would be grand." Russell held out his hand when they stood. "I'll wait for your call."

When he nervously looked at Burke, Rose had that anxious feeling again. "What's wrong?"

"Nothing, we think. It's just that we're trying to keep Moore in our sights. But if Desmond Flaherty double-crossed him... Well, if you don't mind, I'd like to have an officer keep tabs on your house."

"You don't think..." Rose couldn't finish what she was thinking.

Russell quickly walked up to her. "Miss Culhane, I don't think Moore would be that stupid. But we'll just make sure there's someone around."

"I'll be staying at the house," Meghan said, standing next to Rose. "But I'm sure if the garda wanted to drive by now and then, no one would argue."

Russell nodded. "Consider it done. Now I'll wait for your call. If anything happens in the meantime, we'll be in touch."

The three of them walked like zombies out of the office. They stood by Meghan's Land Rover for another moment before Rose spoke.

"Well, that was interesting," she said, leaning against the car. "Now what?"

"Like you told Russell. Now we go home," Meghan said.

"I was hoping you'd agree to that," Rose said. "I don't like leaving Aunt Vivian and the children alone."

Meghan turned to Angus. "Do you have to get back to Edinburgh right away?"

"No, I have a speech to give in a few days. I'm as free as a bird," he said with a grin.

"We'll check out of the inn. You do the same, and we'll meet you there," Meghan looked at her watch, "at half past one. Then you can follow us. We'll regroup once we get back to the house. Yes?"

"Good idea. We can discuss this further," Angus said and headed toward his car.

"Let's hurry, Meghan," Rose said. "I don't like this feeling of being away now."

"I know." Meghan opened her door, then quickly pulled her into her arms. "I'm sorry the weekend turned out this way."

"At least we had last night." Rose laughed and shook her head. "God, that sounded so corny."

Meghan gave her a quick kiss. "Corny but true. Now let's quit gabbin' and get home."

Chapter 22

Vivian had her hand on the phone, then shook her head. "You're bein' an old fool, Vivian," she whispered. She didn't want to bother Rose; she was so looking forward to this weekend with Meghan.

She glanced out the window once again, wondering if the red car was still out there on the main road. "My imagination is gallopin' out of control. I need a good cup of tea."

"Auntie Vivian, I'm hungry."

Vivian turned to see Caitlin flounce on the couch. "I miss Rose."

"She'll be back before ya know it. Come with me now. I'll make some tea."

As they walked toward the kitchen, the phone rang. Donal ran downstairs. "I'll get it."

"Will you stop runnin'?"

"Sorry," he said, picking up the phone. "Hello? Rose? Sure, she's right here." He held out the phone. "It's Rose for you."

"Go into the kitchen and put the kettle on to boil." She took the phone from Donal and shooed him away. "Rose?"

"Hi, Aunt Vivian. How's everything?"

Vivian bit at her bottom lip, unsure if she should worry Rose needlessly. "Everything is fine, darlin'."

"I hear something in your voice."

"It's nothin'. Why are you callin'? Are you fightin' with Meghan already?"

Rose laughed. "No, but we are coming home early. I just

171

wanted to let you know. We're on the way, and we'll have a guest."

"That's fine. But why are you comin' back a day early?" Inwardly, she was relieved.

"I'll explain when we get there. Um…Aunt Vivian, just…"

"Just what? What's wrong? Now I can hear something in your voice."

"Nothing. We'll be there in thirty minutes."

"All right. We'll see you then," Vivian said slowly. "It looks like rain."

"Maybe keep the kids inside."

Vivian did not like the urgency in Rose's voice. "I think that's a good idea," Vivian said, trying not to sound anxious. "Hurry home, Rose. Be careful."

"We'll be there soon. I love you."

"I love you, too, darlin'." She hung up the phone and looked outside. She had seen a car out there that afternoon when she and the children went into town. And Sean Murphy told her he saw a similar car in town earlier that morning, and later when he came back this way, it was on the road across the street from the entrance to Peacock Walk. Perhaps it was nothing, but Trahern was a small village and so out of the way it didn't get much in the way of vacationers. So when a bright red car showed up and no one in the village knew who it belonged to—it was news. And word spread fast in a little town. Even old Maddie Quimp told Sean about the car.

"I put the kettle on, Aunt Vivian. Cait and I are goin' out to see Mr. Murphy's—"

Vivian whirled around. "No. It's going to rain, Donal. Stay in."

"But…"

"Please do as I say," Vivian said harshly. "I'm sorry. Please stay inside. Rose will be home in a few minutes."

Donal slowly walked up to her. "Why is she comin' back early?" He reached out and touched her arm. "What's wrong?"

Vivian smiled and cupped his face. "Nothin' is wrong."

"I'm not a child," he said softly. "I…if there's somethin' wrong…"

Vivian searched his face; he looked so much like his father. She saw a look in his blue eyes she hadn't seen before. "What's on your mind?"

He looked confused and hesitant as if he wondered what to say. "Aunt Vivian..."

Just then, Caitlin ran out of the kitchen. "The kettle's boilin' over!"

Vivian jumped; so did Donal. They both laughed. "That child will give me a heart attack one day," she said. She put her arm around Donal's shoulder. "Let's make a nice pot of tea and eat the rest of those cookies and biscuits." She leaned down and kissed the top of his head. "And I know you're not a child. We'll finish our talk, all right?"

Donal nodded and hugged Vivian around the waist.

"I want a hug, too," Caitlin said.

"Come here, ya monkey," Vivian said, pulling Cait to her other side.

They sat at the kitchen table drinking tea and eating lemon biscuits. Vivian watched Donal, who seemed deep in thought, and Cait, who talked to Bunny and tried to feed him a biscuit. When she heard the tires on the gravel driveway, the feeling of relief swept through her.

"Rose is home!" Cait yelled and jumped off the chair. She ran toward the door, then ran back and picked up Bunny and dashed out again.

"I'm tired of yellin' at that child to stop runnin'," Vivian said, sipping her tea.

Donal grinned. "At least she's not wearin' her dancin' shoes."

Vivian laughed along with him and raised her teacup. "Ya have a good point."

Both looked up when Rose and Meghan walked into the kitchen with Cait right behind them holding the hand of a young man.

"Auntie Vivian," Cait said. "We have a guest. His name is Anus."

"Angus," Meghan and Rose corrected her quickly.

"That's what I said," Cait said indignantly. She pulled Angus up to Vivian.

"How do you do?" Vivian said, taking his hand.

"It's a pleasure to meet you," Angus said.

"A Scotsman?" Vivian said, raising an eyebrow.

"Yes, ma'am, but not to worry. I won't ask ya to make haggis."

"As if I had any idea. And we only have Irish whiskey in the house," she said with a laugh.

Angus put a hand to his heart. "That's where I draw the line, ma'am. Good day."

As he turned, Meghan stopped him while Cait laughed and pulled at his sleeve.

"Ya want to hear me play my violin, Anus?"

"Angus!"

Cait rolled her eyes. "That's what I said!"

"Caitlin, let the man breathe. We want to talk."

Cait shrugged. "I'm going to go watch the telly."

"Your chocolates are in the white bag," Rose said to her.

Cait squealed with delight; Vivian grabbed the back of her sweater. "One piece only," she said, then let go. Cait ran out of the kitchen with a quick "yes, ma'am."

"I wish I had her energy," Angus said, watching the kitchen door swing in her wake.

"Would you like some tea?" Vivian asked.

Rose already retrieved the teacups and saucers from the cupboard with Meghan's help. Angus sat at the table and regarded Donal. "We haven't been introduced. Angus."

"Donal. Nice to meet ya." Donal gave his hand a firm shake, which Rose noticed; it had her grinning at Meghan, who apparently saw the manly grasp, as well. "Are you a geologist like Meghan?"

"I am indeed. I teach in Edinburgh." He nodded his thanks when Meghan filled his teacup.

"You're a long way from home," Donal said.

"Yes. I'm helping Meghan." He leaned over the table. "She needs me."

Meghan grunted sarcastically and picked up a biscuit. "Don't let him fool ya, Donal. He's lost without me."

"So why did you come home so early?" Donal asked.

"Yes, good question." Vivian's smile faded when she saw the three of them exchange glances. "Donal, would you like to go watch the telly with Cait?"

"I'd rather stay here," he said, looking down at his teacup. "If it's all right."

Vivian cocked her head, wondering what was wrong with him. She saw the curious look from Rose and Meghan, as well.

"Of course you can sit with us." Vivian patted his hand. "Drink your tea."

They sat in silence for a moment. Rose carefully watched Donal, who toyed with his teacup.

"You saw the car didn't you, Donal?" Vivian asked.

His head shot up; he was wild-eyed as he nodded.

"What car?" Rose asked.

"A red car," Donal said, still watching Vivian, who smiled. "It was there yesterday and twice this mornin'."

"We only saw it once this morning," Vivian said.

"I saw it earlier near dawn," he said, now looking from Meghan to Rose. "I couldn't sleep. So I…"

"Donal, what did you do?"

He set his jaw defiantly. "I wanted to see if it was still there. So I dressed and walked down to the main road."

"Donal!" Vivian said, putting her hand to her heart. "In the pitch dark?"

"I thought I heard a car in the drive. I wanted to make sure. I wasn't seen."

"For the love of St. Patrick, what were you thinkin'?" Vivian asked, shaking her head.

"I was doin' what I should. Rose and Meghan weren't here. It's my responsibility," he said, squaring his shoulders, challenging anyone to argue.

"I understand," Vivian said quickly. "You should have woken me."

Donal leaned into the table. "It was there, just pullin' away when I got to the main road. And I was doin' what Meghan told me. To take care of things while they were gone."

"Did ya get a look at who was in the car?" Meghan asked both of them.

Donal closed his eyes, as if concentrating. "A man. He wore a cap. He looked big. And he was alone. It was just daybreak, though, and a little foggy."

Vivian agreed. "That sounds right. Sean said the same thing. So this is nothin', right?"

Rose chewed at her bottom lip. She looked at Donal, who shook his head.

"Don't make me leave, Rose. I'm not a baby. I think I should know what's happened." He leaned closer. His eyes filled with tears. "She was my mam. I have a right."

Rose reached across the table and took his hand. "I'm sorry, Donal. You're right. You should know. You both should know."

Angus stood and took his teacup. "I think I'll go watch the telly with Cait."

"Tell us what's happened," Vivian said, not knowing if she really wanted to know.

Deep down, she knew there was something very wrong. She was willing to dismiss Desmond's death as an accident but not Kathleen's.

Yes, she was afraid there was something definitely wrong. And as she looked around the table at the collective expressions, her fears were about to become real.

Chapter 23

Rose saw the determined look on Donal's face; he was far too young to look so mature. She realized they had to be told what happened. And now, knowing there was someone watching the house, it terrified her. She reached over and once again took Donal's cold hand.

"Donal, you know your father loved all of you."

"Please don't talk to me like a child. I know what Da was. I know he loved us, so please tell me what he did."

"Your father was doing something, honey, that wasn't well, legal. The long and short of it," Rose said to both of them, "the police think Desmond was into something with some, I don't know, gangster, I suppose. His name is Fergus Moore. They've had him under surveillance and so far can't prove anything, but they think he's smuggling contraband."

"What kind of contraband?" Vivian asked.

Rose looked at Meghan to explain. "It's a long story, but Desmond got himself into stealing from a mining company just over the border in Tyrone."

"Stealing what?" Vivian asked.

Meghan pulled at her earlobe; it was an adorable habit Rose had grown to love—she only wished they had more time to explore adorable habits than this talk of gold. Rose wanted this solved and over with. The uneasy feeling swept through her; she didn't want the children hurt any further. Lost in her thoughts, she nearly missed Meghan's explanation.

"It sounds so fantastic," Meghan said, "but he was stealing gold."

"Gold?" Vivian looked completely stunned.

Rose had to chuckle. "I felt the same way, believe me."

"How in the world? Gold? I had no idea there was gold in Ireland." Vivian sat back.

"Well, the leprechauns might argue with ya," Meghan said.

Rose laughed along but noticed Donal did not; he was staring at his teacup.

"Gold," Vivian said again. "How did he know?"

"We think that's where this Moore fella comes in. They don't think Desmond thought of this by himself."

Rose continued to carefully watch Donal, who frowned deeply as he listened to Meghan.

"Is that why he died?" Donal asked softly.

"They're thinkin' that, yes."

"And Mam, too?" He looked up then.

"We don't know," Meghan said sadly. "They're tryin' to find out."

"The inspectors asked us to think hard and try to remember if we've overheard or seen anything. I told him we'd talk about it," Rose said.

Without a word, Donal stood and walked out of the kitchen.

Rose sighed and wiped the tears from her eyes. "Damn it," she said angrily. "I hated telling him."

Meghan put her arm around Rose and pulled her close. "I know, luv. But he had to know. He's right, ya know. He's not a child."

Rose sobbed into her shoulder. "I know, I know. But he's still so young to have to deal with all of this."

Vivian leaned over and placed her hand on Rose's arm. "Ya need to stop that cryin'. The children need your strength now. Both of you." She looked at Meghan, who nodded.

"Dry your eyes, Rosie," Meghan said, handing her a napkin. "And go talk to him."

As Rose dried her eyes, Donal walked back into the kitchen. He had his hand closed in a fist and held it out to Meghan.

Meghan opened her hand, and Donal dropped something into it. Rose looked and did a comic double take. "Is that what I think it is?"

Meghan held up the small nugget the size of a pebble and a key on a small chain; she examined both for a moment. Naturally, she was more interested in the nugget. "Donal, will you ask Angus to get his briefcase from the car and come in here, please?" She looked up and smiled. "It's all right, son. Go get him, and we'll talk about this."

Donal nodded and walked out of the kitchen. Meghan let out a deep sigh and handed the gold nugget to Rose.

"Okay," Rose said. "This is gold, right?"

"I believe so. But Angus is the expert. He'll tell us for sure."

"Where did he get this?" Vivian asked as Rose handed her the piece of gold. "And how long has he had it?"

"We'll find out," Rose said.

Angus and Donal walked into the kitchen. Angus looked curious and excited at the same time. "I'm assuming when you asked for the briefcase you wanted me to take a close look at something, so—" He stopped abruptly and looked at the gold nugget in Vivian's hand. He immediately sat and opened his briefcase.

"Where did you get this, Donal?" Rose asked.

Donal stood by her, running his fingers through his thick hair and looking as though he was about to cry. "Da gave it to me along with a key. He said we were gonna be rich one day. And that I should keep that and never tell anyone that he gave it to me. It would be our secret, he said. Father to son. Tell no one, he said, not even Mam. I thought he was jokin' like a buried treasure. I never thought..." He stopped before he started crying. "I should have given it to Mam. I forgot all about it. I didn't think it meant anything and now she's dead."

Rose pulled him into her arms and held on as he sobbed. "It's not your fault. Don't you ever think it was." She hated Desmond at that moment for putting a child in this position.

Donal stopped and wiped his eyes as he pulled away from her. "I never thought of it again, I swear. I didn't even think it was real. I just tossed it and the key in my drawer. Knowin' Da, I thought it was fake. If I knew it meant somethin'..."

"Donal," Vivian said. "You did nothing wrong. None of

us knew what your father was doing. And no one had a clue your mother would be involved because of it. You must believe that."

Donal nodded, but Rose could tell he still felt responsible. While they were talking, they didn't pay attention to Meghan or Angus hovering at the end of the table. Angus had several items set out in front of him. Rose noticed he had a jeweler's eyeglass strapped to his eye while he examined the nugget.

Donal watched, fascinated like the rest of them, well, except Meghan. This was probably junior high school geology to her.

"Donal?" Meghan said as Angus examined the nugget. "Would ya like to be our assistant?"

Donal quickly was at her side. Meghan took out another gold nugget from the briefcase. This one was bigger and had more angles to it.

"More gold?" Rose asked.

"Where's it all comin' from?" Vivian leaned in and eagerly watched as Meghan put on her glasses, then took a penknife out of the briefcase.

"Angus, you've looked at it long enough." Meghan motioned for him to give her the nugget, which he did. "Now let's see if it's really gold."

"From what I saw, it is," Angus said, taking off the eyeglass.

"But we need to put it through further tests and make sure." Meghan handed the bigger nugget to Donal. "Hold that in one hand. And yours in the other."

Donal did as Meghan instructed. "Which is heavier?"

"This one." He held out the bigger piece.

"Now take the knife and scrape a bit off the bigger one."

"And be careful," Rose said when Donal took the knife.

Meghan looked at her over her glasses. "We're scientists, Rose. We know what we're doin'."

"Famous last words." Rose sat back and watched.

Donal carefully carved into the cubed nugget. "I can't get anything off it."

Meghan nodded. "Let me do this one. Watch carefully."

"Meg…" Angus warned.

"I know, Dr. Campbell." Meghan carefully put the tip of the penknife to the smaller nugget. "See?"

Everyone leaned closer. Donal watched. "A little speck came off on the tip."

"Worth about five euros," Angus said, shaking his head.

Rose laughed but stopped when Angus raised an eyebrow. "You're not kidding?"

"I'm not up on what the gold market is right now, but that little speck is worth something."

"And the last test," Meghan said. She looked around the kitchen. "Ah, there. Go fetch that iron pan, please."

Donal ran over and took the pan off the stove and ran back to Meghan. She took the cubed nugget and vigorously rubbed it against the bottom of the frying pan. She then took a whiff of it and held it up to Donal's nose.

He sniffed and backed away. "Smells like rotten eggs." He waved his hand in front of him.

"Like something your cousin Rose would cook?" Meghan offered it to Rose, who glared, and Vivian.

"I'm not sure if Rose could make something that smelled that bad," Vivian said.

"So that's not gold or is it?" Donal asked.

Meghan held up both pieces of gold. "No. It's a mineral called pyrite. They look similar. But to those who are not scientists, like us," she winked at Donal, "it's called fool's gold." She held up the pyrite. "This is shaped differently. Its shape is usually like this, cubed, or octahedrons. And some are pyritohedrons. That is to say, pentagonal or five sides to them."

"Um, Dr. Quigley," Angus gently called out. "You'll notice their eyes are glazed over. You're about to lose them. Simple English I believe would help. You're not in the classroom."

Rose knew her mouth was hanging open. She looked back at Vivian, who looked as though she had seen an alien.

"I understood it," Donal said proudly.

"I knew ya would," Meghan said and winked at Donal and motioned to Rose. "I'll leave out the big scientific words for your cousin. Now look at the difference in color." She held up both nuggets. "You'll notice that pyrite is more of a brass color, and the gold is well, golden yellow. And pyrite is usually much bigger, which is probably why miners get so excited when they find it. And gold has no odor and is made up of only atoms of gold, and pyrite has other minerals in its makeup and gives off a sulfurous rotten egg smell." She sat back and examined the gold nugget. "Gold is also softer. It'll flatten when hammered, but I think that experiment would throw Angus into a seizure."

"Exactly right. It's bad enough ya took a penknife to it. So there you have it," Angus said, sitting back. "That little piece is definitely real gold."

"How much do you think it's worth?" Rose asked.

Angus took the gold piece and held it again. "Not even an ounce, I'd say." He took out his cellphone. "Let's see what the going price is right now. I wish I had a scale."

Meghan took the nugget and weighed it in her hand. "I'd say at least a half ounce."

Angus blinked as he looked at his phone. "Then it's worth five hundred American dollars."

"Wow," Rose said. "That little thing?"

Angus turned his phone so all could see the screen.

"Holy Mother of God," Vivian said and blessed herself.

"Donal, did your father say where he got this?" Meghan asked.

"No, he didn't. He just said to keep it safe and never tell anyone."

"When did he give these to you? Can you remember?" Rose asked.

Donal thought for a moment. "It was a few months before he died. He was outside, and I saw him coming around the back of the house. He had a shovel…" His voice trailed off, and his eyes grew wide. "Do ya think he was diggin' around here?"

"He didn't tell you?" Meghan asked.

"No. He was whistlin' and seemed happy, but he was always whistlin'. And that's when we went for a walk up the hill and he gave it to me."

"Did he say anything else?"

Once again, he contemplated Rose's question. "Only that he was doin' the best thing. And then all that I told ya. Oh, and we talked about the history of Peacock Walk."

"What history?" Vivian asked.

Donal shrugged. "Just about Mam's family and how old the house was, been around for centuries he said, and what it was worth. That's all."

Meghan held the nugget out to him; he pushed it back. "I don't want it. He stole it."

No one could argue with him on that point.

"Well, we'll keep it safe," Rose said, taking the gold piece. "Along with this key. I wish we knew where he got this. Do you think he got it out of that stream?"

"That seems like a big piece to find in a stream. Usually, you find gold flecks or dust when you pan it out," Angus said. "Although it's a small piece, I don't think it's from a stream. Someone had to give this to him. I haven't heard of anyone mining gold in Ireland like the olden days of pickaxes and dynamite."

"Well, enough of this now," Vivian said. "Donal, please go check on Cait. I'll get dinner ready. Oh, by the way, Brendan is no longer staying here. He said a friend of his in Donegal is putting him up until he goes back to London."

"Brendan is Desmond's younger brother," Meghan explained to Angus. "He came in for the funeral."

"And hasn't left," Rose added.

"Now, Rose," Vivian said.

"Oh, please. We all agree he's overstayed his welcome."

"Well, he said he would stop by before he went back to London."

"Does he know about Desmond?" Angus asked.

"We told him the other day after we came back from Kathleen's lawyer," Rose said. "He seemed shocked, but like the rest of us, not completely surprised."

"And remember," Meghan said.

"What?"

"When we told him about the missing mineral rods, he said the mining company was in Tyrone."

"So?" Angus said.

"I never told him it was in Tyrone." Meghan stood and walked over to the window. "And now that I think of it." She turned back to them. "What was your reaction when you first heard about mining for gold in Ireland?"

Vivian laughed. "I had no idea. I was shocked."

"I was shocked, as well. I never heard of gold ore that was mined in rods."

Meghan smiled and looked at Angus, who nodded. "I take it Brendan did not react the same way."

"He did not. Rose, remember? He didn't even flinch when I told him how the gold was mined in rods. Not even a question on it. I do not believe the average person knows that, and the logical response would be surprise or at the very least curiosity."

"Which makes you think he already knew," Angus said thoughtfully. "That's not unheard of."

Meghan gave him an exasperated look. "Angus, really? He's a writer, probably spent most of his time with his nose in a book and not a geology book. He's been in London, in the city. Tell me where he would know about this."

"He's lived in London for years," Vivian said, "away from Desmond."

"But that doesn't mean he didn't talk with his brother," Meghan argued. "I can't prove anything, but I have a feeling Brendan Flaherty knows more than he's lettin' on."

"How do we find out?" Angus asked. "Without him finding out?"

Now that was a good question.

Chapter 24

The night's dinner conversation consisted of geology, the earth, and oh, yes, Bunny needed an operation, according to Cait. His poor ear hung by a thread, literally. She made Angus promise to call his doctor friend, who was a real doctor and not a "rock doctor."

Afterward, while Vivian prepared the spare room, poor Angus was witness to Cait's violin and step dancing extravaganza. Meghan made sure his glass of whiskey was kept full. And though painful to the senses, it was a humorous respite to an otherwise sad and worrisome day.

Finally, they got Cait to calm down—her face was as red as her hair. And she and Donal said their good nights and were off to bed. It was only eight o'clock, and everyone was exhausted. Vivian practically fell asleep in her chair.

"I have an idea," Meghan said softly, as not to wake Vivian.

"I don't like that tone," Angus said sadly, staring at the dying embers in the fireplace.

Rose laughed and laid her head on Meghan's shoulder. "What's your idea?"

"Well, Vivian and Donal said they saw a red car. And Sean told Vivian he saw it in town, as well. Angus? How would you like to see the little Irish town of Trahern?"

He shook his head. "Why I'd love to, Dr. Quigley. I'm assumin' ya mean right now."

Meghan stood quickly; Rose fell forward on the couch with a groan. "I think she does."

"Come along, children. Rose, you get Vivian into bed…"

"I'm awake." Vivian opened one eye. "How can anyone sleep with all this chatter?"

"Do you mind if we go into town?" Rose asked, offering her hand when Vivian stood.

"Not at all. I think it's a good idea, if you can come up with something. Let me call Sean and see if he can meet you. Now off with ya. We'll be fine. Just lock up. I have a phone by my bed. Call if you need to. I'm going to sleep." She kissed Meghan and Rose, then gave Angus an affectionate hug. "Your room is all ready for you, Angus."

"Thank you, Vivian."

After they locked all doors and windows, they headed out in Meghan's Land Rover to Trahern. As they approached the town, Meghan slowed down. Rose knew they were all looking for the red car, which they did not see on the drive there.

"This might be a bust," Angus said, looking out the window.

Meghan stopped at the edge of town and parked along the only street in Trahern. "Ya never know. Maybe Mr. Murphy can meet us. If nothin' else, I'm sure whoever's in the pub will have somethin' to say."

They walked down the cobblestone sidewalk to the only pub in Trahern.

"I love this place," Rose said as they walked in.

The low-beamed ceiling and dark wood gave the pub a cozy feeling. It consisted of a bar, several stools, and a few tables set in no particular fashion. They looked like an afterthought of the owner, Terry Quimp, who probably realized not everyone wanted to belly up to the bar.

As they walked through the heavy wooden door, all heads turned. Rose saw Sean Murphy at the bar. He smiled and raised his pint when he saw them. Terry Quimp stood behind the bar, with a towel slung over his shoulder. Rose had to grin at the sight of this big man with a ruddy complexion and unruly red hair. A few other patrons sat at the bar, and surprisingly, a couple of tables had customers, as well.

Sean motioned them over. "Vivian just called to let me know you were comin'," he said, sliding over to another stool. "But it was very fortuitous, as I was already here." He bowed slightly and grinned.

"But for how long?" Rose asked, sitting next to him.

"None of that now, young lady. You Americans have no sense of propriety," he said in glum fashion. He raised his glass but realized it was empty.

"Sean, let me buy ya a pint," Meghan said. "This is my friend, Angus Campbell."

Terry and Sean exchanged curious looks. "A Scotsman?" Terry asked.

Angus grinned and pushed his glasses up on his nose. "And I'd love a pint of Guinness, if that matters."

Terry laughed along with Sean as he poured four pints.

Rose groaned. "This will take forever." She watched the arduous task of pouring the perfect pint.

"But well worth the wait," Angus said to her.

"I like him already," Sean said. "Now tell me why ya wanted to meet with me on this chilly summer night."

"It's always chilly here," Rose said.

Sean raised an eyebrow. "Ya seem to be in a foul mood, Rose Culhane."

Terry placed the pints in front of them—finally. "It's good to see ya again, Rose," Terry said. "I'm very sorry for your loss. Kathleen was a fine woman and a good mother. How are the little ones?"

"As you might expect," Rose said. "They're clinging to each other and coping together."

"They have Vivian, and how long are ya plannin' on stayin'?" he asked as he wiped off the bar.

"I think I'll be staying on here," Rose said, taking a sip of stout. "I'm their legal guardian now."

Terry smiled. "That seems appropriate. I know the children love ya. Well then..." He poured a whiskey and raised it. "Welcome home, Rose Culhane."

"Thanks, Terry," she said.

They all raised their glasses. Sean took a healthy drink as did the others, then slapped the bar. "Now tell me why we're here."

"I suppose I'll start," Meghan said, leaning on the bar. "Vivian mentioned she's seen a red car in town and in the road by the entrance of Peacock Walk. Donal has seen it, as well."

Sean nodded. "We have. Even Maddie Quimp saw it. She's the one who told me the first time. Terry, is Maddie here?"

"In the back. Let me go fetch her."

"Did you ever get a good look at the driver?" Angus asked.

"Not really. A man, that's for sure. Wearing a cap. But the times I've seen him, it's been rainin', so it's hard to tell."

"And he never got out of the car?"

"He did not. Ah, Maddie, there ya are."

Rose saw Maddie Quimp and had to grin. She was older, perhaps Sean's age. She had salt-and-pepper hair she wore up and off her neck and was as rotund as her brother was tall. Her big green eyes sparkled as she smiled, and her rosy cheeks made her look like she'd just run a race.

"Rose Culhane, you're a sight for these sore eyes, darlin'." She ran around the bar and pulled Rose nearly off the stool to hug her. "I'm so sorry, dear," she whispered and kissed her cheek.

When she pulled back, Rose saw the tears well in her eyes. "Thanks, Maddie. Oh, this is Meghan Quigley and her friend Angus Campbell."

"It's a pleasure to meet ya," she said. "Sean said you were askin' after the red car. Let's move to a table, me feet are killin' me, and those barstools numb my arse."

"I like her," Meghan whispered in Rose's ear as they sat at one of the tables.

"Give us another round, Terry," Maddie called to her brother.

"Comin' up," he called back.

"Now let's get down to it," Maddie said. "The red car. I noticed it just the other day. We don't get many vacationers here in Trahern, so when a stranger comes by, they stick out like a sore thumb." She then looked at Meghan and winked. "Like yourself. I thought you looked familiar. You were in askin' questions about Desmond, am I right?"

"You are. I was in here and overheard him talkin' about..."

"Och..." Maddie said, shaking her head. "That one with the talk of gold swimmin' in the streams like trout." She looked at Rose. "I don't mean to speak ill of the dead, but Desmond Flaherty—"

"It's all right, Maddie. I've thought the same about him since the day he married Kathleen."

"I never wished any ill will on the man, and I certainly was sad to hear he died, leaving a wife and two little ones. Thank the Lord above Kathleen had property and the house. How are those blasted peacocks?"

"Still squawking," Rose said.

"I'll never understand why Vivian or Kathleen never got rid of them," Maddie said.

"I think they're part of the property and are always supposed to stay there. I'm surprised the peacocks weren't left some money. A great-uncle or grandfather probably did."

"Well, Sean," Maddie said, winking at Rose, "that's one way to get rich. Marry a peacock."

"I already did, darlin'," Sean said.

Terry came back with the second round of stout. Rose was glad they didn't live far out of town. Though she watched Meghan, who barely touched her first pint, now she had two sitting in front of her. Rose tried not to laugh as Meghan surreptitiously slid her pint in front of Angus.

"Maddie, did ya ever get a good look at the fella in the red car?" Meghan asked.

"I can't be sure, and I don't want to speak out of turn," Maddie said.

Sean frowned deeply. "When did that start?"

Rose hid her laugh in her pint.

"You've got a wicked tongue, Sean," Maddie said.

Sean lifted his pint and winked at Rose. "That's what the missus said just last night."

Maddie roared with laughter and slapped at his arm. Angus laughed along while Rose could tell Meghan tried to keep the conversation on topic. She gently cleared her throat.

"Ah," Maddie said. "The man in the red car looking very much like the fella that Desmond was sittin' here talkin' to. Meghan, I think you and Angus were here one night. Don't ya remember?"

"It was over a year ago," Meghan said.

"I think I remember him. Tallish, dark hair, older than Flaherty. He…"

"He what?" Meghan said.

"He had some quirky thing he did, remember? He would play with a coin, ya know, rollin' it around his fingers."

Meghan sat back. "Ya know, I think I do remember that. I wonder if Inspector Russell would want to know this." She looked at Rose. "Let's call him tomorrow. We can tell him about Donal's gold nugget and—"

"Donal?" Maddie asked.

"Yes." Rose sighed sadly. "Desmond gave him a small gold nugget and some wild story about making it rich and all the history of Peacock Walk. The poor kid felt responsible somehow for taking the nugget and not telling anyone."

"The poor boyo," Sean said. "But the history of your ancestral home is no wild story."

"Oh, I've been told this story for as long as I can remember," Rose said, holding up her hand.

"What's the story?" Angus prepared himself for a good story. "I love history."

"Then you'll love this," Rose said. "Apparently, back in the day, and by that I mean over three centuries ago, the Culhane family business was…" She stopped and stared around the table.

"What?" Meghan said.

"Smuggling," Rose whispered.

Angus's jaw dropped. Meghan's eyes nearly bugged out of her head. Maddie and Sean looked decidedly confused.

"Why the surprise?" Maddie asked. "It's well known you Culhanes built Trahern stealin' from the English."

"It's just coincidental that Flaherty might have been travelin' in a rough crowd who dabbled in smuggling. The authorities think he got in over his head and died for it."

"I don't think it's a coincidence. Tell me more, Rosie," Meghan said, leaning forward.

"Well, my ancestors would steal from the ships and smuggle whatever it was and do whatever smugglers do to get money for it," Rose said with a laugh. "I never really paid attention to the stories."

Terry ran up to the table. "The red car is at the end of the village."

It surprised Rose no one did serious damage to himself or herself as they all jumped up at once, bumping into one another as they headed to the door.

"Put it down," Meghan said to Angus, who had his pint in hand.

Sure enough, the red car was at the far end of Trahern.

"I have an idea," Meghan said. She took out her cellphone and took a picture of the car.

"Brilliant," Rose said.

Then, before Rose could stop her, Meghan ran down the cobblestone sidewalk. Thankfully, Angus stopped her.

"What are you doing?" he asked.

"I'm goin' to go take a picture of him."

"Not so brilliant," Rose said angrily.

Angus grabbed the phone from Meghan. "She's right. I'll do it."

"Angus!" Meghan reached for him, but he ran past her and down the street.

The driver put the car in reverse as Angus held the phone out toward the car. He got almost to the driver's window when the car stopped, then started forward, nearly hitting Angus as it screamed by them and out of sight.

"I got it!" Angus called out as he ran back.

Meghan grabbed him by the collar. "Are you crazy, man? Ya could've gotten yourself killed."

Rose slapped Meghan on the shoulder. "You were going to do it. Don't yell at him." She turned to Angus and slapped him on the shoulder. "And she's right. Are you crazy?"

Angus rubbed his shoulder and adjusted his glasses. "But I got him."

They huddled around the table once again. Maddie was breathless and excited. "That'll teach him to snoop around our village."

Angus looked at the phone. "I got the tag number, but look at this." He turned the phone for all to see.

It was a picture of the driver. A little blurry and not very recognizable.

"I'll swear to anyone that's the guy who was here with Flaherty," Sean said.

Maddie raised an eyebrow. "After a few pints maybe. Ya can't tell who that is."

The rest of them agreed. Never seeing the gentleman, Rose could only acquiesce. "We need to show this to Inspector Russell."

"Tomorrow. We need to get back."

Rose heard the urgency in Meghan's voice. She grabbed her arm when Meghan stood. "What's wrong?"

"Rose," Meghan said evenly. "Up till now, this fella has been comin' and goin' with no worries. But now he knows we're on to him. I don't want to leave Vivian and the children alone until this thing, whatever it is, is settled."

Rose's stomach churned at the idea of what could possibly happen to all of them. "Let's go. Maddie, Sean, thanks so much."

"Not to worry, darlin'," Maddie said. "We'll let ya know if he shows up again."

"Which he won't, I'm thinkin'," Sean said. "Go home and talk to the garda. Let them handle this now."

The drive home was quiet, mainly because Rose watched the speedometer as Meghan raced down the narrow road.

"Honey, please," Rose said quietly. "No more accidents. Slow down."

Vivian and the children were sound asleep when they arrived home. They checked the doors and windows before turning out the lights.

Angus grabbed his suitcase and followed Rose and Meghan up the stairs. "I'm exhausted. I'll sleep like the dead."

"Please, Angus," Rose said over her shoulder, "no talk of death."

"Oh, right. So sorry."

Rose opened the bedroom door. "Home sweet home. Bathroom is at the end of the hall. Good night, Angus."

"Good night, ladies. I can't wait to see what tomorrow brings. I hope the pictures prove helpful."

"I'm sure they will. G'night."

Rose stood in the dark hall with Meghan. "Well, we've run out of rooms."

Meghan grinned. "I can sleep on the couch."

Rose grabbed her by the hand. "As if that would happen."

They lay in each other's arms; Meghan absently stroked Rose's shoulder. "I wish we were naked."

Meghan laughed and kissed the top of her head. "We don't want to scare Cait should she come in later. It'll be hard enough to explain why I'm sleepin' in your bed."

Rose cuddled closer. "I'll just tell her you're a big scaredy-cat and I needed to protect you."

"Don't kid yourself, Rosie. It's closer to the truth than ya might think."

Rose slipped her hand under the covers, running her fingertips across Meghan's breast. "I love the way your breathing changes when I touch you like this," she whispered, kissing the top of her shoulder.

"You'd better stop that." Meghan groaned when Rose slipped her hand down her torso.

"No sexy panties like last night?" Rose whispered.

"No," Meghan said in a coarse voice. "I didn't want to get ya all aroused."

"Hmm. How's that working out for you?"

"Not...so...good. Damn it, quit your teasin'."

Rose loomed over her, running her fingers across her clitoris. Meghan arched her back into Rose's touch. She kissed Meghan as she slipped two fingers inside. It wasn't soon after she felt the walls tighten around her fingers. "Now, Meghan," she whispered against her lips. "And we must be quiet."

"I don't think I..." Meghan groaned into the kiss as her

orgasm began. She silently writhed under Rose until she couldn't take anymore. "Stop," she pleaded. "I…"

Rose kissed her once again as she eased her hand away. Meghan whimpered and breathed heavily. "That was very nice and sexy," Rose said, kissing her chin, then her cheek, and finally kissing her dry lips. "You were very quiet."

Meghan chuckled. "I tried so hard, I think I broke something."

Rose laughed along; she laid back and pulled Meghan with her. Meghan rested her head on Rose's breast.

"Ah, Rosie." She sighed and wrapped her arm across Rose's waist. "I do love you."

"Good. Because after all this, you're not getting rid of me."

"Thank the saints above for that."

They lay silently in each other's arms. Rose could feel Meghan's eyelashes fluttering against her breast telling her she was still awake.

"What will happen tomorrow?"

"We'll call Russell in the morning and go from there, luv."

Rose felt her move against her, as if trying to get comfortable. "What's wrong?"

"Oh, I thought all of this was just coincidental. That whatever Flaherty was into was none of our concern, and Kathleen just died in a horrible accident. And you and I and the children and Vivian wouldn't be going through all this. And just be happy."

"That will happen. Hell, we're already happy. We just need to get this behind us and solved." She tightened her embrace and ran her fingers through Meghan's hair. "And have the rest of our lives together."

"The rest of our lives," Meghan mumbled, on the edge of sleep.

Rose stared out the window into the darkness. Tomorrow, she thought. Maybe tomorrow all this would be out of their hands. Maybe the questions of what Desmond did with the stolen gold and what Kathleen found out would be answered.

Deep in her heart, Rose knew those questions had to be answered before any of them found any peace.

Chapter 25

"This was very ingenious. If not dangerous," Russell said, holding up the picture Angus had taken. "After ya sent it to me, I had it printed and distributed. It's not a very good picture, but with the license tag, we think we know this fella. His name is Liam Hennessy." He looked up when Vivian set his cup of tea down. "Thank you."

"It was a group effort," Angus said.

Rose and Meghan sat on the couch holding hands. "Who is he?" Meghan asked.

Russell took a drink of tea before continuing. "He works for Moore. Moore owns a construction company in Londonderry. Hennessy is his foreman. We figure he launders all his money through there."

"But we still don't know what it has to do with Kathleen's death," Vivian said.

Russell scratched the back of his head. "No, but there's something there. It's too coincidental, and now we have one of Moore's men watchin' ya. But don't worry. I have my men goin' to have a little chat with him. I don't think he'll show up here again. Moore will get the message."

"What do you think Flaherty did with the mineral rods he stole?" Meghan said.

"I don't know that, either. I visited the mining company. I still can't believe they can extract that much gold out of them." He took another drink of tea. "If Flaherty did indeed take those rods, he'd have to hide them somewhere. And if Moore is havin' ya watched, he must believe you know somethin'. Are ya sure Mrs. Flaherty said nothin' to you?"

Rose could tell Meghan was getting exasperated; she held tightly on to her hand.

"What about the children?" Russell asked.

"We nearly forgot..." Rose told him about the gold nugget and the odd key on the chain Desmond had given Donal. And how he wanted it to be their secret.

Russell listened and scribbled in his notebook. "Who has this key now?"

"I do." Rose reached into her pocket and pulled out the key. She held it up by the chain.

Russell took it and shrugged. "It looks relatively new. Doesn't look like a key to a bank box." He shrugged. "It looks like an ordinary house key or a padlock key." He looked then. "Do you have any boxes or cabinets at your house that require a key?"

"No," Vivian said. "There's really nothing like that."

"No gun cabinets? No file cabinets with important documents?"

"All of that is in a small safe in the library across the hall. It doesn't require a key."

"Keep track of that, please. It may mean something." He scribbled in his notebook once again.

"I'm sure it does, but what?" Rose examined the key again. When she looked up, Rose noticed Russell watching Vivian, who was frowning and looking at her teacup.

"Miss Culhane?" Russell said softly.

Vivian blinked and looked up. "Oh, I'm sorry. I was just trying to remember if Kathleen did anything out of the ordinary in the last few days before..." She took a deep breath.

"If there was anything at all, Aunt Vivian," Rose said.

"I remember her going into Donegal several times, but that was not unusual. But..." Vivian's eyes grew wide. "She said she was going shopping, but now that I think of it, she never came back with any packages."

"Is that odd?" Russell asked.

"Inspector Russell," Rose said. "Meghan and I planned two

days in Donegal. Just two days, and we had a shopping list from two children and Aunt Vivian. I highly doubt Kathleen could have gone into Donegal and shopped without bringing something back."

"So what was she doing there?" Angus asked.

"Would you mind...?" Russell hesitated. "If we knew where she went in Donegal, that might shed some light on this. Would ya mind if I took a look at her credit card statements?"

Vivian quickly stood. "You mean if she purchased something, it would tell us where... I know where they are."

"Do you think they'll show anything?" Rose asked him when Vivian left.

"Maybe, ya never know."

Vivian ran back in, holding a small stack of envelopes. "I've gone through a few things, but honestly, it made me too sad."

Russell took the stack from her and divided them up in three smaller stacks. "This'll go faster if we all look." He handed a stack to Rose, Meghan, and Angus.

"What are we looking for?" Rose asked.

"Anything that might tell us where she was," Russell said.

When they heard the back door slam, Vivian jumped. "For the love of God..."

Cait and Donal ran into the living room and stopped abruptly when they saw the stern look they received from Vivian.

"Sorry, Auntie," Donal said breathlessly.

"What are ya doin'?" Cait asked, wedging herself between Rose and Meghan, who laughed and moved out of her way.

"Readin', ya bulldozer," Meghan said.

"What are ya readin', Rose?" she asked, giggling as Meghan tickled her.

"Caitlin?" Vivian said. "Go upstairs with your brother and wash up. Ya two have been around Mr. Murphy's sheep, I'm sure."

"Aww, Auntie," Cait said.

"Do as you're told, Cait. Go on now," Rose said, bumping her with her shoulder.

Donal was watching Russell curiously but took Cait by the hand and dragged her upstairs.

"Donal seems to be a bright young man," Russell said, leafing through the pages. "Hello…" he whispered, holding up a page.

"What is it?" Meghan asked.

"A bill from a store in Donegal a few days before the accident."

"Look," Angus said, reading a page. "What's the name of your store?"

"Heather on the Hill," Russell said.

Angus looked up. "So is mine. Dated a couple weeks before. This has to be it," he said thoughtfully.

"Wonder what they sell," Russell asked absently.

"Let's find out," Rose said. "It's a sunny morning. Road trip to Donegal."

The store was on the far end of Donegal on the corner. The business sign hung on a shingle over the door.

"I wish Inspector Russell could have come with us," Rose said.

"Well, if he had to be called away, I'm glad it was to question that Hennessy fella they picked up." Meghan assured her, "We'll be fine on our own."

A bell tinkled as they walked in. The young woman behind the counter looked up and smiled. "Good mornin'."

Rose walked up to the counter with Angus and Meghan standing behind her. "Good morning."

"Ah, an American. Wonderful," the woman said. "Are ya lookin' for your ancestors? You've come to the right place."

"That's what you do here?" Rose asked.

"Yes, ma'am. We find your people and where they lived."

"Very good. I do have a question. My cousin came in here a couple times, and you did some research for her. Could you tell me what she wanted if I gave you her name?"

"Ma'am, we have so many people coming in from America."

"No. She's from Trahern in County Donegal. Kathleen Flaherty."

The woman thought for a moment. "Let me look." She took

out her ledger and leafed through the pages. "No. I'm sorry. No Flaherty."

Rose rolled her eyes. "I'm sorry. Look for Kathleen Culhane."

"Oh, of course. Here it is. Yes, I remember her now. She was very excited to find out about her ancestral home. I have to tell you, I was amazed when I did the research. I'm so glad you came in to pick this up for her. I'd hate to see all this research go to waste. I got what she asked for, but she never came back to get it and I had no address for her. I called her cellphone a few times, but she never called back. You say you're her cousin? I'll just need some identification."

Rose noticed the skeptical look and took out her driver's license.

"I'll go get it. You'll just have to sign for it." She disappeared into a small office and returned with a large rectangular envelope and a cardboard cylindrical tube.

Rose's hand shook as she signed for them.

"Peacock Walk seems to be a very popular place," the woman said.

Rose quickly looked up. "Popular?"

The woman smiled and looked at all three. "Yes. A gentleman was in asking about it over a year ago. He came in several times. I don't know why I remembered that, probably because of the name. Peacock Walk is so unusual." She stopped and laughed quietly. "Your cousin had asked if anyone was asking about the property. She didn't seem surprised when I told her, she was almost disappointed."

"What did he look like?"

"If I remember, he was tall with dark hair..."

Meghan took out her phone and showed her the blurry picture of Hennessy. "Is this the man?"

"No. This man was handsome and quite the flirt."

"Desmond," Rose said. "Did you give any information to him?"

"Yes, as a matter of fact."

Rose was incredulous. The woman laughed. "That's the

same expression the redheaded woman had. Ya must know this gentleman. She seemed excited, then I must admit, she looked… worried, I guess. Yes, I'd say she looked worried. Well, I think you'll enjoy the reading." The woman handed them to Rose.

"Thank you."

They couldn't get out of the store fast enough. They agreed to wait and open the envelopes. The drive back to Peacock Walk seemed to take forever. They all piled out of the Land Rover and ran up the steps. Vivian was in the living room to greet them.

"What did you find?" she asked.

"Let's go to the kitchen table," Meghan said, holding up the tube. "I think we'll need some room for this."

Donal and Cait had just finished lunch. They quickly cleared the dishes off the table.

"What is it?" Donal asked, watching Meghan.

She patiently opened the tube. Rose, on the other hand, nearly ripped the envelope in half trying to get it open.

Meghan grinned at Donal. "A map. I'm sure of it."

"A map of what?" he asked, completely enthralled.

"A treasure map!" Cait exclaimed, kneeling on a kitchen chair.

"Do ya think so, Meghan?" Donal stood next to her and peered at the sheet that Meghan rolled out.

Rose had to admit it looked like the rolls of maps Meghan had on her desk at her house. Angus held one edge of the map and placed a cup on the corner to keep it from rolling. Donal must have seen this as a good idea; he ran and got three more cups along with Vivian and placed them on the other corners.

"What is it?" Vivian asked.

"It's a map of your property." Meghan put on her glasses. "It looks like a topographical map."

Angus nodded as he too looked at the map.

"Where's the house?" Donal asked.

"This was done before the house was built," Meghan said. "Rose, what's in your envelope?"

"It's a small bound booklet about Peacock Walk." Rose leafed through the pages.

"When was the house built?" Angus asked.

"In 1875. Emmett Lesley Culhane built it. Took two years, it says." Rose sat and continued reading. "It says he inherited the property from his father, who had died before he built the house. How the Culhane family got their fortune is unclear, it says. But the common thought was the family, like most in Ireland, had no use for the English, and whenever possible, the Culhane men relieved the English of the burden of money and many artifacts." Rose stopped when Meghan and Angus laughed.

"Sure, I'd have loved to live in those days," Angus said wistfully.

"So would I," Donal announced.

"Stealin' is stealin' no matter how noble the cause," Vivian said to Donal. She then laughed. "Though I don't suppose it mattered that the English came here uninvited and robbed..."

"Aunt Vivian?" Rose said softly, then continued, "Upon his death, Emmett started the construction upon his father's explicit wishes to build the house on the exact spot. The house got its name from Emmett, who..." Rose stopped and laughed. "Procured a dozen Indian peafowl from a gentleman in England. It is unclear just how Emmett Culhane paid for the birds as no bill of sale could ever be produced. He had learned that in the Far East peacocks were used to guard homes and property. Thus the beginning of Peacock Walk." She looked up at the rest of them, who studied the map on the table. "What does the map show?"

"Well, I'm not a cartographer." Meghan looked up when Rose cleared her throat. "Oh, sorry. I'm not a map reader. But if you look here." She pointed to a section of the map. "This section is shadowed in, tellin' me that there is somethin' there, some structure. But if ya look at this map..." She unrolled another sheet and laid it alongside. "...you can definitely see this map was drawn up after the house was built. The house is now directly over that shaded area."

"What does that mean?" Vivian asked.

"I'm bored," Cait said in full pout. "I'm going to practice my violin." She hopped off the chair and ran out.

"How can ya be bored with this?" Donal shook his head.

"What do you think, Donal?" Meghan asked.

Rose watched as Donal studied both maps. "I'd say Emmett built this house to hide whatever was there before it." He looked up at Meghan. "Do ya think there's something under this house?"

"I don't know." Meghan looked from one map to the other. "But if your ancestors had something to hide, then building a house over it would certainly hide it."

"But if they did that, how could they ever get to what was under there?" Angus asked.

"Good question. Aunt Vivian, is there a basement or cellar?"

"Oh, no, darlin'."

"I don't think it would even be considered back then. Perhaps some houses built close to the cities, but not this far in the country, not with this soil," Meghan said.

"But something was under this house," Rose said. "But what?"

Chapter 26

For the rest of the afternoon, they all examined the maps and the history of the Culhane family, and there was one common thread—Rose's ancestors amassed the family wealth by thievery.

"Looks like I'm gettin' into a shady family," Meghan said thoughtfully.

Rose playfully glared when Meghan and Donal laughed. "Let's get serious here. We need to figure out what we know."

"I know," Donal said. He got a pen and paper off the desk. "We'll make a list. That's what our teacher makes us do in class."

"Good idea." Meghan rubbed her hands together. "You'd make a good scientist."

This made Donal smile proudly. "I'm all set."

They all looked toward the ceiling when they heard the screeching of *Three Blind Mice*.

Donal winced. "Does she have to do that still?"

"Let her be," Vivian said. "She's busy. Would ya rather have her hoofin' it in front of the fireplace?"

"So what do we know about the maps?" Meghan asked, motioning to Donal's paper. "The house was built over some obscure structure."

"And there is no basement or cellar." Rose leafed through the booklet. "And my ancestors had nefarious dealings, which is how they got the family fortune."

"And they hid it under the house," Donal said absently as he scribbled.

Meghan whirled around to him. "What did you say?"

Donal looked up. "I-I said they hid it under the house. Isn't that what they did?"

Angus laughed. "The mind of a fourteen-year-old. We're out of our league. Of course that's what they did."

"But without a cellar or basement, how would they get to it if they built the house over it?" Vivian asked.

"There has to be another way," Meghan said thoughtfully.

"A tunnel," Donal said with a shrug. "Like the pirates."

Before they could say another word, *Three Blind Mice* got louder. Cait walked down the staircase while screeching away at her violin.

"Caitlin, please!" Vivian called out.

Cait stopped in the doorway. "I got lonely."

"Darlin', we're talkin'. If you want to stay, you'll have to stop that…"

"Screechin'." Donal kept his head down as he wrote. He looked up then. "I meant playin'."

Cait pouted but walked over to him. "What are you doin'?"

"Grownup stuff, Cait," he said seriously.

"Then why are you doing it?"

"Cait." Meghan grinned and took her hand. "Come sit here and look at the map."

"Why?"

"Because I need your help." Meghan kissed the top of her head.

Cait preened and looked at Donal, who rolled his eyes.

"So where were we?" Rose asked, sitting next to Cait. She put her arm around her shoulders. "Hi."

"Hi," Cait said, concentrating on the map.

The fact that the poor child had it upside down was obviously not a factor to her. Rose decided not to tell her.

"So if there was a tunnel, where would it be?" Meghan took the other map and examined it. "I have an idea. C'mon. It's a sunny afternoon. Let's go outside. All of us. Rose, take your history and, Cait, why don't ya let me have the map for now, darlin'?"

Cait pouted but handed the map to Meghan.

"I need your help once we get outside, and ya can't be holdin' a map." Meghan turned to Angus. "There are measurements on these maps that show the distance on the property. We can step off the yardage and may be able to determine it."

"Determine what?" he asked.

"Where the tunnel is," Meghan said with glee. "If there is one."

They all stood in the driveway in front of the house. Meghan and Angus held the maps while Rose and the others looked on.

"All right. If we look at this map with the house after it was built, we can see the house itself is pretty much sittin' right over this structure on this other map before it was built. But see here…" She pointed to the shaded area that was not covered by the construction of the house.

"What does that mean?" Rose asked.

"Hold on, let me make sure we're headin' in the right direction." Meghan looked from the maps to the house and back again.

"What does she mean?" Donal asked Angus.

"We have to be in the same direction as the maps so we can tell where this shaded area on the map is. North, south, east, or west. See?"

"That makes sense," Rose said.

"This is exciting," Vivian said with a laugh. "Like a treasure hunt."

Cait jumped up and down. "We're going to find a treasure!"

"All right. We're heading the right way. So by this map, that shaded area is to the left of the house. Angus, get the calculator on your phone, please."

Angus did and handed the cellphone to Meghan; she gave him the maps to hold. She punched in some numbers while glancing at the maps.

"What's she doin'?" Donal asked.

"Figuring how far from the house to the area that is beyond it. We'll pace it off, and…you'll see."

When Meghan finished, she looked at Angus. "Go to the southeast corner of the house. Your pace is what, Angus? Four feet?"

"Sure enough. How many do I need?"

Rose and Vivian exchanged worried glances. "Need for what, honey?" Rose asked cautiously.

"Just one second, luv," Meghan said to her. "We need about one hundred feet. So I'm thinkin' twenty-five paces."

"Right." Angus ran over to his position.

Everyone watched as Angus walked twenty-five paces and stopped.

"Grand," Meghan called to him. "Stay there." She then looked at the maps and calculated again.

"Is it my turn?" Cait asked.

"In a minute, darlin'," Meghan said. "Okay, Donal, your turn. Take a few long steps but don't strain yourself. Walk normal."

Donal did a few paces and stopped. Meghan watched him and nodded. "All right. I need ya to go to the other corner of the house in the back there. Walk just like that and count off about forty paces."

"Can I go next?"

"Sure," Meghan said absently as she watched Donal. "All right, start your paces."

Donal did, and after forty, he was almost in alignment with Angus but was much closer to the edge of the trees.

Cait pulled on Meghan's shirt. "Me next?"

Meghan looked down and laughed. "All right. Can ya count to ten?"

"Of course I can."

"Then go where Donal is and walk ten paces toward Angus. Can ya do that?"

Cait scoffed as if it were a ridiculous question. She ran to her spot and did as instructed. "Right here?" she yelled.

They heard the peacocks squawking in the distance.

"I wondered where those peacocks went. She's the only person that scares the peacocks and not the other way around," Vivian said, shaking her head.

"Yes, Cait," Meghan called out while laughing. "That's fine."

"So now what?" Rose asked as they followed Meghan, who took the maps and stood by Angus.

"If my calculations are correct, then Angus and Donal are standing right on the edge of the shaded area in this older map, which means if there is a structure still below the house, the beginning of it is in line with Angus and Donal. This is an old map, but it might be an entrance if Donal is correct and there's a tunnel under the house." She ran over and retrieved two large stones. She put one where Angus stood; Angus took the other and placed it in Donal's spot.

"What about Cait?" Vivian asked.

"Oh," Meghan leaned in. "I was just givin' her something to do so she didn't feel left out."

"Very clever, Dr. Quigley," Rose said with a laugh.

Donal ran up to Meghan. "So what do we do now?"

Meghan pulled at her earlobe. "I'm not sure. At least we have it marked off."

"Do you think we should let Inspector Russell know what we're doing?" Rose asked.

"I'd feel better tellin' him if we had more to go on," Meghan said. "Right now, we're just guessin'."

"But with Desmond and Kathleen going to the map place, surely that's something."

"Ya might be right, Rosie."

Rose noticed Angus walking around the area where the stones were, then farther away from the house, closer to the trees. He examined the ground, crouching down and lifting the dirt and leaves. He looked at the surrounding trees and the area before standing and dusting off his hands.

"What are ya thinkin'?" Meghan asked, rolling up the maps.

"I'm not sure. I have to think on it."

"We'll talk about it over supper," Vivian said, shooing them all toward the house.

"What about me?" Cait yelled. There she stood in the same place with her hands on her hips.

"For the love of..." Vivian said. "Caitlin, stop your silliness. Come along now."

Cait ran up to them. "But…"

"But me no buts," Vivian said. "You and Donal, go wash up."

"We're always washing," Cait mumbled as Donal pulled her along. "I'm gonna wash the skin right off me hands!"

Inspector Russell called just as they finished dinner. He had talked with Hennessy, who naturally denied any wrongdoing. There was no crime in what he did. But Inspector Russell made it very clear he knew what Hennessy and his boss Fergus Moore were up to. And when he mentioned Desmond Flaherty, Hennessy seemed to get very nervous and tight-lipped, Inspector Russell told Rose when he talked to her.

She told him about the maps and what they had found out about the store in Donegal. He seemed very interested and would stop by so they could talk about it. It wasn't until Russell inquired about Brendan Flaherty that Rose realized she hadn't given him another thought since he decided to stay with a friend. She wondered if he had gone back to London, though he said he would call Vivian when he did. Right now, he was the least of their worries.

"Vivian, if you keep cookin' like this, I'll have to buy new clothes," Meghan said through a wide yawn. "Now, Angus, tell us why you were sniffin' the dirt earlier."

Angus laughed tiredly and sipped his whiskey. "It's probably nothing. But the ground in that area didn't seem quite right."

"Right?" Rose asked. "In a geological way?" She put her head against Meghan's shoulder. "I don't know why I asked. I won't be able to understand your answer."

"Meghan, you'll understand. The earth in the area we paced off was all grass, and it looked as if nothing had been done there other than what's done by nature."

"And a good landscaper," Vivian said. "We have someone come around once or twice month."

"Do they trim the trees or just take care of the grass?" Angus asked.

"The lawn close to the house and the flowers, but of course they do nothing in the back." Vivian laughed. "Sean Murphy's sheep take care of that."

"Get to the point, Dr. Campbell, before I fall asleep," Meghan said, putting her head back.

"My point is, there seems to be an area right in front of the tree line, close to where we paced off that looks as if it were manicured at some point. Almost like it was kept clear for some reason. And why would ya want the woods kept clear in only one spot?"

Meghan lifted her head; so did Rose. "Are you suggesting?" Rose started. "I don't know what you're suggesting."

"All I'm saying is that the ground cover in that area looks new. And I don't mean last week new. I think that area should be more overgrown than it is."

"Like maybe over a year?" Meghan suggested.

"Give or take, but I'd have to do soil samples from that area and the woods. That would tell me for sure. I can get basic results back in a few days. Some take a couple weeks."

"Damn. It's too dark to go out there now," Meghan said. "Tomorrow morning. First thing, we survey the area."

They all decided on an early night. The next morning couldn't come fast enough.

Chapter 27

"Typical," Rose said, looking out the bedroom window at the dense morning fog. She grinned when she felt Meghan's arms encircle her waist. "Good morning."

"G'mornin'," Meghan whispered against her ear. "Come back to bed."

"I'd love to, but we have to play in the dirt, remember?" Rose turned around in her embrace; she kissed her lightly on the lips, then…not so lightly.

Meghan staggered slightly as she pulled away. "That was uncalled for."

"What? It was just a kiss." Rose traced the line of Meghan's jaw with her fingertips.

"It was not. It was a 'take me right here' kinda kiss. And we have to get…what are ya doin'?"

Rose leaned against the windowsill and pulled Meghan with her. "Then do it."

"Be careful what ya ask for, Rosie." Meghan shivered and kissed her, slipping her tongue into her mouth. "This will have to be quick."

"I don't care," Rose said. Suddenly, her entire body was on fire. She took Meghan's hand and guided it down her body.

Meghan untied Rose's robe, slipped her fingers between her parted legs. "God, I love the feel of ya."

Rose could barely breathe when she felt Meghan's fingers toying with her. "Hurry, Meghan. I can't…." She arched her back when Meghan entered her with two fingers and sensually rocked her hips slowly at first. Meghan thrust deeply, and Rose nearly flew out the closed window. Meghan's kiss muffled her cry as she came. She then sagged against Meghan when she slowly withdrew her fingers. "I want to go back to bed."

Meghan laughed. "So do I, luv. But as ya said, we have to go play in the dirt. C'mon now, at least we can have a shower together before anyone wakes up."

They quietly ran to the door. Meghan poked her head out. "Coast is clear." She grabbed Rose by the hand, and the two of them giggled as they ran down the hall.

Rose opened the door... And there sat Cait on the porcelain throne, little feet dangling, and half-asleep with her wild red hair all over the top of her head. Her blue eyes flew open; the look of terror was laughable.

"Rose!" she shrieked.

"I'm so sorry!" Rose said, slamming the door.

"I guess the coast wasn't as clear as I thought," Meghan said.

Just then, they heard the toilet flush. In the next minute, the door opened. Rose pointed to the sink. Cait rolled her eyes and headed back to the sink.

Meghan laughed and kissed Rose. "You shower first. I'll wait for ya."

The fog had not lifted by the time they ventured outside. After the peacocks were tired of squawking, they ran off into the woods. Donal hovered over Angus while he sifted through the soil. Rose figured it was a large portion right in front of the trees.

"How big is this area?" Rose asked Meghan.

"It has to be about ten feet by six from what I can tell that Angus is examining."

Angus gathered his equipment and dusted off his hands.

"What do you think?" Meghan asked.

"I can't be sure, but I really think this is loose earth that was definitely put here on purpose, Meg."

"Rose." Meghan looked around the woods where the peacocks were meandering. "What did ya say yesterday about the peacocks?"

"That Emmett got them from an Englishman and used them to protect the property," she said. "I guess they've been here all these years."

"And where are they mostly concentrated?"

"Right here in this area," Rose said, looking around. "You can't think Donal is right, and there's a tunnel beneath where we're standing?"

"Crazier things have happened." Angus looked at Meghan. "What're you thinking?"

"Let's try this for a scenario, which I think we've all thought of. Let's just say it out loud. What if Flaherty heard from the villagers and Kathleen about Peacock Walk and all the smugglin' going on a few centuries ago? What if he went to the shop in Donegal and found all this out?" She held up the rolled maps. "And he indeed found an entrance, and that's where he hid the mineral rods of gold? And maybe he was working with that Hennessy fella and Moore for that matter. We all figure Flaherty found out there would be big money in this. Perhaps he stole the rods and hid them under here in the Culhane tunnels."

"Why hide them?" Angus asked. "If he was workin' for Moore and stole them, why not give them to him?"

"Because Desmond had a greedy streak," Rose said. "He was always looking for the quick easy money."

"But he would have to have known Moore would come after him," Meghan said. "No, I think he probably did give Moore the rods." He looked at Rose and Angus. "But perhaps not all of them."

"And Moore found out and had him killed," Rose said.

Angus didn't look as though he agreed. "What are you thinkin'?" Meghan asked.

"Why kill him? If he wanted the rods back, killing Flaherty surely wouldn't do that."

"That's a good point. But you know we don't have to solve that. We just need to see if there is a tunnel and an entrance." Meghan looked around the property once more. "If there is and we're right, then we tell Inspector Russell, and he can take it from there. And we'll be done with this."

"I agree," Rose said. "I want this done with. So what do we do?"

"We need to know if we're right," Meghan said.

"There's one way to find out." Angus looked at Rose. "You and Vivian are the owners. If there's any digging to be done, you'll have to approve of it."

"Agreed. But what I don't understand is how Desmond did all this, if indeed he did, without anyone noticing. Surely, the children or Kathleen would have to see him digging. Aunt Vivian would have noticed it, as well."

Meghan scratched the back of her head. "That is a good point. But that again we'll leave up to Inspector Russell."

"I just got a call from Brendan," Vivian called out as she walked up to them. "He's in London. Left last night. He wanted to thank us for the hospitality, and if we ever needed him, just give him a call."

"No offense, but I'm glad he's gone," Rose said. "I have a feeling he'd just get in the way."

"Well, he said we'd know where to get in touch with him if anything comes up about Desmond."

"I'm sure if Inspector Russell needed him, he'd have already talked to him," Meghan said.

"So what are we doin' out here again?" Vivian asked.

"We're thinkin' there might be an entrance or some structure right in front of the trees where we marked off yesterday. Angus seemed to think the earth and soil there have been recently added."

Vivian raised an eyebrow. "That sounds mysterious. You think Desmond did this?"

"We're not sure, but there's no other candidate," Meghan said. "We just need to do a little diggin' to make sure."

"And since you and I own the property, Aunt Vivian, it's up to us to give them the go-ahead."

"Well, go ahead," Vivian said. "If it gets this over with and we can all get back to our lives, then have at it."

Rose laughed and hugged Vivian. "I love your attitude. I feel the same."

"When will you start?" Vivian asked Meghan.

"Might as well start now. We've plenty of daylight left. Donal can help. But let's call Inspector Russell first and let him know what we're doin'."

"I've got his number inside. I'll go call him," Rose said.

"I'll go with you."

Meghan and Angus surveyed the area while they waited for Rose. Meghan looked at the map. "We can start right there." She pointed to the area close to the trees.

"Good a place as any," Angus said. "The soil is very soft there. I think we can at least get a few feet with just shovels. I hope we don't need anything bigger."

"I can't imagine we would. If Flaherty couldn't do it by himself, I doubt he'd hire someone to come dig up the property. My gut says we're right, and if it's there, it's not too far below the surface."

"If there are tunnels under this house, they'd have to be deep."

"But maybe not the entrance."

"That's possible." Angus laughed softly. "I never thought you and me, being geologists, would be digging for gold and tunnels and not fossils."

"It is a little exciting. Like excavating on an archaeological site. But with our luck, we'll find nothin' and be back to square one."

Angus slapped her on the back. "That's the spirit!"

They were laughing when Rose walked up to them. "It worries me when you two are laughing. Inspector Russell is in court the rest of today. I told him what we were planning, and though he said he couldn't stop us, he didn't seem too happy. He said Hennessy is still in custody. Something about a warrant already out for something. I didn't pay attention. I told him we'd be in touch. He said we would definitely hear from him tomorrow."

"Then there's nothin' left to do," Meghan said.

"Right. Let's get the shovels." Rose rubbed her hands together and looked around. "Where are the shovels?"

"Caitlin has the right idea," Angus said, tossing another shovelful of dirt behind him.

Meghan wiped her sweaty brow and laughed as she watched Cait, in her overalls, sitting atop the small mound of dirt. With her red hair piled on top of her head, she had a bucket and a trowel, absently putting dirt into the little red bucket, then dumping it out and starting all over again.

"At least she's not playin' the violin," Donal said, stabbing the shovel into the ground. "How long have we been at it?"

"A couple hours," Meghan said, shielding her eyes to the late afternoon sun. "Any other day, it's cloudy and cool. Now there's not a cloud in the sky. And I swear it's the warmest day ever."

"We'd better hurry, Meg. The sun will be setting soon and we won't be able to see a thing," Angus said as he shoveled more dirt away.

"Do you think you're in the right spot?" Rose called out. She and Vivian sat on the bench along the side of the house.

Meghan glared at her. "Well, if ya'd help, we might get it done faster."

"Hey, I'm helping. I'm keeping Aunt Vivian company. And who just made lemonade for you?"

"And who do you think will make supper?" Vivian said, nudging Rose. "By the way, it's gettin' to be that time."

Angus laughed as he continued. "You've got a wild one there, I'm tellin' ya."

Meghan grudgingly laughed along. "I suppose." She heard Donal laugh. "And what's so funny?"

"Nothin'," Donal said, stabbing the shovel into the earth. He was about to say something when the shovel hit rock.

Meghan and Angus were immediately at his side. Donal stabbed again and again, each time they heard the unmistakable sound of metal hitting rock. Donal smiled as he looked up. "What do ya suppose…?"

They quickly got their shovels and frantically dug all the dirt out around the area. Rose and Vivian stood by them and watched. After they cleared away a good three feet of earth, they saw it.

"Is that what I think it is?" Angus asked.

215

Meghan knelt down and wiped all the dirt away. "I'll be…" She looked at Donal. "You were right."

"Oh, my God," Rose said, kneeling next to her. "I can't believe it."

"I measure a good four feet and five or six," Meghan said.

As she brushed more dirt away, Rose saw the ring attached to the steel floor. "Is that a lock?" she asked Meghan.

"My key," Donal said quickly.

Meghan grinned. "You're right. Rose, you still have the key?"

"God, yes." Rose fished it out of her jeans pocket and handed it to Meghan.

"Well, Donal, keep your fingers crossed." Meghan wiped away any dirt around the lock and put the key in. "Inspector Russell was right, this is a relatively new lock." With one turn, the padlock popped open.

"It worked," Donal said eagerly.

"Yes, it did." Meghan sounded just as eager.

Rose watched her as she slipped the lock off the ring and gave it a tug; it wouldn't budge.

"Need some help," she said with a groan.

Angus and Donal helped her pull on the ring until the iron door opened. "Vivian, do ya have any torches?"

Donal scrambled to his feet. "I know where they are." He ran off into the house.

"I'm comin', too!" Caitlin yelled and ran after him.

"This is unbelievable," Vivian said, peering over their shoulders.

Meghan easily lifted the door and swung it back on its hinges until it was completely opened. They all peered down into the darkness.

"I'll be damned," Meghan said. "I see a staircase. It's narrow and—"

"I found them!" Donal called out as he and Cait ran back with the flashlights. He eagerly handed them over to Meghan and Angus.

After testing them, Meghan took a deep breath. "I'll go first, then Rose. Angus, you follow. Vivian—"

"I'll stay here with the childr—with Cait," she said. She motioned to Donal.

"Donal, you follow with Angus, all right?" Meghan asked with a wink.

Donal could only nod; Rose figured he'd swallow his tongue with excitement if he had to speak.

"But I want to see," Cait said.

"You will, Caitlin. We just want to make sure it's safe," Rose said, kissing her forehead. "You stand guard and protect Aunt Vivian."

This seemed to be acceptable to Cait, who ran over and picked up her trowel, then held Vivian's hand.

"As eager as I am to see what's down there, it's getting dark. I don't like having Caitlin out here. We'll go inside and start supper. Or perhaps go see Mr. Murphy. He said he had some lamb for me."

"But I want to see!" Cait argued.

"You will. Tomorrow when it's daytime and I won't worry about you fallin' down those steps. No arguin'."

"We'll be in as soon as we're through, Aunt Vivian." Rose tried to contain her excitement, but it wasn't easy.

"If we're not inside, we're at Sean's," Vivian called back.

They watched as Vivian and Cait walked away. Well, Cait had to be pulled away.

"I wish she could have stayed," Rose said.

"It's just as well, luv. Vivian is right. I wouldn't want anything to happen to Cait. Okay then, here we go. Watch your step now," Meghan said, leading the way.

Rose was right behind, holding on to the back of her shirt. It was dark and damp, and the stairs were narrow and steep.

"I wonder how far down we are?" Rose asked.

"I counted thirty steps," Donal said, behind her.

Meghan shined the flashlight in front of her. "Last step, be careful," she called out, her voice echoing against the walls.

"This is a cramped space," Angus said. "And I suppose this is the wrong time to tell you I'm claustrophobic."

Donal laughed and stayed close to Rose, who put her arm around his shoulders. "I can't see a thing," she said.

"Good Lord," Meghan said. "Look."

They huddled around Meghan, who shined the beam in front of her. There on the few crates were at least a dozen stone cylinders.

"I never would have believed this," Meghan said, scanning the area with the flashlight.

Angus walked up to them and ran his fingers over the gray stone rods. "Magnificent. I have no idea how much gold is within these stones, but it has to be a substantial amount."

Through the darkness, Rose watched Donal as he slowly walked up and stood next to Angus. "This is what he stole? There's gold in them?"

"Yes. That's what he took. I'm sorry, Donal," Meghan said, putting her hand on his shoulder.

Rose peered between them. "I wonder how he got them all down here by himself and without anyone seeing him?"

"That's easy to explain."

They all whirled around to see Brendan Flaherty with a flashlight in one hand and a gun in the other.

"Really?" Rose asked, throwing up her hands.

Chapter 28

"I was right not to say anything to ya," Donal said angrily.

Meghan put both hands on his shoulders, then gently pushed him behind her.

Brendan laughed quietly. "You're a good son, Donal. Now if you'll all step away."

"What do you think you're going to do?" Rose asked. "You know we went to the police, and Inspector Russell is on his way here."

Brendan shook his head. "Nice try, Rose darlin'. But I know he's in court, and he won't be comin' back here until tomorrow. By that time, I'll have given Fergus Moore those rods and got the money my idiot brother was supposed to get for us, and I'll be long gone. Where are Vivian and Caitlin?"

"They're at Mr. Murphy's. We sent them there to get Cait out of the way," Meghan said.

Brendan nodded. "Good. Then there won't have to be any trouble. I'll take the rods."

"You'll never get them out of here by yourself," Meghan said.

"I won't have to," Brendan said.

Angus quickly walked away from them and stood next to Brendan, who laughed again.

"Seriously?" Rose yelled. "You asshole."

Meghan was stunned. "Angus, no," she whispered. "Why?"

"What other reason, Meg? Money. You know what we make, what we go through," Angus said.

"So you're all right with killing innocent people?" Meghan asked angrily.

Brendan snorted. "My brother was no innocent."

"What about Kathleen?" Rose took a step toward Brendan and stopped when he raised the gun.

"That's the only innocent part of this whole mess," Angus said angrily. "It was an accident, Rose. We had nothing to do with that."

"I don't believe you," Rose said in a dead calm voice.

"Let me explain," Brendan said. "Quickly, then we must be movin' on. My idiot brother truly wanted to find gold. But it was Angus here who had the brilliant idea to hook him up with Fergus Moore and keep me completely out of the picture. When he and Meghan overheard Des talking in that bar, Angus knew he'd be perfect. Promise him money, wave a little gold nugget in front of his face, and hand it to him, and Des would do just about anything."

"I hate you," Donal spat out.

"I don't blame ya, Donal. So where was I? Oh, right. Angus here got him and the fool Hennessy past the security. They took the gold and split up, each taking half the rods. Des said he would lay low with his portion until Moore decided when we'd move it to London. That's where I came in. And it was just that easy." He laughed then. "Too easy."

"Why have you waited so long to take these out of here?" Meghan asked.

"We had no idea about this place. Des had evidently done his research and realized he was sitting on top of a tunnel. He must have gone to that shop in Donegal and got the maps. And just as easy as you, he must have found the entrance. He got all this down here by himself without any of us knowin'. Moore was fine with not knowin' where the stuff was. The less he knew until the time was right, the better for him. Plausible deniability and all that. So he just waited until Des thought the time was right."

"So what happened?" Rose asked.

"Des had a change of heart," Brendan said sadly. He looked at Donal. "That's when he must have given you that key to the lock." He shook his head in disbelief. "When he called me out of the blue, I was shocked. He confided in me and told me the whole thing of what he'd done, not knowing all this time I was the connection in London for the gold. I came to Ireland, tried to talk him out of it, playing the concerned brother, but he'd have none of it. Said he wanted to turn himself in and give the cylinders back. He wouldn't tell me where they were, so I wouldn't be involved. Trusting to the end, my brother was. So I had no choice. Moore was getting nervous, and I couldn't have that. Hennessy tried to reason with Des, a fight typically ensued with two hotheaded Irishmen, and Hennessy, the idiot, killed him before we could find out about all this." He looked around the dark tunnel. "His death then became a tragic car accident."

"What about Kathleen?" Rose asked quietly.

"That was truly an accident, I'm tellin' ya," Angus said. "Please believe me. Yes, she found out about Desmond because Meghan here had to be noble and honest and tell the authorities, then tell Kathleen. I couldn't stop you without exposing myself." He looked at Meghan. "Damn you and your self-righteous…"

"Now, Angus," Brendan said. "The truth is, I came here to talk to Kathleen. I was with her that night. I told her that Des had confided in me and told me what he had done. I was, as I said, the picture of a concerned brother and felt horrible for not saying anything sooner and told her together we'd find out exactly who killed Des. It was a good performance, I must admit. Kathleen believed me. But you know, she didn't tell me about going to Donegal and getting the floor plans of this drafty old house. I knew she had been talking to you, Meghan, so she was eager to call you. It was my intention to stick around and let you and Kathleen do all the work. But then she had the car accident, which threw a cog in the wheel, let me tell you. So I had to regroup."

"It was an accident," Angus said sadly. "The only accident in this whole mess. It was to be so simple, so easy. No killin'."

"You know," Brendan said, sitting on the stair. "I still don't know how, but Kathleen realized how Des found out about the tunnel. And apparently, you found out, as well. How did you? I consider myself a smart fellow, and I couldn't find out. I'm curious."

"It was Inspector Russell," Angus said. "He found Kathleen's credit card receipt from that shop in Donegal. It was very clever. I had no idea this place existed."

"And you told Brendan," Meghan said angrily to Angus.

"Yes, he did. Well, that's enough of this. I wanted to wait until it was dark, which it is, and we've spent far too much time down here. Now let's get organized, shall we?" Brendan motioned with his gun. "Rose, you're a strong woman, as are you, Meghan. You too, Donal. Each of you take as many as you can. We'll make as many trips as we need."

"Angus, don't do this," Meghan pleaded with him.

"No more talkin'," Brendan said. "I don't want to get ugly, but I will. There's too much at stake here."

Meghan looked at Rose and Donal and nodded. Silently, they each could carry only one stone cylinder. Brendan moved out of their way.

"Angus, here," he said, pulling out another gun from his pocket and tossing it to him.

"This is unnecessary," Angus said, catching the handgun.

"Let's hope so," Brendan said. "You go first, Angus. I'll bring up the rear. Move it."

Angus shook his head and picked up a rod, then mounted the stairs. Rose went first, then Donal, with Meghan last. Brendan poked her in the back with the muzzle of the gun.

"No heroics, Meghan," he whispered. "I'm not a gentle soul like Angus. I will kill all of you. I promise ya that."

As they reached the surface, Brendan was the last to appear. "Very good. Angus, go get the truck. Then we'll make one more trip down there. Go on."

From out of the darkness, they all heard it.

Donal looked at Rose, who looked at Meghan. The screeching sound of *Three Blind Mice* seemed to come from all over the dark woods.

"What the fuck is that?" Brendan said. He walked past Meghan, trying to see in the darkness.

That was all the distraction Meghan needed. She threw the stone cylinder as hard as she could at Brendan. It hit him square in the back; he stumbled forward and fell to his knees.

Rose was stunned, but Donal was ready to do the same as Meghan when Inspector Russell appeared out of the woods.

"Drop it, Dr. Campbell," he called out.

Angus whirled around when the headlights from two squad cars lit up the area, nearly blinding them. Angus quickly dropped the gun and raised his hands.

Vivian ran out of the woods and hugged Rose, then Donal. Meghan picked up the gun and presented it to Russell with a shaky hand.

"Good timing," Meghan said to him. "I think I wet meself."

Russell grinned. "You did just fine."

It was a flurry of police then, whisking Brendan Flaherty and Angus Campbell away.

"Caitlin!" Vivian called out. "You can stop now."

Cait ran out of the woods with violin in hand. A police officer ran right behind her.

"I did it! I told them I could help and I did! You were just like three blind mice without me."

Chapter 29

Rose sat on the couch with Cait on her lap. Donal sat between her and Meghan, who had her arm around Donal's shoulders. Vivian ran around getting tea for Inspectors Russell and Burke.

"It's all too fantastic," Vivian said, shaking her head. "To think of what could have happened."

"We're all fine, Auntie Vivian," Donal said.

Between Rose and Meghan, they recounted what Brendan told them in the tunnel. Meghan sadly told them about Angus.

Russell and Burke listened in silence until Cait sat up. "Then I came in with my violin and saved the day."

"And whose idea was that?" Rose asked, looking around the room.

Vivian cleared her throat. "When Caitlin and I came in, I was in the kitchen when I saw Brendan walking up the drive. I thought it was very odd. And I got nervous when he appeared to be lookin' for us like he was skulkin' around. The lights were out, so I quickly locked the front door."

"I wasn't scared at all," Cait said eagerly. "Auntie Vivian said to be very still and quiet, and I was. Even when Uncle Brendan came to the door and knocked and tried to open it." She looked shamefaced at Rose. "I was a little scared then."

"I don't blame you."

"When he walked off the steps and around the side of the house, that's when I found Inspector Russell's number and called him."

"Good thinkin'," Meghan said. "I have to tell you, I was shocked when we saw him in the tunnel."

"I got the call from Miss Culhane and immediately called the locals here. They were very good at keeping out of sight until I got here," Russell said. "Not knowing what was going on down there, we didn't want to run down there with guns blazin'."

"You couldn't have. The staircase is too narrow. And at the bottom, there was hardly any room to move around," Meghan said. "It would have been a mess."

"We could hear you," Burke said. "And we heard that Dr. Campbell was in on it, and now there were two of them. We knew we needed a distraction. That's where the young Miss Flaherty saved the day."

"I knew you'd recognize the song," Vivian said, "and they hoped that would do it."

"And it did," Rose said.

"I'll never make fun of your playin' again," Donal said, ruffling her red hair.

"We can assume that Kathleen's death was a true accident," Russell said.

Rose agreed. "She believed Brendan when he said he would help. And after he told her everything he knew, that's when she must have called Meghan to let her know. But never got the chance."

Russell agreed. "And from what we can figure from what Flaherty's brother told you, Desmond must have found out about the tunnels and hid the cylinders there. What I don't know is how he got them down there without any of you seeing it. I suppose it's not important, but it'll nag at me."

"I have a theory," Rose offered. "When did Des steal the stone cylinders from the mining company? I mean at what time of year?"

"I believe in the fall before he died."

Rose nodded. "That's when Kathleen came to visit me that year. They were in Chicago."

"Oh, Rose, I believe you're right," Vivian said. "It was Desmond who said I should go along for a vacation. Oh, my God. That's when he had to do it."

"Yep. I thought of that last night. It nagged at me, too. I wondered how he would do that if there was a tunnel. And now that we know there is and the timeframe, that had to be it."

"And being alone here, there would be no one around to see him. Very clever and very plausible," Burke said.

"And then your father had a change of heart," Russell said to Donal. "He may have started off in a bad way, but he tried at the end to do the right thing."

Donal nodded but said nothing. He leaned against Meghan, who tightened her embrace.

"What happens now?" Rose asked.

"Fergus Moore is bein' picked up for questioning as we speak. I think we have enough on him and all the rest. The mining company will get their merchandise back when it's all over. You can go on with your lives now," Russell said.

"That's the best idea I've heard yet," Rose said, holding on to Caitlin. "The best."

Chapter 30

Rose sat on the stone wall that surrounded the grove of oak trees. It was a beautiful autumn day. The trees were changing colors, and the brisk breeze that blew over the green hills had Rose pulling her sweater around her.

In the distance, Mr. Murphy and Salty herded his sheep over the hill. That would stay constant, Rose made sure of that—Mr. Murphy would still graze his sheep on Culhane land, and Rose would be the benefactor of his goat cheese and lamb. He turned and waved to Rose, who waved until he disappeared out of sight.

Her thoughts now turned to Kathleen. As she gazed at the green hills, she could envision them as young girls running and playing on these same hills, causing trouble and wreaking havoc on the village of Trahern. Kathleen loved Peacock Walk and its history, and she adored being its mistress.

Wiping away her tears, Rose walked over to read the faded inscription on the small gray headstone of the first mistress of Peacock Walk, *Aileen Culhane, 1885.* Rose looked at each one, reading each name throughout the generations until she stopped at the most recent.

The sob caught in her throat once again as she looked at the clean white headstone with fresh earth surrounding it.

Kathleen Mary Culhane Flaherty
1965-2014
Beloved Mother and Wife
Mistress of Peacock Walk

Rose took a deep quivering breath and laid the wildflowers on Kathleen's grave. She felt strong hands on her shoulders then and leaned back into Meghan's warm body. She smiled when Meghan handed her a hanky.

"It's a simple sentiment," Meghan said.

Rose sniffed and wiped away her tears. "It's all that Kathleen asked for. Nothing lavish or pretentious."

"I'm not interrupting you, am I?"

Rose turned and smiled, cupping Meghan's face in her hands. "No, you're not. Ever."

Meghan turned her face, kissing the palm of her hand. "I do love ya."

"I'm so very glad you do. I hope I can do this, Meghan." She looked at the headstone once again. "I hope I can be as good and as loving as Kathleen was to this place."

"Rose," Meghan said. "Kathleen never doubted your love for the children or this home. She told me once that she wondered what would have happened if your parents stayed here in Ireland and she moved to America. She told me you would have been a wonderful mistress of Peacock Walk."

Rose chuckled and wiped her nose. "Kathleen was an old romantic."

"And so is her American cousin, who I adore."

Rose sighed and looked into Meghan's eyes. "So you're sticking with this?"

Meghan laughed. "Ya can't get rid of me now. Donal wants to investigate the tunnels."

Rose groaned. "Oh, that boy."

"And Cait—"

They both closed their eyes when the violin music of *Three Blind Mice* started. Rose winced when the screeching began. "I can't wait until she learns something new."

"Be careful what ya wish for." Meghan held her hand as they walked back toward the house.

"You still have time to run," Rose said, swinging her hand playfully with Meghan's.

"And miss Cait's recital? Not on your life. Besides, I kinda like being in love with the mistress of Peacock Walk."

"Meghan? Where are ya?" Cait's voice called out.

Rose raised an eyebrow. "Then God help you, Dr. Quigley."

Meghan laughed again and kissed her tenderly. "And now I must take my leave. The future mistress is bellowing."

Rose watched Meghan, who ran the rest of the way back to the house. "How lucky can I be?" she said to no one in particular.

As she neared the house, she saw the peacocks meandering in the foreground, foraging for food. Most of them squawked and scurried away when Rose approached. However, one male let out a loud mournful shriek, then spread its majestic feathers behind him. It was a beautiful sight to see.

The peacock seemed to regard Rose curiously for a long moment before he blinked, lowered his feathers, and slowly ambled into the woods with the others. Rose gazed once more at the green hills behind her. She said a quiet prayer to Kathleen, vowing she would do justice to Kathleen's memory and her wish for Rose to be guardian and watch over her children.

She mounted the front stairs, her new life waiting as the mistress of Peacock Walk.

About the author

Kate Sweeney, a 2010 Alice B. Medal winner, was the 2007 recipient of the Golden Crown Literary Society award for Debut Author for *She Waits*, the first in the *Kate Ryan Mystery* series. The series also includes *A Nice Clean Murder, The Trouble with Murder*, a 2008 Golden Crown Award winner for Mystery, *Who'll Be Dead for Christmas?* a 2009 Golden Crown Award winner for Mystery, *Of Course It's Murder, What Happened in Malinmore, A Near Myth Murder, It's Not Always Murder,* and *Recalculated Murder*.

Other novels include *Away from the Dawn, Survive the Dawn, Before the Dawn, Residual Moon*, a 2008 Golden Crown Award winner for Speculative Fiction, *Liar's Moon, The O'Malley Legacy, Winds of Heaven, Moonbeams and Skye, Sea of Grass, Paradise, Love at Last, Someday I'll Find You, Moon Through the Magnolia, Stone Walls, Second Time Around, Love in E Flat, One Night in Paris, I Love You Again, Buoyed out on the Foam of the Sea,* and *Build Me a Dream*.

Born in Chicago, Kate moved to Louisiana, and this Yankee doubts she'll ever get used to saying y'all. Humor is deeply embedded in Kate's DNA. She sincerely hopes you will see this when you read her novels, short stories, and other works. Email Kate at ksweeney22@aol.com.